ALL

Leone Ross was born in 1969 to a Jamaican mother and Scottish father. She spent her early years in England before moving to Jamaica, returning to England in 1991 to study for a master's degree. She is a journalist and lives in North London. This is her first novel.

ALL THE BLOOD IS RED

Leone Ross

ARP
Angela Royal Publishing

Published by ANGELA ROYAL PUBLISHING LTD
Suite 53, Eurolink Business Centre, 49 Effra Road, London SW2 1BZ

First published 1996
1 3 5 7 9 10 8 6 4 2

A CIP catalogue for this book is available from the British Library
ISBN 1-899860-15-0

Typeset by Nick Awde/Desert ♥ Hearts
Printed and bound in Great Britain by
Biddles Ltd, Guildford and King's Lynn

For David Williams

'Don't threaten me with love baby . . .'

Billie Holiday

Mavis

De firs' bwoy I ever love did have a coconut head an' a mout' like a Julie mango. Sweet an' soft, like him oil it up an' rub it every mornin'. Him madda call him Adolphus St Dominic Franklin when him born, but him always seh we mus' call him Frankie, like him puppa did name. Not dat him did ever clap eye pon him daddy since him lef' an' go ah foreign. Bwoy, Jamaican man wutliss like a dog when dem ready.

Frankie used to tek me down by de gully side an' turn up me face an' kiss me, an' bwoy, to dis day ah can still 'memba how me did feel. Like me couldn't stop tremble an everyt'ing on fire. Is like the mouths fit together good, y'know? Him would stop an' look inna me face hard, an' touch me lips, like dem was pretty like fe him own. Look like him wan' fe dead. We never use to kiss too long, because me was holdin' me breath. Wasn't like I never know how fe kiss — me an' me sister dem used to practice ah nighttime on each other han' corner — was jus' dat de gully side did stink. Nuff dog an' goat use to go down dere an' dead off, an' you could smell dem all up de side ah de gully. Me never want de stink-up smell fe spoil de sweetness of de kiss, so me scrinch up me nose every time. Frankie laugh an' tell me seh is because me stocious.

We would kiss till me Auntie Myra come up to the top ah de gully an' start call me: "Mavis, woy! Mavis, woy! You nuh see seh you madda deh call you?". Dat time me know seh mamma was jus' startin' to t'ink about askin' weh de school uniform deh, whether me bathe me sister yet, an' by de way, who is dat bwoy you ah spend too much time wid, MIND HIM BREED YOU, me nuh want no more pickney inna de damn yard. Of course me auntie always did call me long time before me madda start excite up herself, so everyt'ing always did get done at de right time.

Auntie Myra was like me bes' friend dem time deh. She gimme one lick pon me ears, but jus' a likkle one, to show me seh she know me deh 'bout, an' den she laugh, a big belly laugh, like dem pregnant woman, an' send me inside.

One evenin' me an' Frankie ah kiss an' ah talk bout t'ings. Him was dropping nice lyrics, seh him want to married to me, how we can save up money when him finish secondary school an get a job, an' tell me how me hair nice, seh it smell good, an' me eye dem big an' pretty. Den him grab me titty an' start squeeze it. Well, what a rass!

Me was so 'fraid. Firs' time me ever 'fraid ah man. Me never know where to put me eye, but me never like it. Maybe if him did jus' slip it nice an' gentle, like him never mean it, maybe me an' him woulda married now. Maybe if him was kind. But him jus' a knead up me chest like me is Christmas bun mixture. Me ah try tell him seh me nuh like it. Me tell him seh me jus' want to kiss him up, love him up nice, y'know?

Me seh, de bwoy get so vex me t'ink him was goin' to pop up. Him face swell up an' de blood start rush all 'bout in it, like somet'ing in deh ah try get out. Start cuss me seh me ah idiot, tell me seh him ah big man, an' how me ah play like me is a pickney. Me was so vex me box him cross him face.

Fe one second me swear him was going to lick me back, an' even though dat never scare me like how when him grab me chest, me was 'fraid still. Me jump up an' walk off, ah gwaan like me nice. Dat's when him call to me.

"You see you? You need a man hol' yuh an' give you a back-ways fuck! You hear me?"

Me ah try walk, more 'fraid, ah look if me see anybody roundabout can help me. An' me vex too, vex 'cause me couldn't understan' where it all run weh to, weh de feelin' gone. Why de bwoy ah gwaan so. Me jus' watch de hill side in de distance, walk me walk, try keep calm.

Den him say it. Me never know what it mean.

"Bloodclaaht wetty-baggie gyal!"

Later on me ask me Auntie Myra what him did mean. Me never put it direct-like, cause me never want her know seh Frankie ah dis me. She never know. You know how Jamaican people love mek up word like dem is dictionary. She light de kerosene lamp, gimme one of her likkle lick dem an' tell me seh me musn't listen to nastiness. Me ah toss inna de bed ah wonder.

Is next day me fin' out.

One girl me know tell me seh all de bwoy dem did start up wid it, seh is de popular word dese days. She say is like when a gyal gwaan like a idyat, like she wan' sex a man, but when him really ah look it, she jus' ah giggle up, gwaan soft, gwaan like she really nuh want it. A gyal who cyaan mek up her mind 'bout dem somet'ing deh. A gyal who cyaan deliver what she promise.

Even now dat me is a old woman, me still feel shame. Can still hear Frankie ah cuss me by de gully side, dead rat an' dog ah fill up me nose.

Jeanette, June 14th, 1996

They beat like drums, the fists. I could hear them from inside the courtroom. I could see them too, in my mind, heavy, striking over and over again, until they sounded like some terrible rain. I remember so many things about that day, but in quiet moments it is the fists that come back to haunt me, pull at me.

Luckily, these moments are rare.

When they do come to me, I always imagine their colours. Nicotine stained over deeper brown. Yellow lowlights in their palms, or chapped from the cold, or shining black with blue. Tales of their owners' lives mixed into the edges, intimate in whorls and heart lines. They beat out a rhythm that I feel in my blood. I wonder how many of them were women's hands, and what *they* were beating for, whether they were hammering for me or for him, whether they truly felt they should be there, breaking nails, splinters falling on the courtroom steps. I couldn't hear the chant, although I was told there were many. Just the fists, unified. I wonder if he heard them too, and how they felt to his heart. Did he rejoice in them? Was he frightened? Did he feel his bladder tighten, wonder whether he would shame himself among them, he, their hero? Did he want to be with them?

Did he feel justified?

This is the story of how new hands came into my life. Not curled into fists, but cool against my cheek, hot against my hair. It is the story of how my hands too, remembered how to unfold into an old freedom, and I reflect on this now, honour it as those fists have melted, linked with others, open palms touching, bare, vulnerable.

When I hear the fists now, I turn away from them.

Alexandrea, June 14th, 1996

I know now that she was terribly brave. After all, I didn't have the courage to do what she did. But then, I spend my life pretending that everything's okay. It seems to be my speciality.

What stays with me is the guilt. It took me so long to see what was obvious. It took me too long. I saw Michael the other day and he told me that she was fine, looking extremely good, driving all the men crazy as usual. I shouldn't even say that. We're all responsible for how we feel. If they're crazy, that's down to them. He says that she has bad days, but it's been a while, and of course, he helps. My brother has always been good with pain. He had enough practice with me.

What I remember most is how angry I was. Smashed up everything in my room afterwards. And wondered whether the jurors were all people like me. God knows that before my brain started working, I would have done the same as them. I watched them over those few days, trying to climb into their heads. I can remember them so clearly: if I was any kind of artist I'd be able to sketch them. A big, broad woman with a face like a ham and flat, brown braids that she flicked out of the way. She chewed a pencil. A Chinese man, with a never ending stream of light blue suits, creased and polished to a high shine. Or maybe it was the same suit every day. Bill Waivers, sitting beside me in the gallery, snorting derisively at every word. I spotted him crying later. Wouldn't have thought he was capable of it. I bet he didn't even cry at his wife's funeral. Oh, and I remember this nasty looking woman who was completely bored. She rubbed her hands on her trouser suit, as if she had glue on them. She kept foraging up her nostril like she was collecting for Oxfam. Disgusting. There was another woman, gorgeous and sticky with outrage. She would've been down with Jeanette. I bet she still thinks about it as well.

I should go and see Jeanette one of these days. I really should. Michael says that the bump's getting fatter and fatter, and he swears its a girl. He says she was in the bath the other day with their cat asleep on the bump. The baby kicked and the cat was so surprised that it fell off into the water. Pandemonium, he says. When he heard the screams he thought she'd gone into labour. She got a nasty scratch on her thigh.

Still, she's been through much worse.

Nicola, June 14th, 1996

The day before, I daydreamed. Imagined what the courtroom would be like. In my mind, it was a stage and as Shakespeare said, we were all the players. Lead, anti-hero, chorus in the pit, all of that. I'd never been in a courtroom. Ain't no crime in my life. Except *LA Law* and *Kavanagh QC*. The judge had a powdery wig that looked more like a fluffy brain, ripped out of his skull and placed on top of his head, dull greys and browns. Lawyers that looked exactly like the johncrows that used to sweep down to examine unsuspecting, sunbathing tourists in Kingston.

I imagined sitting in the visitors' gallery. I could see what the judge was thinking. His hairy, exposed brain was throbbing, words running across it like fairy lights. One word was throbbing there for all of us to see, even before the trial started: Guilty. Guilty-Guilty-Guilty. Pink red letters. He was thinking about her, not him. The judge was looking at her, not him. She was the guilty one.

It was my cue. I looked down at the script in front of me, but the rass pages were blank, I didn't know my lines. The pause in the courtroom was going on and on, interminably, the johncrow lawyers were mumbling and the audience that was the visitors' gallery were looking, and I wasn't coming in, my mind was empty, and I tried to improvise, but Jeanette was putting me off because she was crying, crying and I didn't know the words. The judge's brain was getting larger and larger, blinking its on-off sign and I had stage fright for the first time, lost my theatrical virginity. Someone once asked me if I'd done that yet, and the judge, hearing no more, was bringing down his gavel to hit his lectern-thing, but he was hitting Jeanette, because she was in the way, and I was getting vexer and vexer and I knew that the reason I couldn't control the daydream was because I was daydreaming in a nightmare, I was asleep and I was yelling

'MIS-TRIAL! IT'S A DREAM!' but it was too late, the gavel was going up and down, and he was laughing, that bastard was laughing as he got off and the judge hammered.

I woke up. Cried. Cried snotty and nasty and ugly, like a pickney. Alex came in and held me, and thank God, there was none of that damn scrape-out-your-throat rum on her breath — at least that was something — and she hushed me, said everything will be alright, alright, every little thing is gonna be alright and it was Marley in my head all the next day as we went into the real courtroom, *don' worry / about a thing / 'cause every little thing / is gonna be alright . . .*

1

September, 1994

The meal, like most aeroplane fare, was served in little boxes, parcels, squares and mounds of pretend food that did nothing to satisfy her appetite. Eventually, Nicola sculpted with them, turning her plate into a miniature Caribbean: larger pieces of bread for Haiti and Cuba, a smaller, well-defined Jamaica, peas for the Eastern Caribbean that fled away, curving down the plate in a sea of the white wine that was left in her glass. She was sketching itsy-bitsy parishes onto the impossibly small Cheddar Jamaica with a felt tip and wondering what she could use to fashion a palm tree when the stewardess arrived, peering down her long, gently carved nose. Feeling stupid, Nicola tried not to meet the woman's gaze as the tray was lifted away.

Sculpting with food was typical of her. Her friends teased her about her eccentricities and strange flights of fancy. The squiggles on the place mats, bus tickets folded and refolded into geometric shapes. She always wanted to be doing something with her hands. Her mother had told her that the devil found work for hands that were idle. It had been one of the last things she had said before she had died. Her death had made such small things precious to Nicola, even though she could not actually remember the words. If someone had told her that her incessant fiddling was a construct of maternal memories she would have laughed. All she remembered of her mother's death was its inanity. It sounded like a TV movie. A walk in the sunlight. The simple lack of what she herself had learned as a child, like all children *(look right, look left)* crossing the road. A simple walk in the sunshine and a moment in time that went wrong. Bang. Crash. Squealing tires. Apologies, a twisted face and the dull halls of Kingston Public Hospital. Her father, weeping. The only time she ever saw him cry. And then, nothing.

9

She had been three, and now she remembered very little.

She was an actress. As the stewardess lifted away the tray she mustered all her skills to smile at her. She wouldn't worry, she promised herself, about the woman returning to her dainty little cubby hole. They all managed to squeeze into it. She knew that at six feet tall she could not have tried. She could imagine them swapping their transatlantic tales among their Sloaney friends. *Ooh, what was it supposed to be?* they would all scream. Fuck them. She shifted her rear on the seat and stretched the long muscle in her calf. She hadn't been to the gym, a place she made her own, for a fortnight. Still, she reassured herself that she had had enough exercise. Swimming in the sea at Hellshire Beach, dancing at Devon House, to the beat of a guitarist who had dared to wear eyeliner to hoots and stares and accusations of battymanism. The holiday had satisfied her. She had put flowers on her mother's grave because it was what people did, and stood there, not sure of what it all meant. As she left the graveyard a breeze crept through, blowing loose petals onto an adjoining headstone. It had seemed right to share, somehow.

Planes were never roomy enough for her, and she dreaded travelling. Privately, she suspected that she was claustrophobic, but wouldn't have dreamed of telling anyone else. It was her own private worry, like a pimple in a personal place that you tried to squeeze when nobody was looking. She found it difficult to fit into enclosed spaces, ever since she had started the elongation process at age eight. Her limbs got in her own way, as well as the way of others. Sometimes she had to pause in the middle of a pub or some crowded street, realising that an errant, silky limb had intruded where it shouldn't: someone's face, perhaps, or more embarrassingly, her knee in someone's groin. It happened a lot on trains. She would cross her legs, or shift to allow a passenger access, and her knees would move too high, dance in men's laps.

Alexandrea, her closest friend, couldn't understand it. Alex was small, and she got in nobody's way unless she wanted to.

The masochist in Nicola enjoyed the mounting tension she felt in an aircraft, the particularly delicious frisson that went with trips to the toilet. Bumping and banging in their ammoniac brightness she would feel a tightening in her chest. Every time she went she thought of bursting into the galley and wailing her way up the aisle. Of course, she didn't do it. It was a dalliance, a fantasy that amused her sense of drama. It was the kind of thing her boyfriend Julius would have disapproved of. His sense of drama was structured by beauty and order. He had a job to do. It had been his self-possession that had appealed to her first, when she had gone to audition for a part in his play. That, and the fact that he was white.

She stretched again, brushing her shoulder against the man beside her. His tray rattled. She had paid very little attention to him during the flight; in truth, she had been relieved that he was not the chatty type. Like most men who saw her, his smile had been wide, so she had dismissed him with her best haughty look. She was a warm woman, but she hated making small talk. It was enough to feel waves of their attraction to her. This comforted her more than idle chatter *(Been away long then? Not really, two weeks. My, you have a wonderful tan! Yes, that's what happens when you sit in the sun)* and in flight talk was the worst. Still, she kept score. If her fellow passenger had not stroked a quick gaze up the tube skirt that hugged golden thighs, the jumper that could do nothing to hide a full bosom, the tiny waist, she would have felt failure. That would have stayed with her. Grinning to herself, she turned to start the familiar apology.

The man's eyes were closed. She saw, with sudden, electric attention that he was trembling. Recognition was bitter and bright in her mouth. She knew the smell. Oysters. Bitter pennies. Marshmallows gone dry in the sun. Come, gism, spermatozoa, whatever name you fancied. She could smell it on him and she could feel the tension in his body, and she knew what the jerk of his shoulders meant. She was frozen by his audacity.

For a single moment she hoped that she was wrong, that he was asleep, that her mind was erring on the side of the impossible. But his hands were under his blanket, one of those sickly blue blankets that all hospitals *(Bang. Crash.)* and airlines seemed to buy in bulk, and this made it seem worse. Time had slowed perceptibly.

The man was masturbating. His rhythm was purposeful. And there, barely there, under the smooth sound of the engine's hum, a sound. Slick, wet, smooth. A sound he was playing to. And the *(bitterpenniesoysters-raweggsmarshmallows)* smell. The sound was horrible *(snick-snick snick-*

snick) like someone tearing a plaster off their knee, but slowly. She wrenched her eyes away, and stared at the seat in front of her. Nervous laughter bubbled in her throat. She bumped into people a lot and laughed in inappropriate situations. Julius had threatened to never go shopping with her again after she had had an attack of whooping laughter in Harrods. A woman had walked in with a dog that looked like a cotton bud on the end of a leash, a dog bedecked in a silver coat that had matched its owner's own silver sheath. The dog had urinated on his mistress' foot and Nicola, suddenly wondering whether the woman was wearing matching silver underwear, had broken down. She had been so helpless with laughter that Julius had had to carry her out of the store.

Now, unbidden, incongruous thoughts tumbled over each other. Was he using a lubricant? Oil? Did he keep a bottle of lotion? She bit her hand to stifle a giggle that was a sob in disguise. British Airways margarine?

The man continued to masturbate as she fought for control. Unable to stop herself, she glanced over once more.

He was looking straight at her.

His eyes were very green, fringed with short, dark lashes. The expression in each of them was unreadable, a dark glaze, frozen mountains that she could not begin to climb. Someone had punched him, and the bag of a healing black eye was shot with purple. His mouth was half open; flecks of spittle lay in his beard. When she told people about it, many years later, she could never remember how long they sat there staring, the blurred movement of his hand just out of the frame. She felt as if God was stabbing her with pins, quick, vicious adrenaline jacking her heart rate up, drowning in his eyes.

He smiled.

She broke away, one foot slipping on her coat that had fallen to the floor, hands scrambling for purchase on the chair, half in, half out, nerves shrieking. He was going to touch her, with those hands, those hands. A scream battled its way up her throat and somehow she hit her panic button, and she *was* screaming, thank Christ, because please, please, please don't let him *touch* her and the passenger in front was on his feet, the whole plane was rising from its slumber, lights were flickering on, fragile, sleepy eyes turning to her, a stewardess rushing up the aisle, and she couldn't wriggle her *damned* long body away, and the panicky realisation that she was getting in the way again thumped in her brain.

All the voice lessons she had so lovingly learnt hit the ceiling, cracking the silence, saving her.

2

Jeanette Anderson studied the table in front of her and wished that she was somewhere else. Some fool had taken a knife to the wooden surface in a vain effort to feign immortality *(Devon wuz here. Booyakka!)* and she supposed he had the right. He would probably live out his life and do nothing more remarkable. Around them the waiters shuffled. The lunch hour was well past and the restaurant was preparing for siesta, girding its loins for the evening rush. She hoped they wouldn't still be sitting there, in this iron silence, when the evening came. They'd probably try to fling them out by then anyway. She wanted to get away from it all, from this known boredom, from the man who sat across the table from her. She didn't want to feel regret. Regret might tie her to him for another three years, and she couldn't bear that. She had fallen out of love with her life slowly. She felt like a stone, a great boulder that had stood for years and somewhere in that time a single drop of water had fallen, glistening on her surface, faltering its way to the centre of her. With the changing months she had become colder, and the tiny moisture froze, hurting her, cracking her open, and she knew that the only answer had been freedom. Freedom to leave this life.

She hated the way it had become a ritual. Wake up, work at the shop down the road that sold bric-a-brac, golden cherubs at Christmas time, chocolate hearts in February, incense all year long, and who the hell cared about what the consumers wanted anyway; the regulars coming in and they knew her name and it offended her; the sameness of going home to Mamma, cut up the onions and the scotch bonnet pepper; Mamma's cheap, bright earrings that she always wore glinting in the light, they were so bloody naff; and are you going to see your sister again tonight, you know she not bringing up that pickney right; and then walk home in the dying gloom, meet up with Charles, Charles who she'd chased solid for three weeks, using every single flick of hip and eyelash, every brain cell, every bit of punani power to get, and didn't he see that single teardrop inside her freezing and expanding every day, didn't he see that she could be more than this, more than their twice weekly sex ritual, put it in, take it out, cuddle, and there no *more*?

"So that's it?" he offered. The question lay between them as the third waiter asked if he could refresh their drinks.

"*No.*" Charles put a hand over his glass. She could feel him thinking if this woman's leaving, the bitch *sure* ain't getting a next drink outta me. He was vindictive when he was hurt.

"That's it," she said.

He dipped a finger into the glass and swirled the liquid there. "How long have you known?"

"About uni? A month or so."

"No, Jeanette. Known about *me*, leaving *me!*" His mouth twisted into a single, solid line. She reached out a hand to restrain him, but he shook it off. "Why you never tell, me, eh, Je?"

She looked at him. "I'm telling you now."

He leaned back. His mouth worked. "You leaving for university doesn't mean we have to done."

"Don't," she said. He let her place her hand over his and she felt an old feeling. It was never that she didn't want him. Just that she wanted more. "Don't make this difficult."

"Well, I'm fuckin' sorry I'm making it difficult for *you!*" His face was a mass of mixed emotion. Misery, rage, bewilderment. He leaned back again and glared at her. "You always were a bitch."

She raised an eyebrow. "Fuck *you!*"

They sat in silence. He refused to look at her, one knee twitching in agitation. She fought back apprehension, tried to find words. Had been, all afternoon, since she had told him that a place in London waited for her, a chance to *be*. But there was no-one to make it better, no-one to explain that her leaving was due to no lack in him. What moment could have made it different?

The truth was that she didn't know what people meant when they talked about love. The flowers and chocolate hearts hid some kind of secret that she had never felt let in on. Dull affection she knew. She could feel a tightening dampness between her legs as he looked at her, but pushed it aside. She had wondered if that was love, the first time they laid down together, touching the puckering milk on her thigh as she pondered afterwards. And when she was able to walk naked in front of him, the first time she had let the breeze fall free on her body in front of a man, she had wondered again, is *this* it then?

She didn't know how to answer him because she had never had the answer. She wished that she could be happy, marry him, settle down, do what seemed so easy for others. How cruel that she couldn't.

"Is it that bad?" she asked "Is there nothing left?"

He smirked. "Friends? You want to be friends, Jeanette?" He signalled for a waiter, and two leapt forward, shoes scuffling. He flung some notes on the table. "I'm leaving," he said, and rose to his feet, the collective sigh of the waiters soft behind them. He was a short man — a scarf round his head, pliant shoes on his feet — who liked an occasional spliff and t'ing, could wine till you cry, was polite to her mother, could lift her giggling niece above his head until she hiccuped herself to sleep and he wasn't enough.

"Why you have to be so? Stay with me a while."

He laughed. He couldn't stay. If he did, he would find himself at her feet, clinging to the smell of her, and he wanted to save one thing for himself. He wanted to remember himself strong. But he couldn't help pausing, to ask. "When you going?" he said.

"Friday," she said. Long plaits in front of her eyes like a wave. *Let it stay there until I go, please*, he thought, *so I can't see her eyes*. If he didn't see her eyes he could hold onto himself until Friday. He could stop himself begging.

Jeanette watched him walk away into the dust of the high road. She took a deep breath, tucked her aloneness around the edges of her body. She'd keep it down until she got to London. She'd savour the wait.

Life was about to begin.

3

Alexandrea turned to the contents of her flat and sighed. The boxes were neatly packed and labelled for the bathroom, the bedroom and the kitchen. Jackets hung over the door, carefully encased in plastic; each plate and precious ornament had been folded in newspaper and then encased again in beige or yellow or green tissue paper, so she had yet another way to identify them on unpacking. She picked up the final piece, a little statuette in chrome and miscellaneous metal. It had been a Christmas present from Nicola, a small figure behind a desk with a typewriter on it, a diminutive, personalised name plate beside it on which her identity stood in black letters: Alexandrea Watson. Journalist. Nicola had bought it in a shop in Oxford Circus that made them to order, for accountants, butchers, farmers, anything you wanted. A minuscule pencil holder held equally dainty, silvery pens. Beside that, a little newspaper. Nicola had found a photo of the singer, Sade, and the manufacturers had obligingly stuck this to the model. Above it, the name of the paper: *Black London*.

Alexandrea smiled, ran a finger across the words. Already, her days as an arts reporter at *Black London* seemed far behind her. Perhaps she would ask Nikki where the shop was, get them to change the name plate to Television Researcher. That, after all, was what she would become on Monday morning.

She walked around the flat, her bare feet soft on the cheap, but good quality carpet. She and Gerry had quarrelled over the colour; he had been sure that its dull yellow would clash with everything else, but she had known it would brighten their home. He'd had to admit she'd been right. Not that it made any difference what he thought now. He was gone.

The small bin bag leaned against the door. It looked forlorn, all on its own, but she couldn't bear to have it standing beside anything else. She reminded herself for the third time that morning that she should dump it out in the skip at the back of the building. She moved forward resolutely, but found herself on her knees, fumbling for the knot she'd tied into it. She knew it wasn't a good idea, but still, moments later, its contents littered the floor.

Letters. Some fading at the edges, all still faint with the smell of his aftershave. Gerry had thought it cute to send her pongy letters through the post. She had been embarrassed every time the postman slipped one through the door, but relieved too that Gerry understood her need for just that kind of declaration.

Other lovers hadn't understood that under her ambition was a massive neediness. They had given her books, practical things for the house, clothing. Only Gerry had known that she wanted poetry, flowers, sticky toffee and expensive chocolate, and yes, she admitted it, the stuffed dog that stood, melancholy, next to the cinema tickets for the film they'd seen on their first date, and tulip petals, dried and strewn through the rest of the things. Perhaps he had known nothing at all. Perhaps he was just tedious that way. Perhaps all his ladies — past, and, she felt a pang as she thought it, present — had soft toys and tulips. It wasn't imaginative. He hadn't been imaginative.

She filtered through the remains of their relationship with a heavy hand. He had forgotten a shirt, soft and willing, the colour of bricks. Of course he had had to leave it. She'd been wearing it in bed the morning she had woken up and found him gone. Just a note, scribbled in his manic handwriting, that she uncrumpled and looked at:

I'm sorry. Have to go.
Will call.
Your Gerry.

Of course he had signed it that way. He signed everything that way, the terribly bad poetry he'd left on her pillow, or on the fridge for her to laugh at. They had all sounded like childish nursery rhymes, banal, repetitive, rhyming. But she had loved them. She loved him. Bleary-eyed, through sleep, she'd thought the Dear John letter had been another one of these offerings, and had sat in their bed, reading it, trying to understand how dreadfully wrong this poem had gone, and what could it mean? Then the finality of the words had hit her and she hadn't known what to do. Who was she without him? Friends didn't even know her name anymore. They had become an amalgam dubbed Alex-and-Gerry. It sounded like one word: Alecsungerry. Who was she without people looking over her shoulder, expectant, for him, and who was he without the same? Was he somewhere else now, a new entity, Michelle-and-Gerry, Lisa-and-Gerry? Was it that easy?

She poured it all into the bag and sat back on her calves. The pain, huge and somehow radiant, had not gone away. Of course, it lulled to an impassive ache when she was working, or when she drank. The drinking was a little something that was teetering on the edge of a problem, and in August, on her birthday, she had resolved to take it in hand. She had poured the lager and the whiskey and the vodka down the sink, overpowering their *(my)* little kitchen with the smell. Hadn't drunk since. And she had stuck to that for a whole month. But Lord, it was only the second day of September, and she wanted one. Just a small one. No, actually, a massive pint of something that she could pour down her throat and drown in.

Alexandrea was no fool. She knew exactly what she was doing to herself, weeping over dead memories and pouring alcohol down the hatch. Over the ache was a living anger, but she was not the kind of person who accessed that feeling easily. Nicola kept telling her to let it out, cuss the damn fool, cuss him out, even in your mind, for leaving two years of a relationship like some damn fly-by-night, too 'fraid to talk to you about it. He was a jackass anyway and you're too damn sexy to be thinking about him for a minute more. But she couldn't find the words to condemn him. If she dismissed him in that way she would be dismissing all they had had, all the whispered promises and the lovemaking and the shared dreams. And then what would it all have been for? What good would it have been? If she dismissed Gerry as a fool, that made her a fool for loving him. She couldn't do it. Not yet. So she played a tape recording of their days in her head, over and over again, assuring herself that when he too realised that the situation was ridiculous, when he got sick of the playback he would return. Even now, a day away from moving in with Nicola, she hoped he would knock on the door. She imagined him saying he was wrong, that she was right, and how could he ever, for one moment, have thought that a life without Alecsungerry was anything other than empty? She would delight in unpacking, no, she would make *him* unpack, put their lives back in order, and then they would both go and pick up Nicola at the airport. He would apologise, of course, for putting her best friend to so much trouble. It would all work out. Perhaps Nikki would see their love and decide to move in with Julius. And she'd go to work and show them a thing or two.

The fantasy clicked its way through her head, colourful, almost real, as she took the bin bag down the stairs and left it there, a light steam rising upwards from the burst bag next to it, tomato skins and tin cans rotting in the cold air.

4

Alexandrea smiled as she watched Nicola stride out of the customs gates towards them. She had company as usual, four of them this time, hanging on. Two of the men trying to keep up with her were passengers, clutching luggage and boarding passes. The third was an official looking gentleman with a bald head and trousers that clung, awkwardly, to his ankles, ballooning at the hips. He reminded Alexandrea of John-Luc Picard in *Star Trek*. Except clumsier. A baggage boy brought up the rear, admiring Nicola's legs, goggle-eyed. Nearly every set of male eyes in the vicinity had joined his. Nikki's magic was strange: the ability to draw people *(men)* like butterflies, sore with anxiety to please. Alex felt a small pang. Nobody would ever, or had ever, left Nikki. She wondered what that was like, never feeling rejection, never having to wake up to an empty bed if you didn't want one. She chided herself. There were few people she knew who deserved love more. She supposed that her friend got it because she gave it. She was open, her scent invited acknowledgement. It was part of the natural order of things.

If she had really thought about it, she would have realised that if Nicola was open, she herself was a closed bud. Full of potential, yes. But her understanding of herself was overlaid by pragmatism. She didn't just want to flower. She wanted to succeed. At everything.

The tall man standing beside her shifted impatiently. "I wonder what's happened," he said. "That man isn't just chatting her up. Something seems to have happened." They watched the Picard lookalike waving his arms around, obviously discomfited. The other three men nodded. A chorus. Nicola's head was on one side, listening, then she stuck her hand out. Alexandrea grinned again. She could see the man pulsate in pleasure as their fingers touched.

She glanced up at Julius. His eyes were fixed on his girlfriend as if he had never seen her before.

"Does it bother you?" she asked.

He tore his gaze away and tried to concentrate. He knew Nicola's body language. As a director it was one of the things he noticed first. She was pretending, but he saw the tension. He looked at Alexandrea.

"Sorry?"

She tilted her chin in Nicola's direction. "Does it bother you when other men . . ."

"No." He was lying. Ever since he and Nicola had started their relationship he had known he was in a position that most men would envy. But he, too, was used to people looking at him. Even as they stood there he saw a woman staring from across the concourse. He hated it when people recognised him. He felt as if he owed them something, but exactly what was difficult to define. At least Nicola could guess: the glances she got were always about sex. Men wanting it and women hating her for it. When someone looked at him, their impressions were overlaid with their own personal reverie about who he was: famous director, the constant rumours regarding his sexuality because he kept his personal life out of the papers, whether they'd liked the last production or not, his insistence on solitude. He could see the question lit up, electric blue in their heads: WHO IS JULIUS FRASER? It offended him that they should presume anything, having never met him. The woman yanked at the arm of her partner and whispered, pointing. Mercifully, her husband was not as interested in star spotting. They passed on. Julius glanced around him. His publicist had wanted to come to the airport with them, but he had put her off. *At least let me walk as a normal man*, he had grumbled.

"He-llo . . ." Alexandrea tugged at him.

"At least I know what they want from her," he answered.

She looked at him quizzically. "And you don't know what they want from you?"

He shook his head.

"They want to be acknowledged," she said.

"I don't understand." He watched the woman glance back at him.

"Does she just want me to say hello, smile, give her an autograph?"

Alexandrea laughed. "That as well. But in the end, it doesn't matter. She becomes somebody because she's seen you. Watch her at bingo tonight, or talking to her children. It'll be 'I saw Julius Fraser today in the airport. He was standing with a black woman. He wore a green tie and jeans. He was waiting for someone.' And then they'll try to guess who it was, who I was, how you were feeling, whether you looked like a nice man." She paused. "It's a guessing game. Celebrities are our gods now. We look to them for something we lack. You have the power to make them *feel* every time they see one of your plays. And that makes them wonder. It fascinates them. They want to know you and how you do it."

Julius raised his eyebrows. "It's that complex?"

"Aw, c'mon, Julie. Didn't you ever admire someone? Don't you admire any celebrity now, even though you are one?"

"I can't say I do. Oh, sure, I've admired people in my time. But never to the point of hunger. And I've met most of them now, anyway. So have you. You've probably met more famous people than I have."

"That's why I know," she said. "One thing that continually fascinates 'stars' is how they're perceived. And they'll talk about it, if you press them." She grinned. "Like you are now. Oh, look — here she comes!" She stepped forward to greet Nicola, who was walking towards them. "Girl, you get a tan!"

Nicola tripped and fell forward slightly. The men gazing after her looked bleakly on as Julius steadied her. She flung her arms around him and put her face in his shoulder. Despite himself, he glanced around. No-one was looking.

"What's wrong, sweetheart?" He kissed her quickly.

"Oh my god, there was this *man* and he was jerking off beside me on the plane and I just totally freaked —"

"WHAT?" Alexandrea bristled. "Did he hurt you? Did he touch you? Are you alright?" She plucked at her friend's long, toffee-brown dreads. Nicola turned to her, bending for a hug.

"I'm alright. You should see de bloodclaaht ugly bwoy! Me nearly bawl. Woke up the whole rass plane."

It constantly amused Julius that even though she was a foot shorter than Nicola, Alexandrea often took on the role of her protector.

"— then they took him into another part of the plane and handed him over to the police as soon as we landed. That man I was just talking to apologised and said that next time I flew they'd bump me up to first class —"

She was getting more animated. He pushed aside his anxieties and pulled her into his arms again. She looked at him. Her eyes were too bright. "Calm down," he said softly. "Calm down. You're okay . . ."

He felt her relax slightly. Alexandrea looked away.

"Am I?" Her eyes were large, pupils expanded.

"Yes." He soothed her with the word.

"Yes." She shivered. "Damn you. You always make me acknowledge what I'm feeling." She tried to smile. "As for firs' class, dem mussee t'ink seh idyat don' travel in style too. Like I'm safe from the wankers of the world just because there'll be personal TV's and champagne, to rass."

"You've got the accent back," Alexandrea observed.

"Weh you ah try say, gyal? Me is a Jamdowner, born an' bred!"

"Yeah, but you get Cockney when you tryin' to chat up British men though!"

Nicola drew herself up to her full height. "It's hard being me, innit?"

The two women broke into laughter, clinging to each other. Julius took a firm grip on the baggage trolley and watched them giggle. Nicola was a long drink of water. The skirt hugged a tender waist and legs that looked a mile long, stretched flames of muscle and gold. Once they had been on a train and a black American man had leaned forward to him as they had stepped on to the platform. *Throw that ass into the air and it'd turn into sunshine,* he had joked, leering. Julius had spent moments imagining how good it would have been to throw the Yank's head into the air and watch that turn into sunshine, but he had controlled himself. Nikki had smiled.

Alex was neat. Tiny ears set back against a small, well-formed skull. Hair a silken helmet that forced you into the depths of her eyes. A body cut from a single, dark-hearted stone. Nothing superfluous. She skirted five feet tall and was tougher than she looked, antiseptic where Nicola was redolent. And quick. Sometimes he felt as if she could see inside his heart. He was glad that she had never interviewed him, and could understand why she was good at her job, why she specialised in celebrity profiles. Once she turned her searching gaze on you you were hard pressed to lie. Or insult her with superficiality. He couldn't understand why she was switching to television research. She was a writer. An observer.

Nicola was pulling at his elbow. "Tell me, how's the move going?"

Alexandrea scowled. "Trust you to leave us with all the work."

"You mean you didn't spend all my hard-earned money on a removal van? What happen? Because I know that Julius hand join church!"

Julius teased. "Please don't speak so much Jamaican in my presence. You know I don't get it."

"He's just trying to stop me from telling you that he paid for the whole thing," Alexandrea said.

"Julius! You didn't! You know I hate it when you —"

"Oh be quiet, you ungrateful cow. The man's doing you a favour." Alexandrea swiped at her friend's rear end.

"But —"

"Nikki, shut up!" They were in unison. Nicola laughed as they walked towards the exit. "Me see seh the two of you gang up on me while me gone, eh? What else you been doin'?"

They linked arms.

*

Five hours later the two women collapsed onto cushions in the living room of their new home, panting, smiling in tired glee. Nicola's three cats wound their way through the pile of boxes in the hallway, playing rough and tumble. The living room stretched out in front of them, large and airy. In one end, Alexandrea had piled throw cushions in deepening shades of blue and yellow, but here and there were other colours: a large blood-red heart, an indigo one of indiscriminate shape, another like a huge orange sun. A television, VCR and stereo crouched at the other end, next to stacks of CDs where jungle mixed with blues that rocked with soca and danced to disco from the eighties. A weirdly shaped vase held court on a side table. Shaped like a snake, the sunlight flew through it and created iridescent patterns against the wall. Alexandrea had insisted that it be placed there, a present from a favourite cousin. They had a cheerful argument about it. Their friendship had always been punctuated with arguments. The softer Nicola battling the harder Alexandrea. What they had in common was words.

The house was large, an old brick-layered monstrosity that Nicola had discovered through an estate agent before she'd gone on holiday. The two of them had fallen in love with it on their first viewing, Alexandrea delighting in the large garden at the back, poking around, imagining what it would look like when the weather changed and she could get the trowel out. There were three bedrooms, but the last was so small that they had decided to change it into a study. Books had been unpacked onto shelves that Nicola banged together, both of them knowing that with the PC sitting on the small pine desk it would be Alexandrea's domain. She would be able to look past the slanting roof and smile at her gardening efforts.

By unspoken agreement Nicola had bagged the master bedroom, upstairs at the front of the house, with big bay windows that she could sit in and dream. The movers had sworn and sweated getting Nicola's bed up the winding, antique staircase. It had been the staircase that had sold it to her. Wrought iron with cunning patterns cut into the frame, she could see herself poised at the top step, then descending gracefully. "If you don't fall flat on your face," Alexandrea had pointed out, laughing.

Strip board floors had been polished to a high shine downstairs, with a champagne carpet in the master bedroom and dove grey in the smaller room. Nicola would have been happy to fling the red sheets she already had on the bed, but her friend had hintfully bought her a cream set. Alex liked things to match. The house had both dining room and living room, but they had decided to convert the original living room into a bedroom for a third flat mate when they found one. Nicola had insisted on this as there was no way that a lack of money was going to keep her from this house or her fantasy stair descent. All the rooms were large and airy, wall to wall cupboards in the bathroom, washer and dryer in the kitchen, a clothes line stretched across the garden. Their landlord, who had been living there, was recently divorced. He'd cried when he left.

Nicola got up to snap on a lamp, and then, on impulse, took a bottle of white rum from the refrigerator. She began to sprinkle it on the back steps, the scent filtering through the fading winter day.

Alex regarded her with frank amusement.

"What are you doing?" she asked.

"Old Jamaican tradition. You have to christen the house."

"Are you sure you got it right? That *stinks*!"

"Of course I've got it right." Nicola flapped a hand at her and sploshed a little bit more. Alex was not convinced.

"Aren't you supposed to rub the rum on your chest and then sweep the spirits out of the house with a broom?"

"Cho, gyal, me know what me doin'."

"Rubbish. I tell you, you need a broom. I brought one from my flat."

Nicola turned to glare at her. "Who live in Jamaica for fourteen years?"

Alex smiled. "You. But I'm sure I read somewhere —"

Nicola advanced on her menacingly, the bottle held aloft. Alex began to splutter, scrambling to get out of the way, but her boots scraped ineffectually at the carpet.

"You wouldn't dare!"

Grinning, Nicola tilted the rum. Wet patches scattered across Alexandrea's T-shirt. "Bitch!" She dived for Nicola's feet, making her stumble. They toppled on the edge of disaster as the cats ran from under foot. Nicola finally managed to kick the lighter woman off and, clutching the uncapped bottle, collapsed once more on the sofa, laughing uproariously. She took a swig and choked mid-giggle. Alex pounded her back, slightly too hard.

"I don't know where I'm getting the energy from. I'm pooped."

Alex propped herself up on one elbow and looked at her.

"Your eyes *do* look like pissholes in the snow . . ."

The other woman grimaced. "Out of the mouths of babes and best friends!"

Alexandrea examined her top. "I won't be your best friend anymore if this stains," she said.

"I'll buy you another one."

"After swanning off to the Caribbean I doubt you've got any money left."

Nicola looked away, momentarily embarrassed. It was true that her bank balance had been depleted by the trip home. She was hoping that Julius' play was going to take off in a big way. Alexandrea guessed her thoughts.

"Hoping for the big one with *Summer Alienates*?" she asked. Nicola pretended that the production was like any other, but she knew her friend better than that. Nicola wanted this to make her one of the major players. She had watched her ambitions grow over the last couple of years. Others wouldn't have seen it, but Alex knew the nature of the beast. She herself had wanted it since the tender age of six. Power. If she had power she could make sure that no-one suspected her insecurities. Work balanced the emotional needs. She wouldn't have been able to articulate it, but she knew that if she was a good journalist she could forgive her heart its foibles, its bad choices in men. Give her power and it wouldn't matter.

Nicola was staring at the wall. "Julius would be really pissed off if it failed," she said.

"Forget him for a moment. What about you?"

Nicola closed her eyes. "I don't want to think about it. He said it was stupid for me to go off to Jamaica three weeks before we opened, and I'm beginning to see why. I didn't want to say it to him, but I think I'm forgetting all my lines." She changed the subject abruptly. "How have *you* been? And I mean *really*?"

"Fine," Alexandrea said. She'd woken up out of a million dreams about Gerry while Nicola had been away and each had left her as sore as the last. She felt like a stuck record, playing the same phrase over and over again.

Nicola noticed that Alex was biting her thumbnail, something she did only when she was under pressure. There had been a lot of that recently. Physically, Alex looked much the same, but there was a fragility in her that hadn't been there before. Alexandrea had always been the leader, decisive, articulate. But she found it hard to finish sentences now. She would drift away mid-conversation, eyes like dark, wet pebbles. The night before Nicola had left for Jamaica, they'd gone out for a drink with friends. A heated discussion had taken place, about explicit lyrics in music. Alex had always been the one who rose to a challenge, but that night she had curled into a ball as the debate raged. Finally she had slipped away. And although she had not drunk anything — specifically refusing the cocktails — she had looked as if she had wanted to. It had been odd. It was as if Gerry had broken something small but essential. A cog, a wheel, removed a pin or twisted a lever. She tried to be light. "Any pretty boys at Monique's party? She always has men all over the place. Makes me wish I was single."

Alexandrea sighed. "There was this one guy . . ."

"But he wasn't Gerry, right?"

She had tried so hard for the party: put on a little green dress and the silver earrings her brother had given her for her 24th. And sexy underwear. Rich, peachy lace that rustled when she moved. She had always taken comfort in good lingerie, enjoying its feel, the secret of what was underneath all her own. She was a sensual woman, for all her outward control, and had an erotically charged relationship with herself. She remembered walking into a furrier once just to feel the furs, passing her hand through mink and fox, smiling. Her sheets were always crisp cotton, the best she could buy, her shoes plump with shiny leather, she kept flowers on the windowsill that she buried her face in and perfumed lotion that she would rub into every nook of her body. But at this party even the secret joy of her body couldn't help. Gerry's departure had made her even more insular.

She couldn't bear anybody's touch. Monique's hug had made her start back, and the play just now with Nicola had bothered her, not because of the stained top, but because she had been forced to touch somebody. It was wrong. Nobody was Gerry. His absence echoed in everybody else's fingertips. She couldn't bear it.

Nicola spoke gently. "Sweetie, you can't be wasting your life. I know I might be out of line, but it's been three months. All I want you to do is let someone take you out to dinner. Just to talk. Let them tell you you're pretty."

"He wasn't my thing," Alexandrea said. Her throat hurt.

"Did he have a job?" Nicola joked.

Alexandrea rolled her eyes and tried to smile. "Yes . . ."

"Treat you good?"

"Mmmm-hmmm."

"Was he good-looking?"

"If you like that kind of thing." She didn't want to have this conversation. Apart from the fact that he hadn't been Gerry, despite the fact that he had worked in advertising, his eyes had been blue.

Nicola had a look of triumph on her face. "He was white, wasn't he?"

"Nikki —"

"Bwoy, you don't have to feel no way. I know you don' check for that. Look how long I know you. I just think, well, when you feel better, you could give it a try. One day. Just to see. Look at me and Julius. He's irie. We get on. We're compatible, we want the same things, we have the same interests. Doesn't matter that he's white."

Alexandrea felt the old tension rising in her, the same way it did every time they had this discussion. The thought of dating someone who wasn't black offended her. Julius was nice, but she could just imagine the pitfalls. How could he understand the basics? How could she walk with him through London as a black woman, feeling the pressure, and not go home and hate him, even for a moment, for what he represented? She bit down the thoughts. They'd never agree on this one. Never.

Nicola was continuing, the cats now piled on her lap. "Boy, I'm trying to understand. But it doesn't make any sense to me. I know you want a brother man, but there are negative sides to that as well. The average black British man is so busy trying to beat down Babylon he don't have no time to sweet you up."

Alexandrea wondered how she knew. She'd never seen Nicola with a black man. Not even for five minutes. Irritation prickled her, and she knew the subject had to be changed. Her smile was weary.

"I'll have to keep putting up with the shit until I learn better."

"Oh, Alex . . ."

"Forget it, Nikki. I have to get ready for tomorrow anyway. First day at work and all that." She rose to her feet.

"Let me help . . . ," Nicola said.

"Nah. You're tired too. I'll see you in the morning."

Nicola listened to her patter up the stairs. Eventually she headed for her own room.

5

Nicola Aster Baines looked at herself in the mirror. It was a nightly ritual that was so precious, so private, not even Alexandrea knew about it.

The mirror was her special possession, for a myriad of reasons. Her father had given it to her. It had been the night before her second audition at the Royal Academy of Dramatic Arts and she had been quietly hysterical with fear. She was all of seventeen, set to read a part that she had written herself. She knew that she could be an actress, she knew it. And she needed a role she could make her own.

She had been engaged in rewriting herself for several years before that evening. She was slowly becoming the person she wanted to be, the person she could become if she tried hard enough, concentrated hard enough, believed enough. And she had written this person down, on a piece of paper. The character's name was Mona. Mona was sassy, sexy, strong. She always had men at her elbow. She had dignity, poise. She made people's heads turn. In the short monologue Nicola wrote, Mona was talking to herself after being beaten by her lover *(after a time it doesn't hurt there are no tears but he chips away at me and I long to be born again and to be fresh and new, a fresh soul with no memories)* and the most important thing for Nicola was that Mona was *beautiful*. She was *bursting* with it, and when she moved through the room people could sense her beauty as if it were in their pores, not just their eyes. This was why Nicola wanted to be Mona; she craved acknowledgement, and Mona *showed* them, all of those kids who had teased her for being a bloodclaaht bean pole, and a red neigar, and a brown gyal whose main sin was that she thought she was nice and when she got to England, cold England that bit at her skin all the time, and puzzled her, it was worse because she was too fackin' tall and too fackin' big for her boots and not white or blonde or blue eyed or anything that the ads said were pretty (*I want to be so new that there will be no prints on my fingers, my eyelids only soft folds and my genitals a simple question mark*).

She supposed that her own personal pain was hum-drum, really. All kids got teased at school. Mostly about the way they looked. Look, that's the fat girl, the black girl, the hairy girl, the pimply girl, the girl that's a right slapper, the girl that sucks dick, the girl with the big nose. There was always something and she knew that she had fitted right in as the tallest girl in the class, the first girl to wear a bra, the first girl to think she was *nice*. But that was the problem. If she had ever thought she was nice she could have hidden underneath it, shielded the blows. But she had never thought she was nice. She wanted to get to her knees in the classroom, if only to be on everyone else's level, not to tower over everyone else, not to be noticed. She wanted to have different hair, not the kind of neigar, nappy-headed brownish stuff that her mamma struggled to comb out every morning. *You're a St Elizabeth red neigar and there isn't one thing you can do about it,* her mother had scolded her. *Be glad that you're not too black, and don' sit on that cold floor, you'll get a cold in you dan-dan.* But she had known that she was ugly, bean poley, red-skinned. So she had begun to rewrite it all in her mind. She wouldn't be Nicola anymore. As Mona, she would turn heads. Mona didn't care about tangly hair. She just went dread. She stepped out as Mona five minutes before the audition. The examiner who had watched the piece was impressed. Very impressed. He watched the tall, black girl grow, flower on the stage, passion making her face shiny and anger making her face beautiful. *My God, she might just be something,* he thought. *She might just be a Great Talent.* He didn't realise that much of his impression was based on the rounded curve of hip and breast in front of him. Regardless of his lasciviousness, he was right. Nicola was a Great Talent. When she left the theatre she knew that she had been accepted. She knew because suddenly she was Mona. She had re-birthed herself and could see it reflected in the melting eyes of the men, and the jealous eyes of the women.

But you could re-birth yourselves too, she thought.

It had been daddy's mirror that had given her the final courage to become, and most importantly, sustain Mona. Everyone else had been

33

pleasantly surprised; they thought drama school did it, that she was finally getting her confidence into gear, they had always known she would do it. Only Alex had looked doubtful at the swift change, but she had come to accept it. The old, ugly, scared Nicola that she had had to protect was gone. The world accepted Mona.

Only Daddy had known. He had come into her room with the mirror. It was old, and cracked at the edges, but he had polished it with a loving hand, and mended a break at its base. "Is you grandmother it used to belong to," he had explained gruffly. She nodded, excited but not showing it. It seemed to be an affirmation on his part. He shuffled his feet at the door. She waited. "Ah know sometimes you feel . . . well, not so nice as de odder girls dem —" he tried, harshness coming into his voice. "Look at you! Look at how you look like you gran'mammy!" His voice was an accusation, but she knew what he meant. Granma had been beautiful, in hips and heart, and she was frozen with the delicious possibility that she *looked like that* in his eyes. She wanted more, but he was gone, and she was left with the mirror. Now, each night, she stood in front of Granma's mirror. Looking at the sweeps and curves. Making herself Mona for another day.

There was a knock at the door. Nicola hurried to cover herself. Alexandrea stood there, an apologetic smile on her face.

"Remember Troy Bennett?" she offered.

"Yeah," Nicola said. She moved away from the door, and Alex stepped in, sat on the edge of the bed. They sat together, admiring the welcome home cards that Nicola had been sent, the corner of the room where she had proudly placed the programmes from her six plays, the old posters framed and polished. The cats had followed her upstairs, like silent shadows, patting the corners of the room in curiosity. They remembered. When the two had first met, in middle school, Alexandrea had been asked out by Troy Bennett, who was, according to popular consensus, the *original* bit of alright. Floppy-haired, only just starting to sprout pimples, he had been, nevertheless, tall and strapping, and the hair that waved uncontrollably was like vibrant corn husks. He had invited her to skate at Crystal Palace ice rink, and, Nicola in tow, she had spent no less than four hours getting ready, alternately crying, laughing, and biting various parts of her hands. After they had finally decided that jeans were her best option, at Nicola's insistence they had sewed buttons into her T-shirt. Her breasts were just growing, and Nicola had sworn that the buttons, strategically placed, made her look as if she had permanently erect nipples. Once on the ice, a single damning button had come loose and fallen, sparkling, and somehow *huge*, crashing, it seemed to Alex, into view for the entire *world* to see, and of course Troy Bennett, who hadn't been able to take his eyes off the 'nipples' since he had picked her up, reached out for it, like a real gentleman, stooping on the ice, and halfway out of the crouch, about, say, chest level, had realised he had a bogus nipple in his hand. He had laughed as loud as it was possible for a young boy to laugh, which is pretty loud when you're on your first date with a real boy. A real boy who has corn husks for hair, and actually uses aftershave, even though he had probably stolen it from his dad. Alexandrea had fled, tripped, cracked her wrist on the ice, burst into tears, heard the nipple story relentlessly for the next month, over which period she could not be brought to speak one word to the hapless Nicola, and generally identified it as one of the nightmares of her life.

Like most friends, they told it and retold it, to others and to each other. A celebration of the past, hope for the future.

"Probably what put me off white men in the first place," said Alexandrea wryly. Her quick hands rolled at the joint in front of her. She didn't smoke marijuana, but Nicola couldn't roll.

They spun out the evening slowly, telling mutual memories as the light dimmed behind the trees and the musty smell of weed clung to their home.

6

The bus was enthralled. Jeanette was dancing in the aisle.

No-one could have denied the beauty of her movement. Every twist of her torso, shimmy of her hip made them all, for just one moment, forget. Forget all the things that we have been taught matter. Forget gender. Colour. Fashion. Morality. Religion.

She danced and the dance was unique because it made them remember. She didn't know that she puzzled a small woman with a head of hair so golden that it was almost invisible into thinking about the day she lost her virginity.

Jeanette danced.

A youth, whose trousers were crisp and clean, wondered in embarrassment whether he had any skid marks. A 32 year old typist, huddled in the corner watching the rain, remembered that she hadn't eaten fresh vegetables for a long time and fantasised about the crunch of celery all the way home. There was arousal, one woman who thought of Jeanette for months afterwards, and the man who drove the bus felt inexplicably as if he would burst into tears, even though moments before he had carefully avoided touching an Asian's woman's hand because he had heard that Pakis used the right for eating and the left for you know what.

Jeanette danced, oblivious, the earphones placing the music in her bloodstream. She danced to reggae, but she also danced to life, and a baby who gazed at the smooth brown of her waist, from the vantage point in his pram, smiled and reached out a chubby fist.

She grinned in return and leaned down to tap a rhythm onto the child's cheek. The boy with the skid marks smiled, delighted. He didn't understand why. She straightened again, and danced. It was a strange, moving experience for her audience. They could hear no music, so she danced silently, bending the suppleness of her waist, hitching her shoulders, just so, to blend with the one-two from her hips and the three-four from her feet, clad in Doc Martens that didn't dare to drag her down. She danced silently and she made them dream.

Everything was the dance: she shifted to ease the heavy knapsack on her back, and even that was a part of her choreography. Under her slashed T-shirt the muscles in her back swayed and righted. She tightened her stomach to compensate. The cold of the sleeted day didn't seem to touch her. The passengers warmed to her, huddling behind coats and gloves. What was most touching about the way she moved her body was her lack of self-consciousness: she was dancing for no-one but herself, the movement was in itself an end, a reason for being. She was unique, singular. She was something different for every person who met her. She was a chameleon and she didn't know it.

No tilt of the bus or whisper of the passengers entered her field of consciousness for the time that she danced. She was the same when she made love. Charles would look down at her and wish her eyes open, but it never happened. She would share with him in the beginning, conceding to his warmth, taking him into her body with passion and a kind of graciousness, as if she were inviting him into her house. As quickly as he was inside her, he would feel her politely excusing herself as release rocked through her body. She hummed when she came; he had never heard the tune before. When he asked her for its name she laughed at him. *You're a mad geezer. Everyone else would be loosing themselves in my fanny, but you? You hear music?* It was another example of her instinctiveness, her ignorance of the effect she had on people.

Ever since she had climbed onto a London train that morning in the wake of her mum's tedious warnings of the necessity of a constant appreciation of God the Father and querulous questions about the state of 'her purity', she had heard the voices in her head *(now you free girl, you free, you can free up the system)*. The closer she got to London, the more the delight threatened to blow off the top of her head and scatter her plaits to the four winds. She wasn't unkind, but she was a woman of extremes, and over the last months of her young life she had felt the bit between her teeth, restraining her, even more bitter because the days to freedom seemed so long.

Ah now she ah go get weh! her mother's neighbour had warned in tremulous tones. Everyone had said her mum was wrong to loosen the apron strings, that she'd get into a bad crowd in London, but it was such rubbish. As if there weren't bad crowds everywhere, if you wanted to be with them. As if Manchester wasn't stuffed to the gills with smackheads and angels alike, like anywhere else. *Everywhere I go, drugs and innocence,* she thought. *Drugs and innocence.* She didn't know why the sentence should whirl its way around her head so.

She opened her eyes. The conductor had promised to give her a nudge when they got near the uni, and now he was obliging. She stepped off onto the wet pavement. The bus rolled on, its occupants trying not to look at each other. The woman with the golden hair didn't know that her fingers had disappeared into her paper. Two women kissed next to the girl who wanted celery.

Jeanette sucked her teeth. This was the third bloody time she was coming in to this damn university to try and sort out accommodation. She had been promised a place on hall, but didn't you know it, the system had fucked up, and here she was, sleeping on her cousin's friend's sister's house floor, with Mamma calling every day to ask her how she was doing. *I'm developing a damn backache, innit? What you think I'm doin'?* Of course she would only talk to her mother like that in her dreams.

"Can I help you?" The registrar's assistant was all smiles.

"I have an appointment to see Miss Reid."

"And what is it regarding?"

Jeanette could feel another kiss-teeth coming on, but restrained herself. "It is regarding the fact that you forget who I am every time I come in here!"

The assistant looked shocked. "Well, there's no need to take that tone!"

Jeanette could feel the woman looking at her, at the top that bared her stomach and the cheap gold chain through her belly button and the shorts that left her batty out-ah-door and the 22 hole DMs and the long plaits, with the silver and blue ribbons threaded through them. She felt a savage stab of pleasure: at least the stupid cow was actually seeing her. "Look, luv. I don't want to be rude, but she knows why I'm here. It's the same reason I was here yesterday, and the same reason the day before. I-need-accommodation. Why the hell do you *think* I want to see the housing officer?"

The woman turned to her filing cabinet, lips pursed. "Name?"

Jeanette sighed. "Jeanette Anderson."

"Year?"

"First."

"And the name of the course you're doing here?"

"Jesus Christ. Do you think I'd try and lie my way into your poxy accommodation?"

The woman's lips tightened. "Course?" she repeated.

"Bloody Psychology, alright?"

"Pardon?"

"Psychology." repeated Jeanette, through gritted teeth. "Foundations of Modern Psychology. Biological Basis of Behaviour. Childhood and Adolescence. Thinking, Memory and Language. Laboratory work. Oh, and this may be of interest to you —" The woman looked up. "— Abnormal Psychology. It'll probably teach me why they employ old farts like you in the first —"

"Jeanette?" The housing officer was standing in the doorway of her office. "Can you come in here, now?"

With a glare at the simpering assistant, Jeanette stepped into the room and shut the door behind her. The assistant listened attentively. She was such a rude girl. Of course she had remembered her. She did every time. She was hard to miss. She had presence. But she was so forceful, so loud. Coming up to the desk in her bovver boots and her outlandish hairstyle, and that irritating 'Alright?' She was at a loss to explain her deep feelings of annoyance; in five years she had seen a lot of angry students and a lot of heavy boots. She sighed. There was something about this little miss. She sighed again. She could see a cloud of paper rise and fall through the misted panels of the inner office. The little so-and-so had probably thrown them up in the air. Another cloud floated upwards with the sound of angry voices. She decided to give it two more minutes then call security. She tapped the desk as the sounds carolled from the office.

Psychology indeed, she thought.

*

Bill Waivers was 62 years old. He'd been in what he called the 'ale an' ailin'' business for thirty five of those years. No-one had ever had their way with Bill Waivers, that's to be sure. Not his wife, gawd rest her soul, not any one of them daughters of his, or his strapping son, come to that. So Bill Waivers marvelled at the way this slip of a coloured girl had him wrapped around her little finger. He smiled to himself, rasping a thumb across stubble. And he hadn't even got his leg over. Not that he wanted to. Well, not really. She was a kid, innit? At the end of the day he felt he was doing her a good turn. That was another thing. As long as he, Bill Waivers, had lived and breathed he'd never done anyone a favour that he could remember. As it happened, she was the only one.

Jeanette. He'd known a girl called Jeanie once, but Jeanette said she wasn't no relation. Not that she could be of course, not coming from the West Indies, and all that. Jeanette who'd been tending bar for him for three weeks, spilling his good pints all over the gaff, getting the hang of it. He had roared at her, good natured like though. Didn't want to frighten her. Not that she frightened easy, that one. He remembered the day she'd come banging into his pub and demanded a pint, just like that, in the broad daylight, and him not even opened up yet. She had just barged in — he supposed it was his ruddy fault, he'd left the door open for some air to go through — and she had been steaming like hell, ready for a punch up with anybody. After thirty five years behind the bar, Bill Waivers was no idiot, but he knew when to throw them out and when to let them drink, so he'd given her a pint and watched her stew, puff those stinking fags of hers, and had amazed himself by listening carefully to her business.

She was a right one, and no mistake. She was a looker, with all that hair down her back, like one of those birds in a magazine, and her skimpy clothes. She dressed like a slag, but then, that made her a hit with the customers, innit? A pretty bird like her could afford to show some meat.

He grunted. Not like her indoors before she died. She was a good woman, Lord bless her and all, but she'd had more chins than a slanty-eye's telephone directory. But, back to Jeanette. Before he'd known where he was he'd offered her work for board. And they'd been snug in that for nearly a month now. She'd tend bar with his daughter Mary come the evenings, and in the days she went off to that university up the road.

He would never have admitted it, but he felt like family to her: she was feisty and deserved a bit of luck. He smiled as he heard her footsteps on the stairs. Not that he'd let her see him smiling, of course. She might get sarky.

"Alright, Bill?"

"I keep tellin' you to call me guv. What's wrong with yer? Wax in yer ears?"

She laughed in his face. "Why don't you come and have a look?"

He turned his back to her, reaching out for a stack of glasses. "Dirty mare. Keep yer hands to the punters."

Jeanette began to sort out clean ashtrays. She could smell the sour stink of the place on every part of her. The smell of a pub was like no other she'd ever come across; her mate Eve had told her that she'd tossed around Europe seeking that smell every where, but no luck, not in French wine bars or Italian eateries or Danish red light districts. That lotsa fags as many as you can smoke ten pints of lager and a curry farts breath of the hardworking and not so hardworking lads on a night out stink.

It was the only thing she didn't fancy about working at The Wine and Sow. The smell seeped into her pores, it stuck to her clothes, it crawled in her armpits like fleas, malignant, insistent, stirring her at night while she tried to sleep. She was afraid that they could smell her at uni, in between lecture courses and tentative new friendships. When she tried to get clean she couldn't. Turn on the water for a bath, fill it up with all the Body Shop stuff that you could, and it was still beery belches and cheese and onion that poured out into the tub. It was comforting, but only comforting in the way that a bad habit was as it happily ate away at your liver or your intestines.

The smell was the only thing she couldn't stomach. The rest was wicked, and no mistake. She wouldn't have told anybody, but she felt like a queen in this pub. Uni made her feel good, but in a different way. Working bar in this place was *naughty*, it was just the kind of thing that would have made her mum drag Christ down from Calvary to complain. She laughed. The way she heated up this place come Friday night, Jesus would probably have been well informed: *Jeanette? The barmaid from The Wine and Sow? 'Scuse me, luv, I'm well in there.*

Not that they were all dirty sods. Even then, she enjoyed all the punters. They were so different, but so similar at the same time. She knew that Andy had a missus, and was straight as a die, but Steve got corked every weekend and was spending all his savings. Pete was a sweetheart, really, with his jokes: they were vulgar, but she felt as if she had been let into a very old men's club because she was privy to them *(why did the sheep shagger lead the sheep to the edge of the cliff we don't know go on then mate because the sheep pushes back geddit?)* and they were so easy to please, it was touching. So simple. All it took was a smile, letting a slap on the bottom go by, a laugh and a joke. They lit up like Christmas when she smiled, and it was as if there was no other woman in the room.

She knew that many women wouldn't approve of the way she allowed them to get grubby and familiar. But they knew the score: she was working bar, and a bit of slap and tickle didn't mean that she was going to get angry. As long as they knew when to stop, she was happy. They knew her name, some of them knew the names of her courses, took an interest. That was fun. She'd get to nattering so much that Bill would have to call her back to service.

She liked them all. They were good to her. But God knew, this couldn't go on. The stink of the pub was getting to her, and the pokey room Bill'd let her have could hardly hold her clothes, let alone her books. It wasn't the place to study. And she wanted to be making a wage from Bill, not just working for board. With that and her grant she could look for a bedsit or flatshare. She started sweeping the floor.

That was when Mary came back with a copy of the morning paper.

Mavis

Ah remember de firs' white man me ever see up close. Him was a teacher from England an' him did come out fe teach literature at me school. We never know it was goin to be a white teacher; de teacher before was black, an' she did jus' go 'bout her business an' lef we. Me hear seh she ah breed fah de principal, but me never coulda prove it.

De mornin' we was sittin' an' standin' an' rampin' in de classroom an' suddenly de place hush up an' silent. Him look like Jesus, standin' dere in de door. Long brown hair an' ah dashiki top like him wan' look black. Me never know why him woulda wah do dat. De hair fall on him shoulder an' when him lean ovah de desk in de days we woulda look up in him eye an' see de sky. An' we used to laugh because him wear sandals, dem show off him long toe dem, an' sometimes one odder clumpy foot shoe look like me granny boot. Him breath smell like icy-mint. Him have a small scar pon him cheek. Me cyaan remember whether is de lef' or de right one. Sometimes him woulda jump up like him mad inna de class an' dash weh de book dem an' talk out Shakespeare an' odder English t'ings from him heart, like him know alla dem. De girl dem did grumble because dem 'fraid seh dem wouldn't ready fe tek de tests, but me did like watch him. Me never business wid de tests. Woman nuh really fe do dem t'ing deh. But him did mek de book dem sound nice. Me never undastan' Shakespeare till a white man read it to me. Maybe das why him coulda do it so good; maybe black people too fool-fool to read dem white t'ings.

Him did love de young girl dem. De firs' time him try somet'ing was wid a girl name Charmaine. She was tall an' yellow, an' kinda fool. Eighteen an' still ah go high school inna fourth form. Him use dat mek excuse, tell her seh she need extra lesson ah him yard. Of course she go; she did love him off like the rest ah we. Even though she fool 'bout de school work, she wasn't a idyat when it come to man. Every time she go fe de class dem she carry her likkle brother wid her, seh she haffi babysit. De brother wasn't one ah dem renk pickney, him would siddung every time an' min' him manners. But de teacher couldn't get fe try nuttin'. Ah guess if it was one ah dem dutty black bwoy like Frankie him woulda try feel her up same way in front ah de pickney, but him have some decency 'bout him.

Charmaine tell me seh de house where him live always clean an' tidy, an' she couldn't believe dat him cook an' clean for himself: no helper at all. De man all wash him clothes! But Charmaine seh all him do is stir-stir dem round inna de bath. One day she ax him if him want her wash out some t'ings before she do de lesson. I guess dat she was goin' so long an' nuttin' nah gwaan dat she let herself down. Get careless wid herself. T'ink seh because she yellow an' pretty seh she can jus' smile an' she nuh haffi sex de man. Or maybe she want him. Anyway, she leave her brother in de livin' room.

Jus' as she ah rub up de clothes an' hear dem scrups-scrups wid de soap, de white teacher come behind her an' turn her an' kiss her. She seh it was funny, because him lips feel so thin an' maaga like s'maddy jus' come an' suck de air outta dem. Her mout' jus' ah slip offa fe him own. She put her hand up in him hair an' tell him seh it soft, an' him start get crazy, kiss up her neck an' squeeze her crotches like him goin' to dead off. She seh she really never wah do it, but me nuh believe her. She did well want him grin' her. De man pretty like Jesus, what more she want? Gyal like dat always b'un up inna Hell, ah talk foolishness like she have sex wid de Lawd! Me know seh she widen out her foot dem. She realise seh de reason him eat so much icy-mint is because she can taste de rum on him tongue, an' when him wet up her neck wid de saliva she feel like bees woulda bite her because it was so sweet-up an' sicky-sicky wid de liquor. De whole of her back bruise afterwards an' her head wet up because him bend her over de bath-water an' nearly get bleach inna her hair.

Ah used to sit inna de class an' watch him an' wonder if him know dat de whole ah we know 'bout him thin lips an' him dirty clothes an' him clean house. About ten ah we him was fuckin' one time. Not me. Maybe me foot too tough. Part ah me woulda like deh wid him, doah. At least if me could touch him hair. Sometimes me did want to give in to de sin, throw everyt'ing away an' jus' do de t'ing, stop de wetty-baggie gyal business an' jus' skin out wid s'maddy.

Me sit inna de class an' dream seh me have pickney for de teacher, an' when dem come out dem have icy-mint eyes an' in me dreams dem come out on a wave of red rum an' de teacher ah stan' at de bottom of de hospital bed tellin' me how (you have a pretty pussy such a pretty pussy) *him love me. Alla de gyal dem want to breed fah man like dat, you see. If we couldn't get a man like de teacher, dem like de puss-eye bwoy dem, wid red skin an' clear eye. Mi madda always caution me seh me nuh fe bring home no bwoy dat too dark* (How you fe prosper if you pickney dem black like you) *but even though she woulda like fe see me wid a pretty brown bwoy, she know seh me not good enough to get a white man. Me prove her wrong later on, but dat's for another time.*

Me t'ink seh white people strange. Me wonder if dem ever t'ink 'bout de fact dat dem white, and me wonder if dem t'ink 'bout it, whether dem heart glad ovah it. You woulda t'ink seh dem feel good fe wake up inna de mornin' an' see seh dem white, look inna de mirror an' see seh dem white. We all know seh de Lawd did bring down punishment on black people fe mek dem black, dat is a punishment in de eyes of de Father. De whole ah we mus' remember dat when we look inna de mirror. Ah remember de biggest disgrace me ever see inna me life was one time when me ah walk through Brixton, ah walk up inna de place ah smell de stink, pick up de yam an' seasoning weh me need an' me sight a stall wid de biggest abomination. De man ah sell picture of a black Jesus! Me couldn't believe it, never see such a t'ing inna me life! Me start cuss de man like a dog, seh him ah blaspheme, but him facety, come cuss me back, tell me "Sister, Jesus was a African prince!" Jesus never even feel to go dem place deh. Is ongle de goodness of him heart why him continue to love we even though we curse him name. An' de man ah call me 'sister' like me an' him breed inna de same belly. Me did call down scandal pon de man dat day.

One of de t'ings me nuh undastan' 'bout white people is how dem deal wid pickney. After God put him mark of love on dem, dem go outta street an' breed up wid de ole black bwoy dem an' get mulatto pickney. Ah can undastan' why de bwoy dem ah run it down, but you t'ink seh de white gyal dem woulda prouder dan dat. But no, me dear. Dem spread dem legs. Ah suppose all people haffi learn. Me did learn say spread-leg business ah nastiness. Never bring anyt'ing but trouble. What it good fah, eh? Some likkle sweetness an' de man dem do dem t'ing, an' baby probably come an' den you haffi deal wid dat. Of

45

course, was a time when me did love it, feel sweet dat de man dem outta street did want me. But not now.

Not now.

7

The curving shimmer of Endeavour Productions gleamed at Alex, and soaked the bleak morning into its concrete hide. Late September crackled and laughed at the world, as if the cold was a merry joke that it was playing. She wished her first day could have been one of those oppressively hot summer ones that seemed less rare in London now, days when the moisture in the body rushed to meet the humidity of the air around it, and you could feel them crash together in mid air, an explosion that set off the process again.

The menacing building looked far less inviting than a summer park. She could have eaten peaches and watched the white people. It was fun, seeing them toss off their clothes at the first ray, turning crimson, tying bandanas around their heads, or big bouncy hats of straw or cotton, tutting how hot it was. She got into conversations with strangers, joining in the clamour, commenting on the weather. The answer to her gentle grumbles was always the same, especially if the white person was older: *Oh, but you must be used to this in your country* or *Well, you don't need to be sitting in the sun, do you dearie?* She would play this like a game, to see how many would give her the same answer. Most of the time she got annoyed at their ignorance, at their pride in their ignorance. Other times she felt bewildered. She'd been born in Bermondsey, and felt like yelling it at them. Occasionally they just smiled and nodded at her polite conversation, and she would play with all the theories in her mind *(A: This white person agrees with me that it's hot, full stop. B: This white person thinks that I should be used to the weather because I am black, but is too polite/hypocritical to say so. C: This white person doesn't want to be talking to a black person. D: This white person hasn't seen me because I am black, and has merely grunted because they heard a noise. E: None of the above.)* because she was intrigued with them. She didn't understand. She watched them as if they were sheep. As remote and different as that. Crowded into the tube she felt like the only human. Until she spotted another black face, could exchange a single look of mutual understanding. Julius, of course, was human. But she could not see herself being able to know him as anything other than Nicola's man. His blindness, like all their blindness, made depth impossible. Sheep.

"Baaa-aaah . . . ," she muttered to herself, letting Endeavour swim back into her vision. A man across the road looked at her curiously, and she felt embarrassed. Taking their turns, came pride and fear. She was proud to be here. Sixteen thousand a year wasn't big money in this business, she knew, but it was a far cry from what they had paid her at *Black London*. She was proud that she had got this job, with no experience.

Fear danced around her feet, keeping them from moving forward. She remembered her interview two weeks ago. The show's producer, Jenny Tasdell, was loud, confident and friendly. Alexandrea had looked around for evidence of the show's presenter, Ruby Fleur, but there was no sign of the shifting, changing, nut-brown woman who fronted the programme twice weekly. She concentrated on Tasdell, who had bad skin artfully covered up with base, and the longest, thickest eyelashes she had ever seen. Tasdell leaned across the desk and clasped her hands in front of her.

"Let me give you an example. Suppose we were doing a light hearted show, say 'My Hair Is My Crowning Glory . . . Sometimes'. What kinds of ideas could we incorporate, who would you choose as guests?"

Alex took a deep breath. Images floated in front of her eyes and she wanted to close them. *(Braids and beads and plaits and tongs and cream don't itch your scalp what a natty head to afro or not afro that is the question braids and beads and plaits —)*

"Alexandrea?" Tasdell had prompted her and she wondered how many seconds had passed. The producer wouldn't give a damn about the good-hair bad-hair issue, whether or not you should relax or go natural. Maybe she would have liked to know that Ruby Fleur's hair was not her own, thick and straight and black down her back *(ever put your hand in her hair and felt the stitches, Jenny? I bet you haven't)* like a waterfall. Straight off the heads of women in Thailand and China. Dead hair. She and Nikki had taken the piss out of Nikki's friend Linda when she had trilled about Naomi Campbell's short back and sides: "Have you seen Naomi's new 'do? Imagine being brave enough to cut it all off, when you've nurtured it for so long . . ."

"She didn't . . . she didn't . . . cut it off . . . ," Nicola had stuttered, trying to keep a straight face.

Alexandrea had done Linda no favours. She clung to her belly as the mirth poured out. "She just took out the WEAVE!" she gasped.

"So . . ." Linda paused and looked at Alex's head timidly. At the time she had been the proud wearer of Cleopatra Braids. "That's not your . . ."

"Oh, it's mine, alright," Linda looked relieved. "It's mine because I —"

Nicola and Alex chorused together, "— PAID for it!" They had fallen off Linda's sofa laughing. Things had never been quite the same with Linda after that.

Words finally came to her. "We could look at whether blondes really do have more fun. Get Mandy Smith and Mariella Frostrup in to talk about how easy or difficult it's made their lives, find someone to talk about transforming from blonde to brunette and vice versa." It was banal, but she knew it was what they were after. "And, well, no-one thinks about men and their hair, or them having bad hair days." She dug her nails into her hip. "Maybe we should invite Sanjay from *EastEnders* on — he has enough of them."

Tasdell's laughter had echoed through the office. "Fine. How about if we were talking about breasts?"

"Big ones or little ones?" asked Alexandrea, feeling her own chest itch under the cashmere suit she wore. They laughed again. She had figured she had a good chance. She was right.

Poised at a new beginning, she felt vulnerable. She knew that she was too controlled. Her need for autonomy and order was large and, it seemed, growing larger by the minute. She used to think that the older she got, the less inclined she would be to demand that the milk in the fridge was in a particular place, that would-be boyfriends arrive at a quarter of the hour, and wear a suit if they could find one. As she edged towards twenty five years of life she saw her hold on it grow tighter and tighter. The more she worried about the extent of the grip, the more she held on, each feeling feeding the other. She worried that she worried too much. She wanted to know exactly what was going to happen to her, today and every day.

"It would make it so much easier," she whispered to herself, feeling the concrete at her feet. Her heart thudded in her chest as a car zoomed past, sending up clouds of noxious gas that made an invisible layer on her face. If she had known that the car was going to pass she would have been able to make *preparations* for the smog. It would make her life precise, she could plan so much more effectively. She would have known not to buy Gerry two hundred quid's worth of Karl Kani if she had just had a list *(10:25 am. Wake up. 10:27 am. Sneeze. 11am. Wander through flat and realise with dazed clarity that the man you made love with last night is gone. His stuff is here, but there's that note. 11.12am. Read same)* and so on.

"Alexandrea Watson?" Someone put a hand on her shoulder and she jumped, thoughts of Gerry fading. She turned to look at the man. She was impressed, and it was a relief to have a new emotion to cut the churning anxiety.

Tony Pearson. Known well by most. He had risen up the media ladder as fast as anyone could have wished for; at eighteen the BBC had accepted a script from him for the celebrated *This Is Black* drama series that went on to win an Emmy award as well as six BAFTAs. By 25 he was writing nearly a quarter of the company's entertainment drama. The reviews were love letters. He managed to remain 'black enough' for his own too; he had risen and preserved his integrity. It had been a crushing blow for the Beeb when he departed to the small but cutting edge Endeavour stable. *He must have taken a huge pay cut,* she thought. Still, he was their senior producer. Perhaps the fact that he was spearheading black talent soothed him: he had talent spotted Ruby Fleur himself, walking along Oxford Street, just like Naomi Campbell.

He was Alexandrea's boss.

Pearson smiled down at her. He was, she decided, twice as tasty as he was on the society pages. The bottle green suit fit him so well that she knew it was custom made. His legs were long, and here and there was the firm impression of muscle, hip, thigh, buttock. The shirt was crisp; you could imagine it slicing at your wandering fingers. The mouth. Teeth in shining rows. He had moisturised his hair that morning, she could smell him, noted the gleaming shoes. She saw all of this very quickly. It was what she was good at.

"Er . . . Mr Pearson. I'm so sorry. Have we met . . . ? Of course, we haven't. I would have remembered —" She laughed nervously and cursed herself for the fractured sound.

He smiled and she felt her internal camera go in for a close up on the thick curl of wrinkles that fanned the corners of his eyes.

"No, no. I'm sorry I startled you. We didn't meet when you came in for your interview, but Jenny pointed you out when you were leaving the building. Said you were our new researcher." His grin deepened. "You looked a little lost. I thought you might let me escort you upstairs. It is your first day."

She was flustered at the mental image of meeting her new colleagues with Tony Pearson at her side, but collected herself. "Thank you so much. It's just that —"

"Nervous about appearing teacher's pet?"

She was perturbed by his insight. She was wary when people saw too much.

"Don't worry about it. Jenny will be there, but not many others. I'll leave you at the entrance." He took her arm and steered her through the front door, nodding firmly to the security guards and receptionists. Alexandrea was gratified to see them smile, to see this black man shown respect. Not that she could ever hope to get a man like this. Pearson had been married for years; everywhere he went his wife was there too, a smiling shadow. They had done a spread in *Hello!* when they were first married. He had been in his thirties then. Alex had been fourteen, and they had been the first black couple she had ever seen in the magazine. She had admired Mrs Pearson's pretty face. The portraits put her below her husband, looking up at him adoringly. Alex had thought this appropriate. The way you *would* look at a Prince Charming.

The elevator door slid open and he let her step inside.

"Know what floor you're on?"

"Oh —" she had planned to ask one of the receptionists, but the swift movement from outside to the lift had crashed that. Pearson's eyebrows bent together briefly.

"Fourteen. You're on fourteen."

She kept her chin up and her spine straight. Small voices picked at her *(you're stupid, you're stupid, he must have thought you looked a right idiot standing in front of the doors, not coming in, so he had to come and ge—et youuuu, youuuu're stupid, stupid, stupid —)* sing-song and accusatory, and for long moments she fervently hoped for death. These voices had long been with her, old enemies, worrying and nagging. They came during times of stress, and she could have handled them if she didn't feel overwhelmed in that department. She had all but got rid of them at *Black London*, her first job, straight out of university, interviewing famous people and though they had tripped her up once or twice *(you just asked Seal a question you should know the answer to, what kind of journalist are you, he knows, everyone knows that you're stuuu—uupid . . .)* she had fought them off, listening to them becoming dimmer and dimmer with every successful piece of work she wrote. More intriguing, were the moments when the tension inside her exploded into confidence, even arrogance, when her back was against the wall. A light would push past the Stupid Voices and words would pour out of her into the waiting computer. Sometimes it shoved out through her mouth, and she was cheeky, mischievous, spirited. It had been an occasion like this that had got her fired from *Black London*. The editor had been telling her for at least the fortieth time that she deserved no more money, none of the arts journalists did, even though there were only three of them slaving, dashing around like rats after stories, the music journalist running a high temperature but not daring to go home, all of them exhausted, and she'd risen to her feet and given the woman in front of her detailed instructions on how to fit an AppleMac past her anal sphincter, *sans* lubricant, and that had been the end of it, really. She'd been jobless, but she had glowed for days afterwards.

"I read some of your work at *Black London*," said Pearson.

She didn't know whether it was a compliment or not, so she kept her lips firmly together.

"I was very impressed by your interview with Wesley Snipes. You have a keen eye for detail."

"Thank you."

"Nice little touches. The way you noticed how his contact lenses matched his tie, and used it as an analogy to illustrate a subtle pretentiousness."

She laughed to herself. He had been paying a great deal of attention — and he had his own pretensions. She gulped down pleasure and contempt, used to deflecting compliments. "He was easy to interview," she said. Wesley had been charming, but it had been incredibly difficult to get anything from his lips but haiku-like sound bites. She had sweated raw detail out of him with a mixture of manipulation and flirtatiousness, and lovingly shaped it into copy. She was proud of it.

Pearson's eyebrows drew together again. "Bollocks. You could tell he was a difficult bugger. You just didn't let him get away with it."

Alexandrea tilted her head to look him in the eye. Her shyness drowned in the light. This was her work, her groove, and she could play frank too. "OK, he was difficult. And I cracked him." She ran out of steam as soon as she started, and the last line was faltered. "Thank you for, you know, noticing."

Pearson looked up at the ceiling of the lift, which had slid to a smooth halt. He pushed the CLOSE button, delaying the doors. "Eye for detail. Discipline. Determination. Ego. And a sharp tongue in your head." He moved the finger and the doors opened. "You'll either go far or fuck up badly." She wasn't sure what to say, but he spared her, nodded at the hallway. "Turn left. Then right. Have a nice day."

He was gone. Alex glanced at her watch. She had ten minutes to get to the Ruby Fleur office and *(your Gerry what would your Gerry think of you getting a compliment from Tony Pearson)* her smart outfit seemed garish against the subtler hues of the corridor. She bit her lip, tasting the vaguely metallic lipstick there. Then pouted. The clothes on her back were clean, for God's sake. What more could they want? They had employed her and that could only mean she had some potential. She stepped forward.

8

Nicola stood on the doorstep and hugged the breeze to her shoulders. The sound of the bell echoed in her mind. She had missed him. The way you miss the glass of water that sits on your nightstand when suddenly it's not there, and you are fuddled and confused and feel that something indefinable is not right.

She didn't realise that she was falling in love with him. That would have surprised her. A fine young man in Jamaica had been pestering her with more than usual finesse, and he had finally concluded that she must love off some English man bad, bad. But she was so used to her usual reasons for avoiding such as him *(who needs the race politics in bed with you)* that she didn't realise the growth of genuine feeling. All she knew now was that she wanted to feel Julius. All over. She could hear the shuffle of his don't-care house slippers on the floor as he came towards the door. She smiled, knowing that journalists like Alex would have loved to know these little details about Julius Fraser. She wondered if any hack had seen his down at the heel footwear. It illuminated his whole personality. Soft, warm, run-down, in need of darning and polishing. *(That's what I do for him, I mend him.)*

He opened the door and she stepped into his arms. Muffling an exclamation through the piece of toast in his mouth, Julius clasped his hands at the small soft patch in her back and pulled her into the house.

*

The zoom lens on the journalist's camera recorded it all tenderly, kissing the image of Julius' crumb-covered cheek, capturing time. The journalist paused and then depressed the shutter once more. Twice, three times as the pair came together, belly to belly. He captured the arch of her calves and the angle of his jaw. A second later he preserved the minutiae of pores on her skin, made grainy and rough by the paper he soaked it onto. The shutter noted the tilt of her hips and the openness of her smile, and la-de-da wasn't it all fine and dandy mate, wasn't it like a song.

"Why do foo-ools fall in lurve . . . ," the journalist hummed to himself, *sotto voce*. The click of the camera faded into the chuckle of a squirrel. He thought that Julius Fraser *would* have squirrels in his property.

"And that's the way, folks, of the world," he muttered. "They get squirrels and I take the photos of them that's got 'em." He smiled.

*

Nicola listened to Julius carefully. As usual, he was talking about his baby, *Summer Alienates*, his latest offspring, his voice swerving with pleasure, his brow creased in anxiety.

"So, do you think you're ready?" he asked, abruptly.

She stroked her own hand, wishing he was touching her, and returned his stare. An hour in front of the mirror that morning had given her back her confidence. "What do you think? You saw today's rehearsal. Has the vacation hurt me any?"

Their fight over the Jamaica trip had been bitter. She hadn't told him why she needed to go, she hadn't even told him how her mother had died. She told no one, so it had been there between them, his ignorance, and his fear of favouritism. Julius, despite the rumours that slipped and slid around him, had never, before this, slept with a member of his own cast. Oh, they had wanted to, he knew, many of the fledgling actresses (and actors) out for a break and a piece of his pie. But he had feared notoriety, disgrace, all of his career.

Nicola had surprised him. With her talent, of course, which was unmistakable, but also with her warmth. They had become careful friends, talking theatre, film, beauty, late into the night, he always making sure that there were other people around so their communication couldn't be misconstrued. He was charmed by her clumsiness, and secretly collected the scribbles she made on old napkins. But she had known, one day he had slyly inched one from under her empty glass. It had read, simply: *Try.* So he had tried, later, in his office, when for once nobody was there, and he hadn't known that she was amused at his anxiety because it was she who had made sure no-one would be there. They had started to touch each other over the table, and he had wondered whether they were going to have sex like kids, on the floor, and hadn't wanted it that way, not really, he felt he was past all that, and she had said the right thing, as she always seemed to. Again, simply: *Take me home.* And he had explored the newness of her brown, anxious body, swollen with desire, in his own bed, where he had lain for several nights wondering what she'd be like. He'd counted the beauty spots on her. Fifty-two, he said. She'd insisted there were fifty-nine, and once more it had been the right thing, he felt jealousy, which was unlike him, an otherwise confident man, because who was it who had known her so well that he had found the other seven? So she showed him.

He was irked by her privacy. He would try to reach past a certain place with her, and she would stop him with another right word, put him off track. He had begun to realise that he knew very little about her, that the growing intimacy between them over the months had been about *her* gleaning information, taking his secrets. She gave the impression of great openness, but it wasn't true. She was this golden-brown person, who, when you scratched the surface, only yielded more golden brown perfection. He had never met her parents, as she refused to discuss them. Meeting Alexandrea had been only recent, and he knew that even if he had questioned her — and his sense of decorum would not let him do this — but if he had, he suspected that Alex had very little to tell, even after ten years of friendship.

That was why he didn't want her to go back to Jamaica. Not merely because of *Summer* rehearsals, but because he felt that she was going to something he was kept from. Something that might lure her away before he had a chance to crack her puzzling secrecy. Something that would make it even harder than it was now. That, and the way she had announced, *announced*, for God's sake, not even asked, that she was going, and he had been astounded by her nerve. Was he being taken for a fool? She would lose it, that edge that she needed for the first night, the blood-feel that had to be whipped up into a frenzy of waiting and mixed with the feeling that came when the hairs stood up on your neck before you stepped on stage. Surely, like all actresses, she needed that. But no, she had asked that her understudy step in for two weeks. He had raged. It was out of the question, people would talk, it would fuck up the flow, the cast would hate him, her, the gossip and anxiety would spread like a cancer and the whole thing would fail. He had raged *NO*, and like most men for whom power has always been there, from the reality of being the first son, to a growing brilliance that all around him had come to take for granted, he had thought she had accepted it. But Nicola had thrown it open for discussion at the next day's rehearsal, she had put it to a *vote* for Christ's sake. As if he had ever run his ship that way. And unanimously, he had watched the talented bunch of professionals vote that she could go, they would manage. It was as if they wanted to make her comfortable. He had watched them defy him, in effect, taking their vote, and as she had turned to him, with her gaze *(like no other)* she had smiled at him like she was smiling now and he was a teenager again, knowing that his face reminded all comers of the long muskiness of a dachshund, and he had nodded, mute, if the majority was fine, he was fine.

He hadn't thought that it could get any worse, but she had made it so, stretching, no, running gleefully over the line.

"You all know that Julius and I are lovers."

It was a statement, not a question. He had seen the whispers, and having never done it before he had been at odds as to how to deal with it. In his arrogance and fear he had left it to the murmurings of the corridors, but she, Nicola, had been there again, speaking out. The nods made him want to die, but it had been alright. There were smiles with the nods. For him, for her. "Julius doesn't want me to do this because he's concerned that it will be seen as favouritism," she had continued. A chorus of disagreement, the understanding, bobbing of heads continued. "So, I won't go if it is a problem for any one of you," she said, folding her hands. She had won them all. And in rehearsals today she had flowed. They all had, defying his theatrical experience. It had been fine. Fine in the way that a man turns towards the fire that he has nearly fallen into, and greets its heat.

Nicola leaned forward, plucking at the lines on his brow. She touched a blonde hair on his chin. Once. He forgot the play and groaned. They leaned towards each other over his jam and his toast and kissed lightly, exploring the tiny hurricane of thoughts and emotions between their lips. Teasing, she blew into his mouth mid-kiss, and he gulped in her breath, surprised. He blew back, and they giggled, and he remembered that he hadn't giggled in years.

*

Alexandrea unfolded her hands and sighed, watching the woman sitting across from her on the tube. The child on the woman's lap was dirty, his face a smorgasbord of ice-cream and snot. Her stomach did a slow turn. She forced her mind back to the day at Endeavour. By lunch time her top lip had bled beads of sweat, despite the cool office. Around her, people had been talking about rostrum cameras and edit suites and the researcher next to her insisted on bellowing into his phone.

"What do you mean, he can't come? I must insist that he honour his contract. A car? Well, of course, man. Who the bloody hell do you think we are? The BBC?"

Her dread grew with his decibels. Five other researchers flapped and hummed. Tasdell had greeted her with a coffee, a long list of gay organisations, a brief explanation — "Next week's show is 'Mum, I Want To Tell You That I'm Camp As Christmas'. Get twenty five people from this list to come in as audience." — and had disappeared into her office with a huge Danish and a no-nonsense manner that she had not dared to try and pierce for the whole day. She waded through the list, doing the best she could, struggling to make light of the titbit Mr Bellower had given her when she picked up the phone — "Stress they have no guarantee of speaking. If they make it to the mike, or get Ruby's attention, maybe. But those are not main guests." He seemed to have all the main guests, the ones who were being sent cars. When she spoke to people it hadn't helped that most of them had burning attitudes regarding Ruby Fleur, who was in turn crap, a jewel in the crown, rubbish, the best thing on telly since Cilla, a bitch feminist, gorgeous, and fake. They all wanted to discuss The Episode They Had Hated The Most, and expected her to account for real and imagined mistakes. Alex had fielded accusations as best she could, and tried to stick to the business of accumulating numbers. As soon as she had her twenty-five and reported hesitantly to a senior researcher, she was handed another list, this time for 'My Boyfriend Beats Me, Help Me To Leave Him', and the whirlpool sucked her in once more. Confused and irritated, she had mistakenly re-dialled one of the gay organisations and started her spiel about girlfriend beating. The man on the other end told her she was an unprofessional cow, and hung up. Absurdly, a reggae tune had danced in her mind *(I am the gyal with the wickedest slam)* as a young girl across the table shot her a sympathetic glance. "Some of them are very tough," she said. Alexandrea smiled back, peeling back her layers of reserve. It was clear she'd need a comrade in this war. The girl, a redhead, waved a cigarette pack in her face. "Fancy a fag?" she'd said. They'd broken into laughter.

She turned her mind back to the journey. It was opening night for Nicola, and she wasn't looking forward to it. If it had been anyone else she would have given it a miss and gone home to a hot bath. But she had promised, and to stop now would have been the lowest travesty. To make it worse, she had never seen Nicola on stage. It was an embarrassing reality between them. At *Black London* she had been too anxious to do a review of her friend's work, fearing partiality, and fearing even more that she'd hate the small, but worthy things Nicola had done before. Now it was easier. She could sit and enjoy the thing like any normal punter. More importantly, this was no two-penny production. Julius' work was waited on all year, and to be in his cast at all meant kudos. To lead could make Nicola's career.

Realising she had time to kill, she got off at Leicester Square and wandered down towards Piccadilly Circus, peering in windows that were already brimming with Christmas gifts. She stopped in a sweet shop in The Trocadero and bought a pound of fruit gums in the shape of plump red lips. She thought they'd do for a post-mortem, however the night went. She watched a drag queen wriggle his way through the crowd and wondered how he managed to navigate his bright blue stilettos. The queen caught her eye and smiled, his mouth a slash of scarlet lip gloss.

He was wearing a flimsy gold jacket over a t-shirt that was hilarious: QUICK, PHYLLIS! GRAB A DYKE AND DANCE YOUR WAY OUT, IT'S A RAID! She muffled a smile and the man strutted on. She hoped he wasn't heading for a nightly prowl of yobs. She found the stage door in a little back alley, where a harassed stage hand checked a list and waved her to a door with an obligatory star.

She twisted the knob then walked in, and stopped, a gasp in her throat.

Nicola was in full make-up. The room was littered with mirrors that cast her image, crooked, satin-painted, reflections of reflections of reflections, curving chin here, a cheekbone there. Her eyes filled her face, lashes brushing brows, casting delicate shadows on her mouth, sticky and slick, like varnish. Alex had a confused impression of the character that lurked within the script and then it was gone as her friend turned towards her, filling the mirrors anew with the more familiar stretch of her long, golden back, where glitter and moles marked its surface. Her smile was almost shy.

"Hi," she said.

Alexandrea stared.

Later, she stared some more, as she watched her friend, simply, purely, become someone else. She noticed tears on faces as Nicola marched and writhed across the stage, ripe, juicy and, in the final act, drained, taking the audience with her for every nuance, every emotion. As the curtain fell she found herself rising with everyone else, rising to her feet as they clapped, and stomped, and Julius was called on stage and raised Nicola's hand to the ceiling, to the rhythm of the cheers and the whistles, and she wanted to know how it felt, to change, to be what you are not, to make others feel. Her own work could never challenge this immediacy. She was glad. It was too much power.

The package of jelly lips lay in her purse, an empty reminder of a celebration she could not have foreseen.

*

The papers arrived at their usual, designated time, thumping onto the hall floor, alarming the cats, who performed a hunting dance around them before getting bored. Alexandrea wiped the sleep from her eyes and grappled with one of them over a cup of cocoa. Nicola hadn't woken up yet and she wanted to scan the reviews before the other woman got to them. She thought that Nicola would probably be asleep a while longer; they hadn't got in until three in the morning, Alexandrea drunk on cheap red plonk and Nicola just high on the evening. She did not feel good about the alcohol. But everyone had been celebrating, and she had taken the glass as if hypnotised, sunk herself into the cardinal depths. It had started off as one, but she seemed to remember giving up on glasses and chugging back the bottle. The evening had started differently. When she had managed to fight her way through the craziness backstage — people seemed to have come from nowhere, clapping each other on the back, embracing, kissing, darlings and sweeties flowing on the air as press hounds congratulated, snapped photos and recorded quotes — it sounded like a convention of *Absolutely Fabulous* fans. Alex couldn't see Nicola anywhere. She spotted Julius with a mike in his face and waved to get his attention.

". . . and really, I am awfully glad it's gone so well, and hope the critics feel the same way as tonight's audience. Yes, Nicola Baines is an excellent new talent, quite extraordinary, really. We will see some great work from her . . ." He paused as the cameraman fiddled. "Is that it? Thanks, chaps." He grinned at a chorus of inquiring voices.

"Miss Baines will be out shortly to give you her impression of the evening." He gesticulated at Alexandrea, who stepped forward.

"Who's this, Julius? Your new girlfriend?" asked one journalist. Julius frowned and pulled her into a protective circle of crew members and their PR people.

"Not at all. This is a friend of the cast and crew. If you'll excuse me . . ."

"This is the first piece you've written in which the female lead dominates, Julius. So, which came first, Miss Baines or the play?"

Julius began to turn away, shooting an angry glance at his publicist, who stepped into the fray. A capable, calm woman with a shock of thick hair and a velvety smile, she bared her pretty teeth at the press circle.

"Gentlemen, you all should understand by now that Julius' work is cerebral," She paused. "— rather than physical. Miss Baines will be out to answer questions soon. Of a professional nature."

The persistent journalist grinned. "It's just that we can never get anything on him, Becky," he said ingratiatingly.

Julius and Alexandrea dived further into the protective recesses of the theatre. He looked at her. "Well, most revered best friend? What did you think?"

She widened her eyes. "Unbelievable. I hoped she'd be good, but I didn't expect . . ."

"*That* good, eh?"

They grinned in mutual delight. The press crowd stirred. Nicola had arrived. She had scrubbed her face bare and put on a long sheath of white cotton. Her locks were up and away from her face, wrapped in lavender. Cameras flicked on and bulbs brightened as her co-lead joined her. A plastically handsome man in repose, he had become jagged on stage. Julius pulled a protesting Alexandrea forward, and the four posed. She had a moment to worry about her hair and jacket before the bulbs went off again.

Now she looked down at the picture in the paper. They all looked good, a bit luvvy, but reasonably human. She felt a jolt of alarm. Gerry would probably see this. She could see a bra strap peeping through the fabric of her top. Perhaps he would see her and think about calling. He never had. Before she moved, she had made sure several mutual friends — his friends, really — had the new phone number, gritting her teeth at their amused acceptance. They had all known what she was doing. Maybe he'd call. It wasn't impossible was it *(but improbable kinda unlikely this is the man who left you a note for God's sake)* maybe he would, maybe he would call, just to see how she was, to see how she was doing, to hear about the job *(to say he still loves me that I'm lovable)*.

The phone rang loudly, making her jump. It was so sudden that for a moment she felt it was him. He'd speak to her the way he always did, and even though it had been three months his voice would soften the way it used to when she first knew him, the way that made her feel as if she were the only woman he ever could see or feel and she remembered how at first when she called him in the middle of the day from work for nothing in particular his voice would brighten and lift like he'd been spending all his time at work waiting just for her *(and you remember how it changed in the last months after he wasn't working anymore and he didn't sound as glad as he used to, not at all, sounded like you were a nuisance).*

It was Julius. Her disappointment was so great that she had to ask him to repeat himself.

"Get Nicola," he said.

"Julius, what's happened? What's wrong? You sound —"

"Just get Nicola, Alexandrea."

Nicola was at the door. She stretched and yawned.

"Is that my honey bunny?" she asked.

Alexandrea handed her the receiver. "He sounds *weird.*"

Nicola pushed her hair out of her face and flung herself onto the couch. "Darling, how are you on this morning after the night before?"

The sound of urgent hissing at the other end of the line.

"You too *rass* lie!"

More frantic hissing.

"But weh dem say? What it say?"

Alexandrea listened intently. Nicola always broke into patois when she was excited.

Sizzle.

Nicola looked up at her, and Alexandrea noticed that she still had a dusting of glitter on her face.

"Alex, love. Do me a favour, go an' get the paper will you? Wait a minute . . ." She consulted Julius again and named three different tabloids.

Alexandrea pulled on a jumper and ran.

9

He liked the sound of ripping paper. There was something comforting about it, crisp and clean, *right*, somehow. When he ripped his magazines he would get an ear right down by his hands and luxuriate in the sound, looong rips when the paper's edge was clean and sharp; short, rutting rips if the ends were perforated. He ripped out women, short women, tubby women, black women, white women, women who smiled and flirted with the camera. Famous ones: Lisa Bonet doing her sultry thing. An Asian model called Yasmeen whose legs, he was sure, could wrap several times around a man's waist. Others: one caught in the headlamps of a car, booted, suited, nobody. Sometimes pictures of adolescents who he knew would grow and refuse to love him like all the others did.

He hated himself. There were hours, days, even, when he forgot this, proceeded as normal, spoke to his friends — for he had them, but none knew his heart — controlled the urge to rip. There were short moments of respite in which he thought he was worthy of this life. Short moments in which the knowledge of his ugliness did not fill his ears and mind. In these moments he did not know that he was smooth, debonair, even, with a light touch and a smile that brought if not passion, at least succour. He did not know that a model agent would have dubbed him no worse than unusual, would have plastered his jet features across saffron pages, loved him as a contrast. God in his heaven would have cried, for the child that He had created was no uglier than anyone else.

When he was calm, he watched women instead of ripping them out of periodicals. He watched them and dreamed, forgetting his face, his features. This was what he hated: his skin, that unknown to him, reflected the plump white roses that he gave his best friend because yet another bastard had left her and she felt like it was all over once again.

His nose, that flattened itself across his cheeks, the eyes that he thought of as shit-brown and no more, that shone as he looked at the sky.

On the days that he remembered, his friends would have been shocked at his constant fear, his constant rage. The litany of self-hatred that wheeled across his brain, the way he saw a trip on the pavement as a character flaw, the way he cried inside when a girl on the street stepped aside to let him pass. It was because he was an ugly man, he knew. An ugly black man.

The blackness in itself did not bother him. He knew beautiful black men. Mostly, they were shades lighter than he, dimpled, with thin, precocious moustaches and light eyes. These black men he acknowledged. But he knew there was no place for such as him, Mandingo warrior, jungle bunny, African prince, Shaka Zulu, black as the ace of spades, black as a dying heart, black as sin as dirt as a night with no moon. He was the real black that everyone feared.

He had not always felt this way. The only son of an older couple, his arrival into this world had been greeted with trepidation, but delight. His mother had never thought she would be lucky enough to breed, and to breed a son. A son. His father was a lovely, quietly brilliant man who worked on the underground and wrote sub standard poetry that would have gotten better in time if he had tried.

It was only when he was thirteen years of age that he realised he was ugly. Because he was always the girls' best friend, their companion, the good guy who got the pats, the thrown away kisses, the tears on the shoulder over other boys. Once, when he was fifteen he had courted one of these friends, sent her tremulous love letters replete with clichés and pretty pictures that he cut out and stuck to the margins. It was in him that she had confided about these letters, playing guessing games all the way up the high road as to who this mysterious admirer could be. She was sure that she would love such a boy, a boy who told her pretty things, who seemed to know her so well. She would kiss him gently, she said. They would do the things this mysterious stranger suggested: sit in the park and people-watch, listen to their plans for their lives, touch each other intimately. People, she said, would envy their love. She knew that grown-ups would scoff, but it wouldn't matter. They would dismiss it as

65

puppy love, but she and he would know. If only he would reveal himself to her she could tell him of these feelings. She practised dream meetings with him, casting him as the mysterious stranger. *Do you think he would like me to say this, Sean? Or this? How about if I touched him so? Would he like it? You're a boy, you'd know. Tell me. Tell me.* After some weeks of this he had become convinced that she knew. Didn't she look at him when he pretended he wasn't noticing? Wasn't she waiting for him to take her in his arms? Every word seemed loaded with nuance. Of course she must know. She could see his heart. She was just waiting. He was terrified, but every day the need to speak grew stronger.

One day he brought her the letter, instead of posting it to her house. Her face changed, loaded with delight. He couldn't speak, his throat was so tight, sore with tears and longing. He reached to touch her and her words poured into him: did he know the boy? Had her love revealed himself to him? He must tell her now, so she could find him. *Was it Joe? Alan? Morris? Let it be Morris. He has such a cute nose.* She'd fancied him for ages. Confused, he had stepped back, then plunged forward once more, stuttering. *It was me,* he said. *Me. Sean. It's me.* And then her face again, comically stricken. He meant that he had helped to write the letters, yeah? *Morris isn't too bright. Sean, you helped him, right? You're good at that.* And then as she realised the truth she had changed.

She laughed.

She laughed until she held her stomach, the soft dip of a stomach that he had wanted to touch, to kiss. She laughed until she had to lean on him for support. *What a wonderful trick, Sean,* she said. *You had me going there, mate. You couldn't think that me . . . that you and me?* There it was. He would not be allowed to love her. Her laughter was ugly, and with every rise and fall of her small breasts he felt it all rush in on him, the horror that he had suspected, the horror that he had turned his back on, his ugliness laughed up at him from her pretty face and he walked away. Walked towards his house. Walked up to his room, past his mother, who asked him if he wanted fried or boiled dumplings for tea. The rage had only just started to boil within him. That evening he bought a woman's magazine and began to rip out pictures, as he had every night since.

But he kept them for himself.

Now he turned his attention to the last precious paper of the day. The picture was perfect, just the kind he needed for his collection. The girl was exquisite, ideal in her unattainability, with her long brown-red dreads down her back and her ass-tight jeans and the perfect kiss she was planting on the man in the picture.

He thought the headline was unsuitable for his purposes, and, folding, carefully ripped it off. It fluttered to the floor, staring up at him like an accusing eye: *GOTCHA!*

*

"GOTCHA!" Nicola stared at Julius in disbelief. "How can they do this?"

His face was grim, his eyes far away and blue. "Because they finally got what they wanted." He turned to her. "Why did you kiss me on the doorstep, god-dammit? You should have known they'd be waiting for something like this! Haven't I told you —"

Alexandrea rose to her full height. "What the hell does that mean?" She waved the offending paper in his long face. "You're the one who's been nagging her to move in with you! They'd have plenty of opportunities to snap the both of you then! And you're not exactly pushing her away in this photo!"

Nicola lifted a hand. "Alex, stop. It's alright."

"It's not bloody alright! He's acting as if —"

Nicola interrupted her. "Alex, be cool. Don't turn yourself inside out." She turned to look at her man. He stared back, shamefaced, but not willing to back down. "Is it that you don't want to be seen with me?" she asked.

"It's not that." His voice was anguished. "You don't know them. They'll make us something we're not —"

"Which is what?" she took the paper from Alexandrea and read. "'Julius Fraser today revealed the real magic behind his successful new play, *Summer Alienates*. According to reliable sources, Nicola Baines, the 26 year old lead in the new smash hit has been spending intimate hours with the elusive director in his Surrey home'." She scanned down the page. "'All we have to say to Julius is: Didn't You Do Well, Mate?'," She put the paper aside. "Seems like they're on your side . . . *mate*."

Julius drew a hand through his hair. "I don't want you to be angry with me. This rubbish just compromises my position."

"How does it compromise you, Julius?"

"Well, they're having a laugh at my expense —"

"And what about my expense? *I'm* the one who's starting a career! Have you thought about that? All that'll happen to you is that you'll have 'cocksman' added to your list of already shining accolades. I'm the one they're characterising as an actress who fucked for a part! You're just reaping all the benefits of a 'young, new talent'!"

His answer was interrupted by the sound of the door-bell. Alexandrea leaped to her feet and went towards the hall.

"Baby, I'm sorry, it's just that nothing like this has happened to me before —" Julius was trying to placate Nicola, but she moved away from him. Her mind was teeming. It was true that she had never totally thought about the implications of her relationship with him. Before this, his obsession with ducking the press had been a glamorous game. Giggling, she had let him haul her into men's public loos when he spotted curious onlookers, always let him answer the phone at his house. Now she could see what the press coverage would make her look like. A whore. A tart. No-one would care about her efforts. They'd be thinking that's Julius Fraser's woman. And what about other parts? Would they think she was sleeping with those directors too?

"Nikki!" Alexandrea was in the room again, whispering urgently. "That's the girl who's come for an interview!"

"RASS!" Nicola held her head. Typical. Sod's Law was in full operation today. "Can't you send her away?" The last thing she felt like doing was interviewing prospective flat-mates.

"Well, I'll try. It's just that she said on the phone that she was pretty desperate." She looked at Julius, worried. "And, well, we do need, you know, the money . . ."

Julius struck the table with his fist.

"Christ! Nicola! *I told* you that I'd pay the balance on this place if it got to be a problem!"

"And I told you to fuck off when you offered!" Nicola snapped back.

"I'm not your bit on the side! You already pay me a bloodclaaht wage!"

"Dear God in Heaven, woman! Spare me the feminist clap-trap! I've got more money than you!"

She moved towards him, cupping his face in her hands. He tried to move, but she was strong, and she persisted. Her face was taut. "I want a normal life. Alex and I planned this ages ago. You can't just expect me to change everything for you."

He laughed. He thought of all the things she never told him, the fact that she gave him nothing, not an inch of herself or her life. Her real life, even though he wanted to know, wanted to share. He looked straight at her soft face. His fingers dug into her arms and she recoiled in horror.

"Normal? You gave up *normal* the minute you stepped on to that stage. You don't want normal. You *want* fame. Don't think I haven't been watching you. You want the front pages, me on your arm, showing off. You want the whole world to want you." He released her and she scrambled back, appalled, but he was raging now, in pain. "The thing is, I could never be enough, could I? Now you've got your front page, sweetheart, have the balls to admit that you want it. You want everything. You want poor blokes to get hard-ons in airports, to jerk off beside you because they think you're beautiful! Get used to it! Do you know how many men will take that front page and go off to the loo with it —"

She slapped him, and the weight of her hand drove his head backwards. They all watched the imprint of her fingers on his face.

"I guess I came at a bad time . . . ," said Jeanette.

Mavis

De firs' time me did really want to do it ah was seventeen years old. Manage to keep meself clean for all ah dat time. Me was livin' in Kingston an' feelin' nice 'bout dat, doin' likkle domestic work for one woman up ah Beverly Hills. She nevah want me to live in, so me did get a place to stay where de man tek money from you an' give you a room. Wasn't nothing special, but at least me have a place fe put me t'ings, an' me try mek it nice, pick hibiscus in de mornin' an' have it up in dere. Three odder girl live on deh, an if me did know seh dem was ah set of ol' whore, me wouldn't ah stay dere, but me was fool-fool, never realise till later, an' by dat time me did get to know dem, an' couldn't gwaan like hypocrite an' scorn dem. De nicest girl in dere was a woman name Susan. She wasn't too young, in her forties, but she tell me seh she was one of de mos' popular. Seh de man dem love her. Dem used to hang round round on de roadside like dem nuh 'ave nuttin fe do, and de man dem come pick dem up. She say it wasn't a bad life. Me jus' mek dem gwaan wid it, me never feel like me shoulda judge dem. Of course me never know de ways of de Lawd den. Never let him inna me heart.

De woman me work fah was stush-up, but me did expec' dat. On a Monday and Tuesday me go dere an' clean up, polish de wood floors, clean up after her bangarang pickney dem done mash up de place ovah de weekend. Wednesday and Thursday me wash out de clothes fe de family. Friday me iron an' every day me cook de food. Me an' de woman get on fine, until de day she tell me seh she ah t'ink bout buy one ah dem washing machine, tell me seh she hate fe see me haffi put me han' inna de cold water all de time. Me was well vex, tell her seh if she feel me nah do de work good, she mus' tell me. We nevah hear anyt'ing else bout it after dat.

She have t'ree son an' a daughter. One time me find de daughter baggie inna de dirty clothes an' me did have to have a talk wid de madda. Dat is pure

70

nastiness, seh de gyal expect me to scrub out de seat of her baggie. Woman mus' learn fe do dem t'ings fe dem own self. Man cyaan expec' fe do dem t'ings. Still, me glad it happen, because after de madda go talk to her about it, she come siddung beside me, ask me how me wash de undert'ings fe her father an' bredda dem, but not she, an' me get a way fe explain it to her. Woman fe have pride inna demselves.

Me always did notice seh de bwoy dem nevah really talk to me dat much. Excep' Mark, de oldest bwoy. Him was eighteen, an' sometimes him come sit wid me when me ah iron, an' ask me about how country stay, where me come from. Him was a nice bwoy, decent, talk to people wid respect. A good lookin' bwoy, an' me was only a year younger dan him. Sometimes me t'ink seh me love him off, but me know seh him an' me is not de same, so me hold it down, y'know? Try not to t'ink about it. One day him come to see me, an' we was talkin'. Him tell me bout him studies, seh him want to be a lawyer. Him start talk 'bout man an' woman business, want to know if me have a bwoyfriend. Ah was feelin' shy, an' me tell him seh me never have none, never want none. Him laugh an' seh dat was foolishness, dat nice girl like me need a bit of lovin'. Lovin'. It sound nice, y'know? Remind me of how Frankie used to talk before him start gwaan like idyat. Den him start kiss me, hug me up, mek me feel nice, tell me seh me look good. I was feeling like me was going to fall apart, like me foot cyaan hold me up. Him tek me into the living room, still ah kiss me, smile up wid me. Tell me some dirty joke, mek me laugh. Me tell him seh him madda wouldn't like it, but him seh it would be a big secret between us. Den him start tell me how much him love me off, how him ah look pon me from me come ah de yard. All dis time me nervous, nervous, feel seh de woman ah go come back ah de yard an' catch us. Den him hold me tight against him chest an' tell me seh him have a big favour to ask me. Me remember how me was smiling up wid him, look inna him face like him sweet like cook food. Him tell me seh him brother like me too, dat is him brother really did see me firs'. Him brother name Simon, younger dan him, about fifteen. Seh him want me to be nice to Simon. I wasn't sure what him mean. Den Simon come inna de room, an' him smiling like seh him get joke. Mark ah push me, tell me seh him want me to be nice to Simon, nice him up like, y'know. Me realise seh him want me to sex Simon. Me never know what to say. All dis time between me legs ah hurt me, like somet'ing down dere want to nyam up me whole body. Me look 'pon de two *bwoy dem, see how dem pretty, and speaky-spoky, stush, like dem nice. Me did feel good seh decent bwoy like dat woulda want anyt'ing fe do wid me. After me foot nuh stay like model own. An' all de time me t'ings jus' ah itch an' scratch an' me cheek feel like it ah bun up. Mark see seh me not sure, him laugh an' kiss me. Him ask me if me still a virgin. Me tell him yes, no man nuh put nuttin' dere yet. Him still ah push-push me towards Simon, den him whisper inna me ear, seh dat if me leave it too long, me insides ah go tough-up, de longer me leave it de more it ah go hurt when me do it. An' me know it woulda sound fool to de church sister dem, but it did start sound nice, seh dem woulda tek me inna dem pretty bedroom, Simon tell seh him change de sheet dem especially for me. Him on de odder side ah me now, wid him han' ah play inna me hair, tell me seh me mus' come look pon de sheet dem, how him buy dem in Miami when him ah dream 'bout me. Mark put me han' inna Simon han', an' him draw me to de bedroom, all de time him ah talk nice, you woulda never know seh young bwoy could talk so sweet. Of course now me know seh man will promise you dem liver an' dem kidney if dem ah go get de crotches.*

Him wasn't tellin' a lie, him bed mek up wid some nice sheet wid pink flowers 'pon it, an' me heart ah beat inna me breast like it want to bruk out. Me ask Simon if it going to hurt, if him ah go hurt me, an' him ah whisper tell me no, no, him not going to hurt me, him have one hand inna me top, put him fingers at me nipple, jus' ah tease, tease me, and yes, between me legs like fire. We start kiss-up, an' him ah shake like me, an' me realise seh even though him ah talk pretty, look like him never do dis before neither, an' dat did mek me feel good. Me ask him if him ever do it before, an' me voice bruk up an' shaky, an' him hol' me an' tell me no, since me come him know seh him have to save it for me, and outside me hear Mark ah turn on de radio an' me know seh me was going to do it, do it, right dere inna pretty bed wid dis pretty bwoy, and me feel like me going to dead.

Simon tek me han' an' put it down near de front of him pants, an' bwoy, den me did frighten an' happy all at de same time. De t'ing inna him pants jus' ah jump up like somet'ing alive, like it ah breathe for itself. Me tek me han' away, but him tek off him pants an' stan' up dere inna him brief, wid de pants at him ankle, an' him tek de han' again an' put it dere, an' him t'ing jus' ah jump, him put me fingers round it, and is de firs' time me hol' one, and me 'fraid, an' feel good at de same time, seh it ah jump an' big up fe me. Den him put him han' inna me baggie, haul down me skirt, push me top past me titty. Him put him finger on me pussy, push it inside, an' me haffi siddung on de bed 'cause me so excited, skirt drop on de floor, one ah me hair clip come out an' fall on de board floor like is thunder, floor weh me shine de very same mornin'.

Den me hear a bang, an' some voices ah talk. Simon nearly dead, him ah haul-up him pants, ah talk to me urgent, tell me to straighten me clothes, an' him madda inna de living room ah talk to Mark, an' me could hear her ah ask him what happen, how him ah gwaan so funny, what is goin' on here, an' Simon ah get urgent, ah shake me fe put on me clothes, what happen, if me is ah stupid bitch or what, seh me mus' PUT ON DE CLOTHES, an' de madda bus' de room door.

All kinda bloodclaaht gwaan after dat, excuse me, Lawd. De madda mek fe box me, an' miss, an' den she try box de son, an' all de time she ah yell an' scream an' bawl how de Lawd Jesus mus' come an' tek her, why she get all dem nasty son, why every helper she get jus' want to fuck, an' how she cyaan get no decent s'maddy inna her yard, how de whole ah we jus' come an' bring all dis stinkin' nastiness wid we. Den she turn inna de bwoy face, ah cuss dem how she sick of all dis damn foolishness, she jus' ah lose helper left right an' centre, an' she grab me, tell me seh me mus' mek meself decent, an' come outta her house, an' next t'ing me know me on de verandah, an' she ah push me, yell down shame on me, but all ah could hear as me ah walk down de road was dat she was sick of all de damn foolishness, how de bwoy dem do it all de time, all de time, all de time, an' me know seh me was a damn idyat fe believe it, an' me ah walk an' all de water in de world ah spring outta me eye inna me face.

10

She reflected that it was only right that Nicola had thrown Julius out of the house. Actually, it had been quite funny. Not at the time, of course. She had felt too alarmed — Julius was no lightweight and he was angry. Too embarrassed — that Jeanette girl had been standing there looking like she was going to hurt herself laughing. Too distressed with the possibility of a break-up looming on the horizon to see the humorous side.

Now, three days later, a badly needed cigarette break in the Endeavour bar finally gave her the time to laugh about it. They were going into the studio later today, and the office was slightly frantic. She supposed that Julius hadn't been collared like that since he was a boy. After Nicola had slapped him, they had stood there, the four of them, waiting for hell to break loose. It had, but not in the way she could have foreseen it. Julius had put a hand up to his cheek and looked astounded. Nicola had grabbed a fistful of his shirt collar and half-pulled then half-pushed him out of the room. He let her drag him half-way down the hall before he realised she was serious, and then he made an attempt to be manly, but it had been too late. He'd lost the impetus, and before he knew it he was on the front step, Nicola had slammed the door and turned back into the other two women. She'd rolled up her sleeves, adjusted her dishevelled jacket, smiled, shook hands with the new flat mate, and offered her some coffee.

The new flat-mate. Alex frowned. The presence of a stranger, she knew, had outraged Julius even more. He was right. She wondered whether the girl would run off to the papers. She wouldn't need accommodation then. Just pack all her stuff into a rucksack, take a plane to Miami on the dosh she could make. She decided that she would have a word with her. She looked like a bit of a non-starter, never mind her degree in Psychology or whatever it was.

She had been annoyed to find that Nicola had taken to Jeanette immediately. She came from Manchester, she said, and Nicola had done a play down there a few years back. Jeanette said she'd seen it and flattered her way into the place. She wondered whether Nicola should have taken Julius up on the money offer. Perhaps it would have brought some peace between them. And it would have saved them having to put up with a loud Mancunian. She was moving in today.

She and Gerry had had fights about money all the time. He never had any, after he quit his job on the construction site. And he'd been dole-struck after that *(while you worked your behind off)* and sat around the house watching crappy television. He hadn't even tried. She realised it was one of the first negative thoughts she'd had about him, and tried it on for size. Gerry as cheap bastard. Gerry as dole king. She couldn't sustain it. He had massaged her feet for an hour after she door stepped Denzel Washington. Dried her tears when she lost all the taped interview with Sade and had to ask the singer to do it again. She had cringed talking to Sade's publicist, but he had been there, smiling encouragingly as she apologised, ironing her suit as she ran around the flat because she had *an hour* to get down there to do the interview again. There had been so many good times. Like when he cooked her dinner on their first anniversary, even though he hated to cook *(cheap pasta, so what)* and yes, well, the time he gave her her first orgasm, that first night when he had leaned between her thighs *(they say a black man won't lick a stamp, and didn't we kill off that myth)* and the time all his mates had been round even though she didn't want them there and they'd gotten into a discussion about 'eating under the table' and they were teasing him in front of her, you do that, don't you Gerry, innit, Alex? He does that for you doesn't he and she had been embarrassed *(and afraid)* when she had seen his eyes and the warning placed in each one and again she had been embarrassed *(and shocked)* at that warning, and she had laughed and smiled and said no, boys, nothing like that required here and they had believed her, probably because they thought she was such a snotty bitch anyway, with her suits and her high flying JOB.

"Alex, I think Jenny is looking for you."

Pearson was standing in front of her. She reflected again on the way he moved silently, popping up, as he had the first time, at her elbow or behind her, when she least expected it. She had commented on this one day, that little devilish light shining through unexpectedly, and he had passed it off, teasing that no wonder, she was always so deep in thought. She knew that wasn't it. He was so silent around her, loud with everyone else, stomping.

It bothered her.

She rose quickly. He was settling himself into a chair. The Endeavour bar was cosy, soft settees for more informal meetings, straight backed, *faux* antique chairs for the power mongers. The bartenders were cheerful, and remembered what you were drinking. She had been careful to tell them she was teetotal the first time she had walked in.

"Do you want a drink?"

She was puzzled. "You said that Jenny wanted me."

He waved a hand. "Yes, but I don't think it's urgent. Have a drink. I bet you like screwdrivers."

It was too close to the bone.

"I don't drink, really. I should go . . ."

He smiled. "Hey, who's your boss?"

She straightened her spine. "I am directly responsible to Jenny."

He shrugged, dismissively. "Who is directly responsible to me. Have a drink."

She could taste the sweet memory of the wine on Nicola's opening night. She rubbed her mouth unconsciously. Valentine's day would test her. If Gerry didn't call her. She sat down.

"I'll have tomato juice, please."

"Watching your weight?" His tone was conversational, lazy, but she had the unpleasant impression that he knew exactly how much she wanted real alcohol right now.

"No, I don't do that, but —"

"You don't need to. You are very . . . svelte."

She shifted uneasily. She didn't like people commenting on her appearance at the best of times. "I'll have the juice." She tried to be firm.

He shrugged and clicked his fingers at the bar man, who hurried over. Alex wondered whether he did that all the time, and whether it had the same effect everywhere he went. It wouldn't in some all-British working men's club. Still, he'd probably never been to a place like that. She hadn't either.

They sipped their drinks. The red liquid flowed across her gums, and she tried to pretend it was vodka. The silence wasn't comfortable, but he let it continue.

"Are you having a good time?"

She was flustered, and then realised what he meant. "Working on the show? Oh, well, yes, it's interesting. We're getting ready to shoot —"

"What did you think I meant?" He was amused. She was saved by the redhead researcher, Sharon, who had become an acquaintance of sorts. She came hurrying up to them, feet flying.

"Sorry, Mr Pearson. Alexandrea, Jenny's looking for you and she's getting . . . frantic."

She got to her feet fast, relieved. They trotted back up to the office, panting slightly. Sharon looked worried.

"Didn't Pearson tell you that Jenny was raising the roof?"

"No, he, er . . ."

"Well, she is. She's banging on about fag breaks being bloody unnecessary, and what the hell are we all playing at." Sharon's face was melancholy. She ran on nicotine, and the non-smoking offices were playing havoc with her.

They stepped into an ominously silent room. Tasdell whirled to greet them. "Alex, where were you? I need your guest list, and I need you to brief Ruby on the crowd. She's read the subject notes, but she needs to know what the likely responses of the audience are. Can you do that now, please? She's coming up."

Alexandrea hit the PRINT button on her computer.

"You haven't printed out yet? Come on, come on. She's in the Yellow Room." The producer looked harassed. Alexandrea felt a stab of alarm. Nobody had told her she was ready to deal with Ruby Fleur face to face. The old need for control thundered in her ears. She'd heard on the grapevine that the woman could be a real battle-axe. Of course she had met her in the first week, but Ruby had barely acknowledged her, deep in conversation with Pearson. She couldn't believe he had invited her for a drink when she was needed up here.

She grabbed her notes off the printer and fled the room. Behind her she could hear Tasdell's voice — "No more bloody fag breaks, did everyone hear that?" — and she felt shame envelop her. If only she was being sent to write a profile. That she could have handled. Celebrity interviews gave her the control, with the clicking tape recorder and the pre-arranged questions, the challenge of noting tiny details, coaxing more than the usual, boring quotes, deciding who to betray or not with the off the record statements made in a second of drunkenness or friendliness or naiveté. They never knew what she would write, and it kept them on edge. But here at Endeavour she knew she couldn't unsettle Fleur. Still, there was always her cool, unflappable mask. She knew to an onlooker she would have been the same old capable Alexandrea Watson, hurrying on important business down a corridor. That comforted her as she knocked on the door of the room.

"Come." The voice was imperious, absent. She stepped in. The woman in front of her was busy stripping a cuticle off her finger with her teeth. Alex looked down at Ruby's hands. A bead of blood had sprung up, bright against the long, obviously false, equally bright vermilion nails.

Ruby smiled, her teeth startlingly white. Alexandrea gazed at them, intrigued by their symmetry. They were literally the most perfect teeth she had ever seen. They *had* to be capped. No-one's teeth were that perfect. These were never-ate-any-toffee-in-my-life or ever eaten at all teeth. If she had been interviewing Ruby, she would have asked this immediately. It was an old technique, one of her favourites. The music journalist at *Black London* had told her it worked in the right circumstances: *Shock 'em out of their little fat wallets,* he'd said. *Ask them about the pimple on their chin, especially if they're a great beauty. Ask a ladies' man if he's gay, if you think there's the possibility he is.* She'd wondered aloud at the wisdom of the counsel: surely any star worth their salt would tell her to fuck off? He'd shaken his head. *Nine times out of ten they love rude questions. Oh, they might make some noise, but they'll respect you for not boring the hell out of them. Do it with a smile, a cheeky one, like you know their secrets. You can do it. You're gorgeous. Gorgeous women can get away with anything.* He'd been right. Perhaps they got so terribly bored with interviews and the predictability: how's the film the play, the book, how did you prepare for the part, where do you get your ideas from, are you aware that you're a sex symbol? They heard it every day.

Alexandrea opened her mouth to say hello and because it had been a bad day so far, because she wanted to be on kissing terms with a bottle of anything, just because, because, because, it didn't work that way. Her little light shone bright and the words came tumbling out.

"Do you wear false teeth?"

Ruby Fleur's eyes widened. Dismally, Alex listened to the echo of the words in the room *(you stupid, stupid, stupid bitch, what, you want to get fired AGAIN).* "What did you just say to me?" Fleur's mouth was a little 'O' of surprise. She quivered. *(Stupid-stupid-stupid-stupid.)* Ruby jumped to her feet and shook her hair back, her whole body outraged. " You want to know about my teeth? Any other questions? The hair, perhaps?" She turned her back on Alexandrea, medium height, rounderful, brash. "You want to know if my bum is disposable?"

"Miss Fleur, I'm so sorry —" She wanted to die. It was ridiculous. If she got fired, how was she going to pay the rent? She was going to prove them all right, that she couldn't make it in the big white world.

"Well, which is it?"

(Stupid girl, in for a penny, in for a pound.) She felt the insane part of her, the small part that didn't care about order, or control, or good manners, the part *Black London* had constantly edited out *(you can't say that Eartha Kitt looks like a small brown monkey even if she does, Alexandrea)* take over.

"Well, since you asked, let's start with your bum. At least I'll have an exclusive when I'm fired on the basis of extreme stupidity."

Ruby stared at her. Her body began to shake. Laughter poured from her like a geyser, solid mirth. She sank back onto the couch, laughing like a banshee. Wiping tears away, she flashed the unbelievable teeth once more.

"Off the record, Miss Reporter, the derriere has had a tiny piece of plastic adjustment, the nails are also false, but the gnashers are all mine."

She looked at her hand and then stuck it out. Alexandrea noticed that the tears had washed away the blood. "Alexandrea Watson. I am so *pleased* to meet you. And no, you are not fired." She flung her hands up in the air. "What a breath of fresh air in this *bloody* place!" She moved forward and hugged the astounded Alexandrea. The embrace was as firm as the woman, and she had a brief moment of comfort *(wish you'd been my mother)* that quickly died. She hugged back. Ruby looked into her face.

"C'mon. Tell me about the heaving masses that are coming to this show."

Tony Pearson could hear them from his adjoining office. He couldn't remember Ruby laughing that way for a long time. Not since that day in Amsterdam when they had crept away from the conference. He remembered kissing that particularly peachy backside, long before the surgeon's knife broke through gristle and fat, long before little Carmen Hoolung had changed her name by deed poll to become Ruby Fleur. They had made up the name together. After all, no-one could get anywhere in life with a name like Hoolung. Fleur was trite, cheerful, as kitschy glam as the programme. He smiled and knitted his fingers together. He liked creating his women. It was fun. Watching the girls dance around his fire. He could hear Alexandrea's thin, pleasant voice through the door. He stroked his chin.

*

"Are they real?" The journalist regarded Nicola's locks with a curious smile. They were sitting on the edge of a photographer's studio where three men were busily putting together a complicated back drop. The journalist was all blonde: dark blonde tresses, lighter blonde trouser suit. Her nails were the darkest thing about her, stubby brown chips that made her pale hands look harsh.

Nicola returned the smile uncertainly. Alex had spent many evenings telling her about the mysterious world of interviewing, but it was strange to be on the other end of it, just the same.

"The last time I looked, they were."

The interview had begun at ten that morning, a mere fifteen minutes ago, and what alarmed her most was that she could feel Mona ebbing away from her. It had taken her several hours to conjure her last night. What with the fight with Julius, the stony formality between them at the theatre, it was hard to play strong woman. Even though she was hurt by their terrible argument, she would not admit her love. She did know that her feelings were very strong. But his face. The *knowledge* there. With that one cruel crack about the aeroplane incident, she had felt laid bare to the world. She realised that in loving her, he *knew* her. It frightened her. He had put his finger straight on her sore spot *(you don't want normal)* the fact that she wanted the applause, she wanted the glamour, she wanted even more than he could afford her in terms of recognition and public acclaim. She had been applauded before, but these nights with *Summer Alienates* were a revelation. At the end of each performance she waited, breathlessly for the thunder to wash over her. And it did, again and again, there had been a standing ovation every night. Only Julius spoiled it, joining her, as he had on the first night, raising her hand. She could see the irony in his smile, the mockery in the little bow he gave her. Yesterday she had stopped him backstage, tried to ask him. Could he not, not *do* that, at the end? *What?* he had said innocently, his eyes blank. *Make a fool of me,* she had hissed. *You smirk at me. I was not aware of any such thing,* he had answered. *If you'll excuse me.* His coldness pained her. She was used to melting everybody, anybody. He was cold *(you don't want normal)* and if he saw her secret ambitions, then everyone must see them, see Mona, perhaps they were laughing at her facade, thought she was sad, play-acting through life, the need for cheers plastered firmly across her forehead, as if in red paint. The new thought that she had fooled nobody had terrorised her and blotted Mona's image from the mirror *(you want the whole world to want you)* and the woman sitting in front of her today was chipping at another part of her. She was a large, creamy cat, with her barrage of questions, reclining and then pouncing, leaving tiny scratches on Nicola's psyche. All her questions were about being a *black* actress: is it harder to succeed here, do you feel there are enough parts for black talent, have you felt stereotyped? What bothered her was the woman's smug sense of her own knowledge. It was as if she was showing off, trying to assure Nicola that she was a professional, not one of these white people who are ignorant about black people, no, she'd studied them, she knew the issues. She looked as if she wanted to be patted for her pains. Nicola felt like a lab rat.

"How do you get them looking like that? I mean, what's the process?" The tape recorder was poised. "We might do a little box of beauty tips from you or something. You might start a trend. Do forgive me. I just thought that the dread locks might be a religious thing. Are you a Rastafarian?"

Nicola was taken aback. "No, I'm not a Rasta. Though I really don't think I'd presume to give women beauty tips." She leaned forward. "I thought we were going to talk about the play."

The journalist laughed. "Oh, we are, we are. I just thought this might be interesting. Are you always this serious?"

"No, I'm hardly ever serious. Except about my work. Aren't you?"

"Quite, quite. What's it like being in a mixed race relationship? You do confirm that you are having an affair with Julius Fraser?"

"Er . . ."

"You did see the pictures? That was you kissing him, without a doubt."

"Yes . . ."

"So you don't *deny* it?"

"No."

"So?"

"Well, what do you want to know?" She felt panicky. She wasn't sure whether Julius was ever going to speak to her again, and certainly didn't feel ready to answer probing questions. What should she say? *Well, everything's fine, but I dumped him out of my house the other day, ha-ha?*

"Well, is it easy? Of course his celebrity status must have its own challenges, but how about your different colours?"

She tried to think. "I don't have anything to compare it to. I've had boyfriends, but I've never been out with a black man before, so . . ."

Pounce. "Is that by choice?"

"Ah . . . no." Nicola's temples ached dully. "I just tend to meet white men in my business."

"But in *Element of Time*, the play you led two years ago, all your fellow actors were black."

82

"Yes, that's true. I didn't fancy any of them. What are you trying to say, I don't like black men?"

"Not at all, not at all . . . ," the journalist soothed. "I just wondered . . ." She snapped off the tape recorder. "I think the photographer will need us in about five minutes."

"Oh, but we haven't talked about —"

The woman patted her hand. "It'll be fine. Now we're ready. Bob, do you have all the gear for Nicola Baines?"

The man nodded. She could feel Mona drifting away from her as the headache got worse.

11

Fascinated, Alexandrea watched the group of people in front of her make television. She was sitting alone, in the glass fronted, black backed booth where staff were encouraged to view programme recordings. Empty brown chairs sat around her. She deserved the break, and Tasdell had wanted her, the new girl, to see how it worked. Above and to her right, a screen showed the waiting studio audience. Alex smiled as one man scratched dandruff from his scalp, ignorant of the camera. Tasdell was seated next to the director , both surrounded by a bundle of technicians. They were all fixated on their own screens, snakes and coils of cable flirting at their ankles, disappearing into strange places, connected to hulks of metal that clicked and whirred. She was excited. The first few weeks had been about what she knew best, talking to people, gathering information, preparing structure. But to see interaction in this other form was odd. What Fleur did was so . . . public. She was performing for a crowd, yet getting trust, on a smaller level, from her main guests. Alexandrea liked to bury into a secret place with the people she interviewed, resenting shared spots or hang-dog publicists that interrupted. She tried to create intimacy, warmth, make them forget that every word was being wound into her tiny dictaphone. When she had first started working she had tried to explain the process to Nicola, and Michael, her brother. "It's like climbing a ladder. You . . . you get them to the first rung, all polite, predictable questions. Then you ease them to the second, as they reveal intimacies and jokes. You know you're getting there when they say you just asked an *interesting* question, when they have to stop and think for a reply. It means they've never been asked that before. The third rung is something else — it's when the words just come out, and you know they've forgotten you're the press, you're just another person, and they're confiding in you, and if you've got it right, they seem to wake up out of it in the end, shake themselves. They get anxious, ring you up afterwards and beg you not to write certain things. Then you know you have gold!"

Michael had looked curious. "Has no-one ever double-bluffed you? You know, you think you've got gold, as you call it, and then you realise that they told the same to everyone?"

She laughed. "Of course. I left Eartha Kitt thinking I had this big old scoop, because she'd talked about her childhood and bawled. I was thinking my God, Kitt cried her eyes out in front of me! Luckily, before I wrote it up, someone asked me if she had cried. Apparently she does it at the drop of a hat."

That of course, was where research came in. If she'd done her homework, she would have known. She patted the dictaphone in her bag. It was her security blanket. She liked to carry it around. She had got an exclusive out of Laurence Fishburne the day she had spotted him ambling around Leicester Square, looking gloomily at the pigeons. The editor had practically kissed her.

As she watched Ruby she felt more than grudging respect for her. It wasn't an easy job, this. Single-handedly, she controlled the crowd, mothered those who needed comfort, soothed the angry. It was a remarkable thing to watch. On the monitor, a young woman broke down into dry, angry sobs. Her father had declined to appear on the programme, had sent word that if she was a lesbian, he had no daughter. Ruby had tears in her eyes as well. Alex found it hard to decide whether they were real. She hadn't worked Fleur out yet.

She listened to Jenny muttering instructions to the host via her ear-piece. "Okay, Ruby. Move away from her now. We need to get the mother on. Intro her to bring in some support."

Ruby obliged, facing the camera. "Angela's mother, however, doesn't feel the same way. She's here to support her daughter. Eileen, come on out." A small, faded woman was pushed into the lights. Behind Ruby, out of camera range, staff signalled to her to sit down next to her daughter. Ruby's patter continued. Alexandrea grinned. She had to concentrate on so many things at a time, and her timing was spot on.

"You look pleased with yourself." Pearson was in the door jam.

"I'm just intrigued. This is the first time I've seen it all done. Isn't she *good*?"

Pearson glanced up at the monitor. "She is very good. That's why the show works. We never thought we'd be able to crack the US model of chat, but she's done it."

He sat down beside her, their knees colliding in the small booth. "I'm glad you're enjoying the experience."

"I am." Ruby was trying to calm an irate man who was berating Eileen, for not leaving her husband. "How the hell is she going to just leave him? It's not that simple!" The man was refusing to shut up, his voice getting more strident. "Oh sh— oh dear! He won't let it go! *C'mon*, Ruby!"

Pearson was unperturbed. "Watch."

Alexandrea was suddenly aware that Pearson's large hand was leaning softly against the back of her chair, an inch away from her shoulder. She looked at him, but he was gazing up at the monitor.

"Look, see, she's got him sat down . . ."

She moved forward on her seat, slowly. She didn't want him to notice her moving. Surely the hand was innocent. And since it was, he might think she was presuming a pass, and really, what could she be thinking of? It seemed vain of her to even think that the hand could mean anything at all.

Ruby introduced her next guest. "Suppose you were married, with two small children, but you know that you've been gay all your life? Steve has finally confessed his agonising secret to his wife, but today he's going to tell his parents why they're separating. Please welcome . . ."

Pearson's arm moved forward, encircling Alexandrea's small shoulders. He squeezed reassuringly. "See, it's all fine. Ruby's a professional."

They sat there. A hundred thoughts churned through her mind. This couldn't be a pass. The man had shown her nothing but courtesy, doused with a little of his own frankness. But if someone walked into the booth, this would look very suspect. She fought several feelings. Perhaps she should say this to him. Or wait until he moved his arm of his own accord? Surely he could see how inappropriate this could look?

Embarrassment filled her eyes.

"Mr Pearson —"

The man removed his arm and stood up, poking his head around the door. He said something muted to Jenny and then turned back.

"They'll probably edit out the shouting man anyway." He gave her a little wave and strode out.

Alex chastised herself. Was she getting so uptight about men that she couldn't take a friendly hug? Her skin crawled. It was Gerry of course, thoughts about Gerry. Pearson was being friendly. It must be a pain, having to stand on ceremony all the time. By the time she left the suite to escort the audience out, she had tucked it to the back of her mind.

*

Jeanette trailed a hand down the man's back and stifled her amusement as he flinched. "You ready again, already?" she hugged her body to him, from the back as they lay like spoons, her breasts pulled flat and downwards against him, her sex damp against his buttocks. She put a hand between his legs. "So you are."

Grinning, the young man rolled towards her. She pushed against his chest with open palms.

"No more just now. You too greedy." She gestured towards the suitcases in the room. "Plus I have to unpack all this."

It had been very nice. He was a friend of a mate on campus, a nice guy, who had offered a lift when he saw her struggling at the door of The Wine and Sow. She imagined that he had arranged to be passing, to show his gallantry. She had mentioned that she was moving. And hadn't she mentioned the exact time too, within his hearing, hadn't she paused at the door, waiting? Bill had offered to give her a hand, pay for a cab, but she had thanked him prettily and the two had laughed together.

"Some lad coming to give you a lift?"

"He better."

Waivers wasn't a bad sort. She knew he'd have her knickers off in five minutes if he hadn't set up the pub as a kind of drunken mausoleum to his wife. She pitied him, really. He'd roll off to his rooms drunk most nights, and she could smell the women and song on his breath. But he never did it in what he still saw as his wife's property. "She's dead, but I know she looks down on me, the old bugger," he'd said, fondness encircling the words. Men were funny. But she had understood. She understood men. She looked down at the one in bed with her. He probably wasn't going to believe it when she asked him to leave, but the time was coming. She didn't want any of the kissy stuff. Charles had given her enough of that.

She supposed that she was now what polite society would call promiscuous. She'd seen the sly looks. She couldn't blame them. She'd been sleeping with nearly every looker that came her way. She reckoned she'd been through at least twenty since the start of term. She didn't feel bad about it; she felt delicious. It was wonderful to have it on her own terms. No-one was getting hurt. Some bruised egos, perhaps, for those who had thought she was looking for that special something. She'd tried to make it clear from the start. It was laughable that most of them didn't believe her. One guy had had the cheek to warn her that she would fall in love with him if they kept up the sex-fest. She saw him sometimes at uni, looking at her all cow-eyed. But mostly, it had been alright. She didn't want to look into it too closely, but she guessed that her academic progress puzzled them too. Perhaps they expected her to be dumb. Even though she knew there were comments about her, she let them go over her head. She made her choices with finesse. One lad had swaggered up to her making comments about free crotch. She'd made him know that he shouldn't even think about it, and had been amused as several men rose to her defence. She knew she puzzled them, but at least they treated her with respect.

It was exciting for her to make choices. Not only about the men she slept with, but how she lived, what she ate, how she managed her money. Mamma had always made sure she never had a chance. If she bought a piece of clothing and had no money left at the end of the month she knew it was her call. Either she did extra shifts for Bill, or she had a problem. But oh, to be able to realise that she could deal with it. That was the ultimate. If she spread her legs, she could deal with it. If she touched a biceps, it was her responsibility. They were all shades and shapes, different paces, different musicals, short, tall, indigo or ivory. And if they didn't deliver she could look elsewhere. She felt it was her right.

Mamma, she knew, would have been scandalised. It seemed like she'd been scandalising her Mamma all her life. Mamma with her iron spine and her hot line to God. She'd have to give Maye a call and have a laugh about the expression on this lad's face now. She could see his erection making a curved tent through the duvet. Funny how bodies didn't listen. How people didn't listen to each other. Mamma had never listened to anyone in her life. She'd been the one who'd had to educate her sister about sex, she, Jeanette, the curious one, the baby. The younger teaching the elder sister. Maye had a fragility that undermined her common sense. Mamma hadn't understood the day they'd had to go to her, one daughter trembling, the other, her chin jutted out, and it was her who'd had to speak the dreaded words, that Maye was a little bit up the spout, a touch preggers, you know pregnant, don't you, Mamma, you've done it twice. Sixteen years old and pregnant, facing the mother of matriarchs, stiff in her glorious widowhood, first husband dead, second husband dead, and she still rode on, speaking to the Lord every day and Jeanette had felt a grim thrill of satisfaction as they hovered by the door, morning sickness killing off Maye, satisfaction because finally their mother was going to lose it, lose control, and wouldn't it be glorious and frightening to see that, but Mamma, well, Mamma had just straightened her shoulders a little more and the dreaded torrent had not come forth. Just something else, her mantra, the little Jamaican saying that she drew out at all times of crisis.

"If you can't hear, you must feel."

She had turned her back, as if the subject was closed, as if her mantra had made Maye barren, and when Maye's baby had pushed her way into the world, she had not been there, she had turned her back, stolid in the knowledge that she had a bad daughter, and she was a good woman. Two marriages and probably not a bonk in between. Jeanette felt a shiver run through her. *(If you can't hear you must feel.)* The first time she'd heard those words she'd been five. Mamma had an old electric heater that she would carry from room to room, huddling herself and her children in one at a time. The heater was standard, bars glowing a bright orange, and

Jeanette had wanted to touch them. Said to Mamma that they were pretty. Mamma had told her no, not for touching, you'll be hurt, you'll burn, but she couldn't quite believe that this thing that tantalised her so much, glowing and dancing in front of her little girl eyes could hurt anybody. Mamma had said no a couple more times and then turned away, and she had seen her chance and reached out to grab and in the seconds between the scalding of her flesh and the moment her hand was still safe she saw that her Mamma was *watching:* she was watching, and she wasn't stopping her and then the whole world was an explosion of the most unbearable pain as she gripped the hot bar *(my god so much pain)* and she was so terrified that she didn't know how to let go. It could have only been a few seconds but she had never felt such pain and Mamma had pulled her away, not before she had seen the mixture of triumph and agony in her mother's eyes, and Mamma had waited only long enough to run her little palm under water and let her daughter see the bubbles rising to the surface of her hand before she was bandaged. With the hiccups of her sobs just dying away, her mother had rassed her on her behind and the howl was more of surprise than hurt and she had heard the words for the first time *(IF YOU CAN'T HEAR, JEANETTE, YOU MUST FEEL!)*

The young man bent to kiss her lips. "There's a dance at the student union on Friday night. Want to come?"

She smiled at him, shadows settled softly, like dark chalk dust in her collarbones, warmed by the generosity of her breasts and the sweat that rejoiced, nestling, in the hollow of her navel. He looked down at her and saw a secret smile at him from between her thighs. She shook her head. Resigned, he pulled on his boxers. She took him to the door, all the while smiling her musical smile. He was secretly amused. Later he would reflect that she fucked like a man, all senses, demands, no emotion except cheerfulness. She had winked at him after giving him a blow job. When he was an older man he would realise that she simply fucked like herself: a woman who liked it. Not knowing this now, his ego smarted at the door. He would have gotten up the courage to remonstrate had her flat-mate not slipped her key into the lock right then.

Alex stopped when she saw the couple. "Jeanette. Hope you moved in alright?" she asked. She noted the robe that scarcely covered the other woman's body. They had been having sex. In the house she'd moved into five minutes ago. Part of her was appalled, part momentarily jealous. She waited to be introduced, but Jeanette beamed and pushed her partner towards the door. They watched him crunch towards his car. Alexandrea mustered a smile.

"Your boyfriend?"

Jeanette winked. "Nah."

"Oh." She felt even more disapproving, unsure of what to say next. Jeanette dived into the silence between them.

"I bought some food. I'm gonna cook for us tonight, to say thank you for letting me move in so quickly."

"Well, I had nothing to do —" Alexandrea stopped, embarrassed. Her big mouth had got her into enough trouble today.

Jeanette studied her face. "It's alright. I know you weren't too hot on the idea. But, fair dues: thanks all the same." She moved towards the kitchen. "Do you have any garlic? Neither of you two are veggies, are you? I'm doing fried chicken and rice and peas."

"Aren't you going to, er, change?" The bathrobe barely skimmed her hips, the legs strong and well formed.

Jeanette grinned over her shoulder. "Nah. I need a breeze-out." The suggestion in the comment was obvious. Alexandrea closed her eyes. "You don't mind, do you?"

"Well, we don't —"

"Nah, I know you're no prude." She began to clatter through pots. "My mother would be proud of me. Still, I'm sure Nikki will diss me and tell me my cooking can't compare to real Jamaican cooking."

Alex's irritation deepened. The girl was too much. She wanted to poke around in their garlic, she had the nerve to predict what Nikki, *her* best friend, was going to say or feel. She knew her reaction was childish, but clung to it stubbornly. It had been a long day, and coming home to a stranger wanting to dirty her kitchen wasn't making it any easier. The girl would have to know the rules if they were going to live together without her going mad. Then she remembered.

Jeanette listened to Alexandrea's careful, diplomatic explanation with a chuckle in her heart: she was to understand that Nikki was *(perhaps)* a rising celebrity, that her boyfriend was *(definitely)* a celebrity, and that the press was giving them a hard time, and that she, Jeanette, was to do nothing to sabotage the good time that was being had by all *(famous or otherwise)* before she arrived. She chuckled mostly at Alexandrea. Alex with her posh accent under which she could hear a hearty dose of down and dirty Cockney. Alex and the way she looked resentfully at the garlic she chopped. Alex and the way she tried to appear in control. She could see that Alex was scared shitless, and it amused and softened her. There had to be a lot under the mask for her to be holding it down so ferociously. She nodded and smiled, smiled and nodded, like an automaton. She knew what the other woman thought of her, what all girls like Alexandrea thought of her with that lad in her bed and a smile on her face. She didn't give a fuck. She was more than what they thought, what her mother thought, what the men thought. She knew that for the first time in her life she was operating exactly as she wanted to, and nobody's opinion could change that.

She gave assurances, looked deep into Alex's eyes. If the older woman was aware of her condescension, she gave no sign. She suspected that Alex knew she didn't care. Perhaps it was more important for her to hear her own voice, calm herself with it. She didn't know how close to the truth she was. She decided that she had to do something to chill the woman out. She chuckled inside again. She'd make it her life's calling. Call it psychoanalysis.

12

Irritated, Nicola grabbed her hair and wound it around her head. It was getting in the way, and she was too stressed to deal with its heaviness.

"Problem, Nicola?" asked Julius. The cast was sitting in a circle on the stage. It was one of Julius' weekly rituals. He liked to discuss a work in progress, iron out mistakes on a personal basis. Nicola's co-lead was arguing the wisdom of turning the music volume down in the third act.

"I can't hear Nicola's last words with that swell. It throws me."

Julius was looking at Nicola. There was solid cold between them, with no suggestion of a thaw, but he knew that hair gesture.

"Sorry, Karl." He flicked at the script. "What were you saying?" Karl explained once more, testily.

"Well, you don't actually need to hear her, man! You know what she's saying and you just take your cue from her timing."

"You don't understand. It's the emotion in her voice that sparks my response. I need to hear it."

"I think Karl's right. It messes me up as well." Nicola shrank slightly from Julius' blank stare. "Just sometimes. Act Three and when Adrian jumps the wall. I mean, my back's to him, so I need the cue. Timing's not enough if I can't hear him."

Julius glared and then muttered in the stage manager's ear, who left the room. He turned back. "Right. Eleanor will sort out music volumes because there has to be a balance between what the audience can hear and what you hear. So we'll see tonight. Let's move on. I'm not sure about the love scene. Phillip still doesn't make the transition as smoothly as he could . . ."

Nicola listened to the sound of his voice. Despite herself, she shifted on the floor, uncomfortable. She didn't know what to do in the face of his restraint. Anger she could manage. But watching him blank her, the formality, the fact that she couldn't seem to *move* him, troubled her. The stalemate had been going on for too long.

She had always wanted white men. If she was honest, she must admit that. White men. The chiselled jaws and tousled hair of Mills and Boons. Their power, the things they took for granted. To belong to one, to walk with one, to be wanted by one satisfied her. The first white boy she'd dated had noticed her at Lime Quay, back home. She had been thirteen, awkward as a giraffe, trying to hide in the brief bikini a friend had lent her. She saw him watching her. His family obviously had money; the yacht he showed her around belonged to them and had been named for his big brother. He told her how good she looked, lay in the sand with her, rubbing it into her shoulders. It had been him who had first started to count the moles that were scattered there. Like all girls, she thrilled to that first sexual attention. But she would not have felt this way about any young, attentive boy. No, what made it all delicious was the new texture of his hair, the angle of his thinner lips, and yes, oh yes, the flush of success when his father took her to school the next Monday in his sports car, and didn't all their faces fall, the girls who made her ugly. He was the prize, the ultimately unattainable, and she had got him, got him so bad that he had cried when she had found another and another *(red gyal think you nice)* and layered on her reputation for distance came another layer. She had heard them talking about her, a shop had opened in New Kingston with a jazzy little name, melting piles of cute miscellany and a jingle on the television. With the cruel tenacity of young ones they sang it whenever she was around *(if you can't get it at Hole In The Wall)* and she had decided that if that was what she was, she'd be worse, give them something to talk about and even though she was a virgin she bought more bikinis, each briefer than the last so she could be somebody *(chances are you can't get it at all)* and she was something with the white boys, they couldn't have them, the *(black)* girls who called her names *(if you can't get it at Hole In The Wall, chances are you can't get It at all)* and after a while her father had found out, some fas' woman up the road had heard them singing it and he had been talking about migrating for months anyway, and her uncle said come out, take advantage of Her Majesty, but that hadn't been a problem because when she got on the plane there had been one thought in her head, that in England she'd have more choice, and when another jealous babble greeted her in the first week of school she had sought them again, the weary look on her father's face deepening. He knew she had a strange mission, and he had tried to prevent it, but eventually he placed it in the back of his mind as he met the unerring flow of Mills and Boon suitors.

Soon she had needed a defence of some sort, so she trotted out the phrases she had heard others use, they're just the lads I meet, I have a lot in common with him, because she couldn't have said I like it, this is my preference. She couldn't even have said I've loved them. She wanted them because she had something to prove, and because she knew a black man couldn't provide that for her. She said it was circumstances. But inside herself it was more complete, more calculated.

No black man would appreciate Mona. None of them could see Mona's complexities, her beauty. They wouldn't understand. In Jamaica black men were what the teasing school crowd had to settle for. She couldn't want what they wanted. In England, they were too busy fighting the good fight, being *black men*, angstful, complaining, the lot of them. Always complaining about their lot in life, how horrible it was, poor them, poor victims. She wanted peace. Romance. Adoration. She was not willing to share their energy. She wanted it all, or nothing, and because she saw them fighting, she knew she could not become their obsession.

Because she could not join the fight, because their rejection of her was so complete, because she existed, she felt, on the edge of everything, not feeling her blackness, but not wanting to be white, she lived with a constant vulnerability. She had waited for the day when someone stood up in a crowd, pointed, called her name, traitor. She sought comfort in Mona, for in the mirror she belonged to no community but her own. The more she ran away, the more she sought out white men. Comfort in their unattainable puzzles, triumph when she had a place beside them. They had to fight for her. They dated her in the face of their disapproving families, they protected her from her own, who asked too much. She played with the stereotypes of their whiteness and blackness, not sure of what else to do. Their love words pleased and pained her, because in being with them, she could feel herself becoming their archetype. It was a temporary disguise. She was defined. It was better than the insult she was in the eyes of her own. Ironically, she had become what they accused her of: they told her to go away, that she was too good for them. So she was. She had been a sacrifice.

She had been existing in a dream before the article in the tabloid had come out. Her sacrifice roared up at her from the page. It was the truth. She was a sell-out, and she felt weak shame where there once had been defiance. She looked at herself and the words of the blonde woman and she was shocked. She felt herself drowning in it. Still, an old temptation was strong within her. If she had been revealed as a traitor, perhaps she would continue. Life would be less complicated than it was now, trying to walk a tightrope of racial consciousness. Why not scream it from the rooftops? *I don't want you, none of you who make life so complicated, you black men, because I don't know what to say to you or how to treat you because if I face you I will have to face myself and I was never taught how to, I don't know the rules because you told me that I was too nice to be among you and I have believed you all my life, I have seen myself as traitor and now I am one, look at me.*

Julius watched Nicola covertly. He knew she wasn't listening. He was about to yell at her when she unfolded her legs and stood, without the aid of her hands. It was such a graceful, forceful movement that the whole company stopped. She ran off the stage.

"Excuse me." He rose and followed her. Damn business for a moment. He pushed at his pride and anger. Her physical removal of him from her house had bitten into him. The outrage of a woman being able to remove him. He had promised that he would not forgive her that. It had been impossible, watching her rehearse, touching her hand every night to the audience's acclaim. Every time he had wrapped his fingers around her own he had remembered the first time he had held her hand, almost as long as his, and she had pulled away. "What's the matter," he had asked. She had looked down, embarrassed, the *joie de vivre* gone. "What is it," he had insisted. And finally, her small voice, "My hands are so . . . big," and he had grabbed her, overjoyed that she had showed something, anything that was more than her carefully crafted warmth, kissed the hands, showed her how strong they were, how deserving of love. Her gratitude was fierce.

He found her at the stage door, putting her jacket on, ripping her hair down. Hearing him, she turned away.

"I'm so sorry. Julius, I know how this will look. Please don't be angry. Go back to the cast, it's going to look bad."

"I don't really care," he said.

"But you have to, this is the kind of thing you were most afraid of, look, we'll break up, it's no good anyway, tell them we've broken up, Kathy can step in and take my place, she's really good and she deserves a break.." She was gabbling.

"There is no way I would compromise this work by losing you."

She looked at him.

"I'm sorry," he said.

He walked forward and stood in front of her, his hands stuffed into the pockets of his jeans. His face was uncertainty, his eyes wet *(and the hairs in the beard blonde)* with something she couldn't recognise. She touched his face. Their greeting. A greeting that was becoming old and comfortable, even now.

"I'm sorry."

And she knew how hard those simple words were for him, this man who had told her he loved her with rare simplicity and passion, told her this with all his might. I love you was easy for him; he believed in tapping into the finer instincts, speaking his mind. But I'm sorry was difficult. That was more than an expression of emotion. It made him a little boy again. They stood looking at each other, her hand on his cheek, cupping him.

"I'm sorry, too. I am a damn stupid, stubborn gyal." He smiled. "Why you go fall in love with me, eh?"

There was a promise there, between them. A promise to try. But even as they made this silent pact, she felt a spot of moisture at her spine, a slow, callous finger creeping downwards. Something. She wasn't sure. Something.

13

The dance floor swayed in front of their eyes. It was a thick carpet of black and gold which winked through the darkness like insane fireflies. Some revellers wore tacky, plastic masks, which they slung across their foreheads in an effort to see across the room; others passed big-head spliffs, dance moves and gossip. People swigged drinks, turned their faces to other faces, seeking themselves in each other. The smoke carried through the crowd like a live animal, wrapping itself around souls.

As they walked into the room, the DJ was busy calling down scandal on a miscellaneous member of his audience: "Bobby? Anybody name Bobby Lawns, here with Alicia Morgan? You baby mother, Monique, is here, and she says as long as you ah do the t'ing with a sixteen year old, she gone about her business!" The crowd roared in mirth, sparks floating up to the dark ceiling where they danced with the blues smoke. The DJ continued, his mischievous eyes now as golden in the queer light as the lace on the woman beside him. "Bobby! You hear? You baby mother ah lef' you! What 43 year old ah do with pickney? Ah bet you never tell her how old you was!" The men in the crowd roared encouragement for Bobby. "Ladies in the house! You think she should lef' him?" The YEEEEESSSS!! hit the men and bounced off them. No-one stopped dancing. The DJ laughed gleefully into his mike. "Anyway, as soon as it come, we ah go wish Bobby a happy new year, eh?"

Alex looked around, wondering if she could spot Bobby and his teenage princess cowering in some corner. No luck. Michael pinched her and she cuffed him affectionately. It wasn't often that she asked her brother to cramp his style by walking with her, but tonight seemed necessary and his girlfriend was away. Michael was always so sweet. She knew some people thought he was a bit boring, mistaking his quiet solicitude for weakness. He had only disdain for machismo; she remembered him watching the other boys in the playground back at school, a look of deep distrust on his face. His delicate way of speaking, gently picking his way through the words as if playing in a minefield, had got him labelled queer early in life. He had never fought back, simply disarmed them with his lovely simplicity, pointed out to thugs that they'd bruise their knuckles on his face, and what was the point? Not that he couldn't move his body with agility or speed; it was when Marie Pritchard had pulled Alex's hair that she saw it first, a carefully calculated flick of the wrist and all 14 stone of the 13 year old Marie was on the ground. Michael wasn't gay either, although he had admitted to experimentation in high school one night when they were eating sherbet under the covers of her bed, giggles muffled from their parents. Her eyes had become very round as he told her of kisses, light kisses with a small teenager he had met months before. And then stories of losing his virginity with a girl down the road, just before the taboos of siblings had taken over and he had decided it wasn't very proper to be telling his big sister anything like this, and it was certainly less than cool to be sucking sherbet at the same time. Even now when he stopped by the house he would sometimes bring her a bag, and they would eat the sweet-sour sunshine together, conspirators of old. He lived with Marisa, a woman he loved as carefully and gracefully as he did everything else.

He nudged her. She had to lean close to hear him over the din. "Julius looks like he's going to die."

She looked over at the man. Julius was smiling bravely, but his hands stuck out at strange angles, his feet tapped to a rhythm that didn't exist in the dark room. If he'd been a less confident man he would have been shrinking against Nicola. She reached for Michael's ear and yelled back. "I knew that any place Jeanette wanted to go, Julius couldn't deal with!"

Naturally this had been Jeanette's idea. She wanted to dance, and she wanted company, and she had wheedled away at all of them until they were part charmed and partly sick of her voice. Julius and Nicola had been thinking of going to dinner, but as soon as Nicola had said she was in, Alexandrea had given her brother a call. After nearly three months of life with Jeanette, she was resigned to the insistent charm of the girl. It wasn't that she disliked Jeanette, just that she seemed so . . . uncontrolled. Her plaits and her arms flapped, her lips were always wet, her laughter always loud. Jeanette had tried various overtures, but few had been successful; the same moment that Alex found herself laughing with her she felt herself recoil at the red mouth, the very health that burst forth from the woman.

To her surprise, Nicola and Jeanette had taken to each other from the beginning. They had a certain uncontrollable love of life in common. She had expected Nicola to feel threatened as time marched on — after all, she was used to being the centre of attention — but strangely the two women had, by some silent consent, decided to rule together. Their unity made Alexandrea feel insecure; usually Nicola sought her level headed advice, but now it was less so: she seemed to need Jeanette's exuberance more. She supposed that since Nicola's relationship was going well she needed play time. And Jeanette certainly provided that.

Tonight the younger girl looked dangerous. The shorts she wore were really no more than a silver leather G-string, over white fishnet stockings. The cheeks of her rear were smooth and deep brown, the thighs fleshy. She wore silver, knee-high boots and her vest was matching, thick white mesh. "Where do you keep your underwear?" she had whispered to Jeanette before they left the house. Julius had nearly died when Jeanette had hauled off the top, leaving her torso completely naked, to show how a bra was cunningly sewn into the pattern of the fabric. Nicola and Michael had doubled over with laughter as she nonchalantly fixed a diamanté nose stud to her face, her nipples mounds of brown sugar. Still, perhaps Julius and Nikki weren't all that good these days: before they had left for the club she had seen Julius pull her friend aside and heard the tension in their lowered voices *(so you don't want to go to black people's things, it's not that I just don't think I'll fit in)* and over the last few weeks there had been a subtle change in Nicola. Once, when Jeanette had made a disparaging comment about a mixed race couple on the high street, she had expected her usual all-the-world-can-be-united-by-love ploy. Nicola had actually ducked her head. Jeanette had apologised, an apology that Nicola had waved away. What hurt Alexandrea most was the fact that she had been trying to get her to examine her penchant for white and only white men for years with no effect. And then along came the Psychology student.

She looked over at Nicola now, her usual charming, beautifully dignified self, flirty in red chiffon that skimmed her thighs, and admitted that this turnabout probably had more to do with what she had come to think of as The Article.

Nicola's first interview had resulted in a banner headline that had so upset her friend she had literally gone off for a couple of days: 'I DON'T LIKE BLACK MEN: Julius Fraser's new girlfriend speaks . . .' Obviously the hack had misquoted her, but it didn't help. Julius had screamed bloody murder down the phone, and the paper had printed an apology, but the deed was done. The photo spread that went along with the article hadn't helped; Nicola had been told it would be a light-hearted look at famous actresses, but the spread was more parody than celebration. Nicola as Josephine Baker, complete with a waist full of bananas; Nicola clad in leopard skin with a jungle backdrop — Alexandrea didn't know who that was meant to be, and indeed how on earth her friend could have been suckered into the image — Nicola as Marilyn Monroe, blonde tresses and long brown legs just looked like someone's idea of a bad joke. Already *Black London* had written a scalding feature that talked of coconuts and oreo cookies and Mars Bars — the culinary equivalent of traitor. Nicola had tried to repair some of the damage by appearing on a few chat shows, but there was only so much that could be done.

Alex looked at Michael bleakly.

He nodded. He saw the looks Nicola was getting from the outskirts of the crowd. People were beginning to recognise her. And to bring Julius here. It was going to be difficult. "We may as well make the best of it," he whispered. She smiled at him again. He had drawn a stare or two from Jeanette, and she had feared the absolute worst. But Michael had removed her playful fingers from his shoulder in a movement that felt more like a caress than a rejection, and Jeanette had smiled, accepted defeat and moved on. Alex recognised a look of regret on her brother's face as Jeanette slid onto the dance floor.

"Don't you DARE!" she hissed.

Michael smiled. "Why don't you like her? She's good fun."

"Yeah, that's all I hear these days. Puh-leeze."

"C'mon, Al." He knew she hated being called that. "You need to chill." They struggled their way towards the table where Julius perched. The place was literally packed, shoulder to shoulder. In a different generation they could have been in a slave galley. Only Michael's deceptively strong shoulders cleared them a way through the undulating mass towards Julius, a drink firm in hand.

"Alright?" asked Michael.

Julius looked slightly relieved. He liked Michael a lot, and Nicola was no help in this kind of scene. She didn't seem to understand that he would have fit in if he could. Things between them had been good, but there had been another, almost imperceptible change. It was as if she was rubbing his face in her blackness. He wanted to talk to her about it, but some part of her had closed off once more. He certainly wasn't naive; he had never dated a black woman before, and had been curious about the challenges, the things he didn't know. His father had read the papers and raised an eyebrow, commented that a coloured girl might be . . . interesting. He'd frowned back at him. Nicola would have to meet them soon and he hoped his otherwise intelligent father wouldn't act the fool. Still, when they had first met, Nicola hadn't seemed bothered about their racial difference. She hadn't mentioned it at all. But now there was something there. She was changing. He thought he was doing a lot, supporting her over the press coverage. She was her usual, complex, loving self most of the time, but occasionally she seemed unreachable. The week before he had gotten her a copy of *Sankofa*, an obscure little film that he'd thought she might like. It traced the pains of slavery. He even thought it would act as the spur to a conversation about their relationship.

Unfortunately, the day had been a long one for him, full of miniature, irritating disasters, and lulled by a large fire in his front room, he fell asleep. Later, when he stirred to consciousness he hardly recognised her. She sat, her face in profile, watching the images on the screen. There was a spasm of pain dancing across her. Her lips were drawn back against her teeth in a grimace that made her ugly for the first time that he could remember. Disturbed, but unable to face or deal with the raw emotion in front of him, he had pretended to be foggier than he felt. He motioned towards the screen. "Who's that character? I don't remember her . . ."

She had turned on him then, and he couldn't see into her eyes, they were so dark with hurt and fury. "Typical fucking white man!" she spat. "Can't tell the difference between one black person and the other? All look the same, do we?" He was appalled and hurt in the face of this person he didn't know. "What on earth do you mean?" Just as suddenly as she had attacked him, he saw a tear swell to fullness in a crease of her eyelid, a tear that grew until it dripped and pattered down her neck. He was on the floor beside her, afraid to touch her, but needing to, and thank God, thank Christ, she had put herself into his arms and cried, and it wasn't the crying that frightened him the most, it was what she said over and over again *(you don't understand you don't understand you don't understand)* and he didn't know what to do but to stroke her hair *(strange how you couldn't really run your hands through dread locks like other hair but you had to run your hands over them)* and look at her, bewildered. He knew intellectually that this was pain about blackness, pain about slavery, but he couldn't understand what it had to do with him, with them. So he held her and tried to climb inside her eyes, tried to clear the darkness away.

But now, now she was laughing with her friends, and he couldn't help feeling a grudging jealousy; when she was here, places like this, she was no longer his in some kind of way, she was of them. He had seen it in their eyes when he had walked in, the resentment, the different way they looked at her when he was with her, and the way that her status somehow changed when he was with her. As if she was tainted with him. He closed his eyes against the sway. He was not so arrogant to think he belonged here just because he was human. He felt an outsider. But, it would be alright, he promised himself. Alright. He was going to be with her. If she loved him enough to put up with this, she would stay.

Michael peered into his face, then looked out at the crowd. Julius envied the man his look of pleasure. Jeanette and Nicola had pulled a reluctant Alexandrea into their circle, and she, too, had finally loosened and flowed. They were bodies of dark bitter earth, darkly-veined stones, chocolates jostled in a box, each with a sweet centre, waiting to be bitten into, their movements together made Michael think of autumn leaves, shaken and flung by the wind, their paths indescribable and eternal, all of them sweating, terrible, lovely, holding each other up, flowing and flowing and Julius watched Nicola kiss them both, fling her hands into the air, the red chiffon a scream against her and it was the most alienating experience of his life. He looked at Michael and knew he saw something different. He felt himself gripped with despair. Perhaps, if he asked, Michael could explain it all to him, guide him, give him ways of meeting her in all places. He felt himself reaching for the man, but drew back when he saw his face change.

"SHIT!" Michael started forward, moving fast. Julius was momentarily confused, then looked back at the women. Even as he did so he realised that the air had changed. It had changed with the song. He could see the deejay across the room, his fingers twirling magic as he mixed.

If a gyal man ah run you down
Ah nuh fe you fault
Tek 'im, tek 'im, gyal!
Ah nuh fe you fault

Tension played thick on the air. A large space had been cleared where the women had been dancing. He searched desperately for Nicola, saw that she was being restrained by a man, a man who pulled at her tall frame as if it was mere paper *(my body, he has hold of my body)* and he could see that she was yelling, and even though he did not hear over the music, the terrible, insidious music that pounded into him, he could see the word she was mouthing, and it was his name, over and over: Julius, Julius, Julius. The crowd had completely swallowed Alex, her frame lost in the hunger for *(blood)* excitement. He started to his feet, still confused, his head dizzy with adrenaline and fury. And then he saw the epicentre of the crowd.

Jeanette had stopped dancing and was facing a larger woman.

Julius saw that the woman held a knife.

The deejay hauled back the record and started up again, too far away to realise that he was fuelling a dispute.

If a gyal man ah run you down
Ah nuh fe you fault . . .

"Yes, my selector! Come again!" The woman in front of Jeanette flung a hand into the air. Her eyes were the stillest part of her, watching her prey carefully. She rolled the knife in her hand for better purchase.

When she had first plucked at Jeanette's braids, the girl had thought it was a mistake, and kept on dancing. The woman had introduced herself swiftly: she was Donald's fackin' woman, and who the fack do you think you are, bitch, tryin' to take my man? Jeanette had groaned inwardly. Donald was the sweet youth she'd given some to when she moved. She had reached out for the woman, trying to explain that she didn't give a damn about Donald, but she was not to be dissuaded.

She had tried some more choice words on for size and spat at Jeanette's feet. Anger had risen in Jeanette, red-hot, stinking anger, and she had laughed in her rival's face. As if by some sixth sense, the unknowing deejay had cranked up the new tune, perhaps feeling somehow, through experience, that the vibe was aggression, rivalry.

Whatever the case, Jeanette looked the woman full in the face.

"You can't do a thing about it." She laughed, smoothed her hands over her hips, sung softly. "Me ah tek 'im, tek 'im gyal. Ah nuh fe me fault . . ."

And then the knife. The fight had died from her as soon as it had come. She was no coward, but she wanted no part of that blade. She shook to think of it sinking into her flesh, the flesh she had so joyfully uncovered for the evening. Their eyes locked. The woman with the knife was in full steam, dancing to taunt Jeanette, her hips a mass of diminutive, intense movements that started deep in the groin. She lunged forward. Jeanette managed to dodge her. The crowd murmured its approval, whipped by the music.

"Dus' 'er out!"

"Eeh-eeh! Facety gyal come tek liberty! Run her!"

The girl moved forward again, and they grappled, the knife between them. The crowd drew a breath. Julius was trying to get through them, but he felt as if he was swimming through mud, and even with his height he felt himself lifted off his feet several times.

The woman jabbed upwards, the stroke more luck than art. Above Jeanette's right eye soft liquid began to flow. Liquid that splattered onto the shadows of her arms. It was happening so fast. She was trying to see through blood. She was amazed at how much of it there was. The girl was laughing with her friends. She'd obviously brought people with her, because no-one seemed to be helping. Despair bloomed. She watched the woman move towards her again and took a deep breath. She seemed massive, looming above her. Blood flowed off the end of an elbow and dripped onto the dance floor. The woman stepped forward into the dampness and skidded, teetering, trying to keep her balance.

Here you go, girl, MOVE your ass! Jeanette thought. She took a step backwards. And then, amazingly, her attacker went reeling back, into the arms of the crowd. A man had stepped into the breach. Tall and slender, he was bald-headed and curved as a whip. Rubbing angrily at her blurred vision she saw Julius and Michael clearing paths in front of them, their arms performing a frantic crawl.

Where were you? she thought. Then decided that fainting might be the best choice.

When she woke there was roaring in her ears. She realised several things simultaneously: that Alex and Michael looked almost twin-like when they were worried, that Nicola and Julius were in the middle of a fight once more, something about a photographer, and that the man who supported her head was not a whip, as she had thought, but more like a licorice stick. He was neatly dressed in trousers and a T-shirt, no homeboy streaks in the head, just a shiny, velvet dome and deep, old eyes. She guessed he was about thirty. She smiled and lifted a blood-streaked arm as the ambulance wailed through the streets. The medic told her not to talk. Her face throbbed hugely into the night lights, the wail of the ambulance raising her pain level to a shriek.

She tried to speak. The man leaned forward. He smelled like mushrooms, mushrooms and incense. She wondered what he did for a living.

"What did you say?" he asked.

"What —" She struggled against the ache. "What's the time?"

He smiled, crinkling his face delightfully. Checked his watch. "It' s five past midnight."

She tried to smile. "Happy New Year . . . for what it's worth . . ."

"Happy New Year to you."

She tasted blood in her mouth. "What's your name, Saviour?"

"Sean." said Sean.

Mavis

De firs' time me do it for money ah was a different person. When you nuh have no money in you pocket dat's what happen. Not dat me family ever have more dan two cents to dem name. Me madda teach me how to mek chicken last fe four pickney fe one whole-ah two week, dat's when she get fe buy de whole chicken rather dan de chicken back. De only part ah de bird we never nyam was de chicken batty, 'cause everybody know seh if you eat dat you chat too much.

When I was a pickney de bes' t'ing to eat inna de world was condensed milk an' bread. Mamma woulda sen' Auntie down de bakery, bring back de warm hardo bread, jus' bake, smellin' warm, an' me lay me head against her chest where she did hol' de fresh bread, feel how it hot an' how she smell good.

An' den she would put me one side, cut a big slice of de bread, open up de milk can, one side one hole, one more on de other, an' pour it over de bread, drip down de side. Ah woulda sit at de front door, mek de sweet milk drip down de side ah me han', an' first me woulda lick it off de fingers, an' den lick de top, roll de thick sweetness around me tongue, den hold meself, look at de bread, how it look nice, like me was the luckiest girl in de whole world. Den me hear me bredda dem ah come, an me have to bite into it quick-time before dem come an' beg me piece. When dem done fuss how me always get de firs' bread-back, dem go inside to Mamma an' get fe dem piece, an' me siddung dere, in de sunshine, listen to de sound dem inna de tenement yard.

Dere was one couple over de way, de man was like him always ah look piece, an' all in de day-time we could hear de man endlessly, all de time, ah cuss her fe lie down wid 'im. Most of de time she give in. De times she never him woulda beat her, beat her slow, licks jus' ah sound through de yard, an' Mamma, who was a big, strong woman, would finally get so vex dat she go over dere an' bang 'pon de yard, an' cuss him how him mus' stop rass de woman, if him nuh tired of de noise. Me feel seh she shoulda lef' dem. After de woman ah gwaan like she like it. Me used to wonder why she nuh lef' him. Sittin' dere wid me condensed milk.

Dem days after de woman run me, me couldn't even afford condensed milk fe mek me smile. All evenin' time ah come an' me ah hol' me belly wid de wind, drink pure peppermint tea fe try full me. Even more dan me belly-bottom every day me ah fret seh me cyaan pay de man rent. Is not like Mamma did have any money fe send me. Is me used to have to send likkle money to she when me have it. De landlord did name Mr. Moore. Him always did tell me to call him Mr. Moore, like him want respect, an' him never call me by my firs' name, even though ah hear Susan an' de odder gyal dem call him by him Christian name, Carl. Christian name. Dat was de funny part. Me did t'ink him was a good Christian, him give me time to pay off de rent, all bring tin bully-beef come give me, because him know t'ings gone bad wid me. But every day dat pass me know seh t'ings ah get worse, an' me never know what to do. Me couldn't sleep ah night-time, de way me body hurt an' me mind jus' ah wander an' ah worry.

Me was gettin' closer all de time to Susan. She used to carry some food for me as well, come up to de room an' chat. She tell me 'bout her life an' how she start inna de business. Is her madda encourage her fe do it. Seh it was generally alright when she start, it pay enough money, an' all you haffi do is mek dem stick it in an' juk youself up an' down an' dem do de t'ing an' get off. She say looks don't matter, even though it can be easy if you beautiful. She say all dem want is a hole, den half an hour later you can tek a fresh an' go back on de road. It was nice to talk to she an' de odder girls, we crack joke like egg all night long. Me never realise dem time deh dat dem was tryin' to teach me, dat dem know seh me woulda come into it soon. Me never know, me jus' laugh at de story dem, mek up me face when dem tell me how fe hol' de man somet'ing dem, how dem haffi gwaan like dem like it too, not dat most of de man dem really care who you is or where you come from. One woman tell me say if you want to make de man do him t'ing fast you put toothpaste in you mout' when you suck dem an' de toothpaste mek dem shoot off quick an' you mout' don't get tired. Sometimes me would feel sick, but de way dem tell it, like dem tired an' need somet'ing to laugh 'bout, you haffi stay deh an' listen. Susan once tell me seh she was considerin' how much of dem nasty man stuff she swallow, seh it mus' be pints by now, an' how another gyal tell her she never swallow, jus' spit it out on a rag and rub it up on her titty dem like she love it, an' it was alright wid de man.

As me tell you, me never realise seh me was doin' apprenticeship wid de gyal dem, me jus' ah pass time, ah try t'ink 'bout how me ah go manage. Den one evenin' Mr Moore come to check me. Him was a big man, not really good lookin', 'cause him mout' too mash an' him eye squingy in im face, but him talk nice, like him have education. Him ah ask me 'bout how t'ings ah go, if me get work, how me feel. Lawd, me shame. Mamma did teach all ah we seh we mus' pay for everyt'ing we ever use, and is three months rent me owe de man. An' him is not me family. Him start tell me seh him feel bad, but is a business him run, dat because him nah get de rent him pickney dem haffi do without t'ings. Me jus' put me face down, feel like me want to dead. Me ah t'ink 'bout him pickney, me never t'ink good to know seh de likkle dollars me was payin' him couldn't mek no difference, an' him have de odder rent dat him gettin'. Me jus' feel sorry, like me ah fool, but me know seh me cyaan go back ah country an' shame in front ah me Auntie and Mamma, 'cause dem never have nothin' to give me, an' me is a big woman, suppose to be doin' t'ings for me family.

Me mek him sleep wid me. Me always hope seh de Lawd Jesus would forgive me for dat, because me couldn't see any odder way. Sometimes inna de night me get 'fraid, because de Bible seh all sinners will not go through de gates of Heaven. An' me know seh me have years of sin to throw at de Lord foot bottom. An' den me know seh if de good Lawd see fit to put me down in de fiery pits, is so me goin' haffi tek it, because maybe Him will tell me seh me coulda fin' another way. Me haffi tek de responsibility fe what me do. Me is a sinner, an' all sinners get what de duck get — dem get fuck. Excuse me, Lawd. Is like me ah use me whole life to prepare for hell an' damnation, because even though de Lawd is a forgivin' God, me nuh really t'ink seh him can forgive me fe what me do. Is not jus' dat me sex de man, is dat even though it hurt likkle bit, me feel big. Me feel big because dis man, Mr Moore, want somet'ing dat me have, likkle jing-bang me, country gyal, ugly gyal. An' when him breathe out, when him grab me up like me ah de bes' t'ing, when him put him t'ings between me legs, me realise seh me have somet'ing can rule all man like him. Is not de fornication ah t'ink God ah go punish me fah. Is because me use it, an' me did know seh me was usin' it, an' me haffi tek what come to me because me did gwaan like me nuh have no broughtupcy. Never listen to me madda, who used to call me from de gully side. She did know what she was talkin' 'bout. Me jus' too hard ears, never want to listen. T'ink seh me is God's gift. Me sex de man, an' den is like s'maddy lif' somet'ing from me eyes. Show me how me fool.

After de man done, him mek me know seh me inna him stable now. Susan dem was tryin' to mek it easy for me, dem ah try teach me cause dem know seh de man was lookin' me to tun ol' whore too.

Jesus forgive me. Me did feel good s'maddy want me. Feel good.

14

The woman washed her hands noisily, and there was a silence in the toilet's pristine whiteness as she applied her lipstick. She hummed a few bars of homogenised pop music and slipped out into the corridor. Alexandrea listened to her go. The tune pricked at her, running around her head at random. She couldn't place it.

She sat on the closed toilet seat, knees up, arms clasped around her legs, heels against the seat of her brown trouser suit. She had taken a piece of toilet paper off the roll and rubbed at her shoe soles before sitting down. She needed to hug herself, but it wouldn't do to go back to work with dust on her backside. A hard piece of chewing gum was stuck to the left sole, and she spent careful time picking it off. It lay in her fist, forgotten. In the other hand she held her tape recorder, her friend, her companion. Headphones at her ears. She was listening to an interview she'd done years ago with Danny Glover. It comforted her. Drowned the blues. She had been at her best.

Angrily, she turned it off, realising that Danny was having no success in drowning out her anger at herself. She put her feet down on the floor, twisting one ankle around the other, wiping at her nose, which was already inflamed and sore. She was so tired of the tears. It was time to be over this, time to stop dreaming about him, praying for him *(he is NOT coming back to you!)* and in the spirit of that thought she put her knuckles into the wall as hard as she could. The pain made her pause, sucking the bruised flesh. Today was one of the bad days, and even though there had been less of them recently, she was alternately surprised and furious that they continued. She would be working, eating, even sleeping and the ache would rise up in her, stolidly, as if it had a purpose, a mission. Smacking her in the midriff. She played the times with Gerry over and over in her head, an insane video tape that would not stop, as much as she pleaded with her mind *(please someone take the tape back to the video store it's overdue anyway)* and she cursed herself for letting him into her life. If only she had not gone to play mas' at carnival that year, if only he'd not commented on her costume, she had been a mongoose, brown on brown, long black whiskers and if only she had not been pleased and flattered by his laughter and the uncontrollable way he'd flung back his head and why the hell had she decided to jump that year anyway, she'd never done it before but her friend Julia had said it'd be fun, and her new year's resolution that year had been to have more fun and she had wanted to do an article from the inside of carnival and it had been good, mostly because they'd sat on the tube together with him recounting all the amusing incidents he'd seen with his own eagle eyes that day, the man that fell off the float straight into a policeman, the little girl who'd been stealing gizzada from straight under the stall holder's eyes and when he had noticed, Gerry had begged for her and paid for the whole lot and the little girl had laughed in his face, cheeky devil, and disappeared into the sea-tide of the crowd and all the if onlys in the world.

Her mother would have been ashamed of her, curious as to why she couldn't hold a man. Her pretty, driven, brilliant mother. Mrs Watson, the interior decorator, eccentric, smart, twenty two inch waist at 50, arm in arm with her perfect husband, the very definition of masculine, a new man before the phrase was even coined. She supposed her parents couldn't begin to relate to anyone's failed relationship. Theirs was so symbiotic, so friendly, still so loving, so out of a bloody fairy story that it pained all those who were witness to it. She remembered watching them when she was a teenager, the way that they touched each other all the time, and she watched other people watching them, seeing their emotional failings reflected back at them, remembering their dashed needs every time Mr Watson kissed his wife, seeing her own loneliness pushed aside every time Mrs Watson came home from work and put herself in her husband's arms with a hungry delight, as if she had played the whole day, killed hours that only had to be killed so that they could be past and she could once more be in his vision.

They had made her sick.

There was something vulgar in their love for each other. Something unsightly, unsubtle, something wild. She could hear them making love at night, sighs filtering through the house, her mother's silver laughter falling through the gaps in her door, her father's voice a distant rumble. Her parents had met when they were sixteen years old, and immediately, her mother was fond of telling her, fitted into each other. Neighbours and relatives had remarked on how used to each other they seemed, as if they had known each other for a very long time. Theirs was seen as a great love, a love that cynicism and worldliness laughed at, but secretly wished for. They were a century of years between them, and still, every time she went home, they thirsted for each other, entertained each other, sparked each other's brilliance. They needed no-one. Not even the daughter who had come out of their love. For the first years of her life it would have helped if she had had a sibling. Perhaps they could have bonded together, presented a united front to the love of their parents, but she had waited three years for Michael, and in many ways, by the time he was old enough to talk, the damage had been done. At first, like all children, she knew no different. She thought that everybody lived their lives feeling as she felt, like a guest in a bed and breakfast. Their physicality embarrassed her, this child who rarely knew the warmth of their arms. She would cringe in shame when they came to school functions, sitting touching each other all the time. Their sexuality burned into her brain; it was all so unnecessary, she felt. She wanted to scream: *You're married, you're married, everyone knows you're together, stop it, stop showing off,* but she was a good girl, and she had learnt that such displays of emotions were met with blank stares. When she went to friends' houses she was at first alarmed then intrigued with their parents' relationships. There were so many other kinds of matings, but more than their variety was the fact that none of them reflected the terrible dependency that seemed to belong only to her mother and father. She saw no pattern in the world, nothing comparable, and was puzzled. A simple fact never occurred to her: her mother felt safest in her father's arms, and he felt safest in hers.

She had suspected, in her childhood, that she was in the way. But her parents had managed to curb that particular fear with occasional pats, sometimes whole days of attention. Still, she never felt as if they presented themselves to her or anyone else as individuals. She would have liked to know them in this way, but she became used to their mutual response. Even today, as an adult, every time she phoned them, they would speak to her on twin extensions, seemingly unable to talk to her alone. If her father answered the phone he would immediately call out to his wife. They united against her from early, shrinking away in the face of her occasional rages, wondering when she sulked or cried in a corner.

Friends had been deeply important to her, proof that she could be seen and yet, unknowingly, she tried to recreate her parents' relationship with all the people she'd ever loved. She knew nothing else. Nicola's natural warmth allowed her neediness, was not frightened by it, but others had suddenly abandoned her, confused by the intensity.

She was three when Michael had come into the world, whimpering gently, his eyes wide open. She felt the need to protect him from their parents. Her mother had cried the night she realised she was pregnant. Huge sobs that soaked the front of her husband's shirt. She knew because she had hidden behind the huge wooden chest in their bedroom, listening. Her mother was inconsolable, pulling at her hair. And then she heard it, the words she had known but had never wanted confirmed: her mother's whisper was ugly, injected with resentment and frustration *(another one, another one, we didn't want the first one)* and she had drawn back, banged her head, and they had seen her. Her mother's eyes were huge, and she kept apologising, telling her they didn't mean it, as if her father had also spoken those terrible words *(we didn't want the first one)* but even as she apologised, she reached only for her husband for comfort. Alex had sat on the edge of the bed, far away, and listened to them speak at her, from a distance. She knew that Michael would be her responsibility, her friend, her family.

Michael had not grown with the same resentments. While he acknowledged her pain, his wholehearted acceptance of others as they were became a protective layer for him. He was a tentative balance in their family, and brought an uneasy peace when they gathered together.

She scrubbed at her face in the basin and reapplied her make-up. She'd been working too hard, and she knew it. To shut it all out. To create some order in her world. Jenny had given the team the rest of the day off and she planned to get into a hot bath, play some very mellow music and to try to beat down the ache. She slipped into the corridor and walked straight into Tony Pearson.

*

Sean was in shock. Every time he looked over at Jeanette he couldn't believe that he was here with her. This was number six, number six, the sixth time he had seen Jeanette. She was with him now, and she was holding his hand, and he could see her in the flash and squabble of the fireworks, excited like a child, squealing with delight every time another colourful explosion touched her eyes. She looked up at him and her smile pained him. His hand sweated in hers. She hadn't noticed, at least he didn't think that she had noticed that he sweated like a pig when he was nervous. That made Jeanette wondrous. The fact that she didn't seem to see any of his glaring, horrible faults. Even on Tuesday, when he had taken her to a restaurant, a place that was as posh as he thought she deserved, cost him nearly one hundred pounds for the meal, but also posh enough for all the waiters to speak their poncy fucking French, and he hadn't known how to speak to them or what to say and he had wanted to cry, and beat them with his fists, because he felt his old enemy creep up on him, the little voice that assured him that he was not worthy of this place or of her, and he could see the other diners looking at him, asking themselves why a woman looking so fine would be seen alive on the arm of a man like that, and he was struggling with the tears and the rage and she had put a hand on his arm, and he had a soaring, beautiful moment of calm as her slender fingers caressed him and she had looked directly into the eyes of the waiter and charmed him into sending over the maître d', the top dog, who spoke wonderful French and equally beautiful English and it had been alright and she hadn't noticed when he dropped a forkful of the hundred pound meal on the sparkling white cloth, and they had talked, he had been witty, and clever, and she had seemed to like him.

Because he was used to being everybody's best friend, he wasn't sure that this was, well, an intimate thing that they were doing. Was it an intimate thing? In his mind in bed at night, with the pictures of the women flapping in the cold breeze that passed through his room sometimes, he tried to imagine what it would be like to be intimate with her. He knew women's bodies well, but it was all theory. He knew the curve of a thigh, the sweet dip of a hip, a dimple in an alien and private place. He could see all of this as he gazed at the ripped women on his walls, but he knew of nothing practical. He couldn't imagine what it was like to touch a real woman, what her earlobes felt like, how she moved or moaned when something pleased her, he knew that they got wet, but he didn't know whether that was dripping wet or waterfalls. He didn't know the sounds, the sighs, the slick rhythm of lovers, the creak of the bed, the carpet burns. Or the way an errant breast can get caught under a flailing elbow and the squeak can be mistaken for orgasm, or the moment when giggles take over desire because a member has dropped out when it shouldn't. He didn't know the irreverent mystery of sex. He wanted to know. He wanted to know with Jeanette, this lady standing beside him, humming at the rainbows and pink showers in the black sky above them. She squeezed his hand again.

"Aren't they beautiful, Sean? They're so beautiful —" she searched for words. "This makes that hard as hell course seem like nothing!" She had told him about her studies, about how much she wanted to help people with their problems, understand pain through science. She was so clever. And so lovely. He had told her all the anecdotes of the kitchen where he was training to be a chef, the unexpected way in which food could be moulded into form and substance, little tips that he could see her using in her own kitchen. This was one of his stock topics of conversation: the stew that had gotten away, that awful bollocking he'd had from the head chef when he put salt instead of sugar into the pineapple upside down cake, the customer who had insisted on bringing her dog to the restaurant, seating it on its own chair, feeding it slivers of chicken wrapped in bacon.

Whenever he saw Jeanette he played a game. It was fanciful, something to pass the time, something to honour her with. He would glance at the women they passed on the street and imagine what their lives were, how they couldn't compare to this woman who was beside him, walking beside him. The lady in the raincoat was no lady — she, he knew, was a worthless layabout, stuffing herself with chocolates bought with a dole cheque, not trying to improve her life, to be educated like Jeanette. And that fat woman, standing at the post office, he saw her as indulgent, refusing, with a kind of deliberate defiance, to take care of her body. She shouldn't be on the same street with Jeanette, her lush body striding through cold pieces of air, warming them up. Even a little girl, with her father. She was a pretty little thing, thick hair in plump plaits, but even if she combed and greased it for the rest of her little life, she could never have hair that could compare to his lady's, hair that sent wistful smells out to him, coconut and jasmine.

If she was his lady, of course. They hadn't even kissed. He wondered whether she wanted him to try. The last firework was dying in the sky, leaving lime-green blood stains in its wake. Perhaps he should make a statement: *look here, are we dealing or not, what's the flex?* Be a man. After all, the making of a man was in his might, his father used to tell him that. His father had also attributed the words to someone else, but he suspected that it was a line from the older man's meandering poetry. Perhaps he should ask his father to write a poem for Jeanette.

She pulled at him, wanting to buy a toffee apple. They ate it together. She hadn't eaten one in years and had forgotten that they were so sweet. He promised to make her some that she would like.

"How can I be dealing with a trainee chef?" she complained, delighted. "You'll probably express love with food, and I'll be huge by the time we've been married for a year."

His smile was calm, but he felt sick and exhilarated at the same time. As they walked out of the park, away from the tilt-a-whirl and ferris wheel, he tried to understand what he was feeling. It was an emotion so long denied that for moments, as she talked merrily, he could not understand it. It was only later, when he dropped her home and kissed her cheek and she made him kiss her lipstick off as well that he remembered.

He was daring to hope.

15

Alexandrea sank into soft, muted cushions and looked up at him, perched on the edge of his desk, one foot swinging. The material prickled into the back of her neck. Embarrassed, she felt her handbag underneath her and scooped it away. He was going to think she was *(stupid)* afraid of him if she didn't get a grip. She wasn't fearful, but the incident in the edit room had left her feeling uncomfortable. Every time he was around, she dropped things, had even lost a whole file when he walked into the office one day. It was ridiculous. She shifted the bag out of harm's way, rubbing the sore place where it had dug into her. Walking into Pearson had shaken her meanderings on her family and Gerry, but she didn't feel capable of fencing with him today. He had noted her swollen eyes without comment, and she hadn't liked that keen gaze on her. They needed, he explained, to have a word in his office.

With three months to go on her contract she wasn't nervous about her prospects yet, but Jenny had suggested that all the researchers make arrangements for a private word with Pearson, to show willing, discuss their futures at Endeavour. It was The Way. She had seen others step to this routine dance, slightly sweating or *laissez faire* bodies, depending on their personalities or connections, hovering at Pearson's door for little informal chats. Of course the man had a calculated reputation; the chats were legendary. Two feet in at Endeavour did not a career make. With short contracts being handed down all the time there was a constant air of vulnerability. And here he was, right now, much as she had imagined he would be, poised like a big cat on his desk, an informal pose on the face of it, but really one that gave him an advantage.

Still, to be asked into his chambers. That was something. She had also heard stories of those that he nurtured: people like Jenny Tasdell and Ruby

Fleur. People who got places. Surely, as a black man it would give him pleasure to make another black face a protégée. Because she was getting on well with Ruby herself she had delayed the inevitable, hoping that their good vibes would assure her a notch on the next series. But she knew she wasn't hustling enough. Now, it seemed, Tony had ideas for her. They had passed another researcher on the way to his office, and the man had given her a furtive thumbs up. She squeezed at the excitement inside her.

It was a very masculine room, shades of chrome and silver reflecting the calm blue of the overstuffed couch he had waved her towards. Through the huge window behind him she could see the sky, clouds doing the soca as a flock of supple birds burst through them. It was the kind of office she would have liked to have. A place for everything, and everything in its place. Neat. Crisp. Like a new book, its edges sharp but pliable.

He got himself a lager from the tiny bar, and handed her a glass of orange juice, the glass an elegant exclamation mark in her hand. He was such an arrogant man; hadn't even asked what she wanted. It was only his charm that smoothed the edges. She sipped and steeled herself. He had seated himself on top of the desk again, the trousers he wore shown to their best advantage. She slipped her smile into the juice. She remembered someone telling her that when a cat purrs, it is not saying 'I am happy', rather 'I am inoffensive'. She was excited, but she watched the man. He was purring. But he had claws.

"So." He clasped his hands together in front of him. "Are you enjoying the show?"

She nodded assent, placing the glass on the table beside her.

"Good, good. Remind me which episodes you've worked on?" He shuffled through papers as she spoke briefly about the work she'd completed, careful to mention the episode in which their main guest had dropped out and she'd found a replacement. Pearson listened, his head on one side. She found herself repeating what she'd said before. The silence from him was so deafening.

"What are we going to do about us?" The question hung in the air between them, a bad smell, a *faux pas*, she couldn't quite understand. He was still swinging one leg. His eyes didn't leave her face. She searched her brain for words.

"What do you mean?" Rosy job descriptions began to fade before her eyes.

He sighed, and she could see a twitch in his jaw. "I mean, what are we going to do about you and me?"

She struggled with the moment. She felt the amazement on her face. She didn't consider herself naive, but if he was saying it, she wanted him to *say* it.

"I'd like you to explain exactly what you mean." She was calm, but she could feel adrenaline streaming through her veins, threatening to reveal itself on the surface.

"Alexandrea, I'm a Caribbean man, and I believe in speaking my mind." He had risen now, walked behind the desk and placed himself in the chair there. He looked nervous, pained even. In the midst of her confusion, she was touched. He looked like a small boy asking for a first date *(this is the common denominator)* and she permitted herself a sweet feeling of triumph *(they're all the same vulnerable boy)* because he looked so unsure, this powerful man! Mentally, she hugged herself. But of course it was out of the question. Didn't he know that he was a marble statue, something she could look at, but hardly take home to bed? He was speaking again.

"I've always admired your work, but it wasn't until the day you came for an interview that I realised how beautiful you were."

When Alex looked back at that moment, she always wondered why a lie hadn't sprung to her lips. Nicola told her she should have told the arrogant twit she was a lesbian, had a boyfriend, anything, just to let him know it was out of the question. Still, here and now, only the truth occurred. She twisted uncomfortably, suddenly realising the depth of the position she was in. Did turning him down mean that she lost her job? Discomfort became panic. What was this man really saying to her? Fighting for time, she gesticulated towards his desk.

"What about them?" The photo of his wife and child gleamed like the rest of the room. The child wore a red jumper. He had chocolate at the corner of his mouth. Beautiful Mrs Pearson was softened by maternity. From the twist of the woman's smile she knew that Pearson must have been the photographer. He touched the picture lightly, his jaw dancing.

Then turned to look at her.

"Is that the only problem?"

"Well, I think it's a helluva problem."

He was looking disappointed now, disappointed and frustrated. She sensed a storm in her own soul. He was so sure of himself. She searched her own behaviour. Had she said something, done something, to make him so confident of her? She thought of his arm around her in the edit room. The man had been testing her, for God's sake. Perhaps she should have pushed him off, wagged a finger at him? She felt her lack of power. If this had been *anyone*, she could have softly rebuked him, told him that he had been mistaken in no uncertain terms. Gerry would have laughed at this. He had always been full of admiration at the way she saw off admirers *(look down your nose at them, baby)* but she couldn't do that now *(you could lose your job, surely not, you could lose your job)* "I don't think you understand exactly what I mean to offer, Alexandrea —" Her teeth felt on edge. "Come to dinner with me this evening. We can talk about the ways you'd like to arrange this . . ."

She rose to her feet, feeling decidedly shaky. "Mr Pearson, I'm sorry if you've got the wrong impression, but I have no sexual interest in you."

He laughed softly. "You don't have to play hard to get, Alexandrea. My terms would be very agreeable."

She faced him, trying to resist the urge to slap his face. How could she have respected this man, admired him? He was a stinking dog, and she couldn't quite believe that she was in the middle of this. "I am sorry, Mr. Pearson. This is out of the question."

They gazed across at each other for some minutes. Pearson's face crumpled. "Then it seems that I owe you an apology. I misread the signals."

"Yes you did." In the face of his regret she began to bend. This could obviously be sorted out. They were both adults.

"I'm sorry." He stuck out a hand. "No hard feelings?" She shook it, felt its weight carefully.

"That's alright." She felt her feet carrying her towards the door, managed a smile, and was in the corridor once more.

*

The sweat ran down Julius' body. It was sweet to her, and she licked it off, her face serious and dark. He was crouched over her, nudging between her legs, a fountain of lightness, a weight that didn't seem heavy. She felt him begin to slide into her, slowly, stroking the tiny grooves along her, hair entangled, plaited as their bellies met and kissed in recognition. She pushed her hips up, seeking, rubbing herself on him, delighted. Their flesh strained, smiled, faster. He lifted himself and put his hands round her ribcage, playing the bones. The long sound in her throat trickled around the sheets that he had kicked off, sank through them, melted with them. He was anxious this afternoon, had been mystifying all day. Anxious as he pulled away from her, as, protesting, she pulled him back near her, as close as anyone could ever be, anxious in his whispers, *do you like this, do you like it, tell me, tell me what you want,* shifting his body to accommodate her, listening closely to her movements and her building tension, *tell me, tell me, baby, what do you want, how do you want it, how shall I be,* as Nicola wondered and undulated beneath him. She gritted her teeth, let spasms grow from her toes, glow in her elbows, make her sweet, sweet, sweet, and she joined in, their murmur was a chorus that was very old, ancient, lovers' tongues, spoken by many, never recorded and she felt herself shaking, the sounds she made touched by instinct only, hips trembling as his mouth followed her, echoing her moans with his own and she couldn't stop herself, it burst from her in the mutual darkness, and as she said it, over and over again, making it new, he was watching her, and every time she said *I love you, love you, love you,* he closed his eyes as relief surrounded him, bubbling, soft, and he couldn't find his own release, it didn't matter, because she had said what he needed to hear, and he was choked, old, young, bare, alive, and all he could say was *yes, yes, yes.*

When their breathing had calmed, he had given her a box. The implications of it tugged at Nicola as she sat in her father's flat. She knew he did not approve. He didn't say it, but she knew it. She looked at him across the little kitchen table. He sat, his arms on the surface, sniffing. He had a bad cold, and she kept handing him tissues. His face reminded her of chamois leather, the coat of a deer, brown like her own, battered as a subway car. The battering stood out like bruises. Some lingered there for the loss of his wife and the life of bringing up a girl child, bringing her to this England-is-a-bitch place, not knowing how to feel or what to say in the face of her talent and beauty and feeling that she could not really be his daughter, he who stood at five eight in bare feet and her fingers that were inches longer than his, her way of talking and that feeling that somehow he had gone wrong with her.

She, in turn, knew that she was a puzzle to him. He had greeted the news of Julius' proposal in his usual, solid way, but she saw new bruises forming. He didn't speak very much, for he considered long and hard what he had to say. Conversation was usually small between them. He preferred thought and action. They spent some time together after her news, he picking slowly at a small lunch he had prepared for them. When she bent to kiss him at the door, he had handed her a sad smile to take away with her. It sparkled in her pocket with the ring. She hadn't put it on. She turned away, but he reached for her, and asked her that small question. It rattled in her head now, as she stretched in her room, bending and straightening, firming her belly and her legs, feeling the pull of muscle against blood *(wouldn't you marry a man that looked like me)* and she searched for an answer in the petals of the roses that were dying in her room, a huge bunch, the only one she had saved from the opening night, soft pink roses that smiled at her from their grave.

16

They sat companionably, back to back, Jeanette's legs outstretched and littered with daisy chains that she tried to drape onto his head, humming songs she heard as a child *(go down Emmanuel Road gyal an' bwoy)* Michael batting off her gestures with his deep laugh, listening to her hard. They had become friends, these two, managing to hop, skip and jump over that thing called sex, admitting mutually that their hearts did nothing when they saw each other.

"I flirted with you out of sheer habit," she told him, and he laughed out loud.

"I can't want you because I'm involved in that crazy thing called love," he told her.

"Would you want me if you weren't living with someone?" she asked, foreseeing his answer and knowing that whatever it was she wouldn't be hurt.

"Probably not," he replied, laughing. She shoved him and threaded a daisy into the gold hoop in his ear.

She was relieved to have a friend, a man who didn't peek between her legs when he thought she wasn't looking. Alex hated the fact that they were friends.

"She feels you're stealing her security," he had explained when she asked.

"What is the problem between me and her?" she insisted, but he hadn't answered her directly.

"Be nice to her, she needs it." was all he would say.

"Tell me about this love thing," she asked, continuing to hum *(fe go bruk rock stone, go down Emmanuel Road)* as he searched for words.

Unable to explain, he turned it around on her. "Why do you want to know? And *what* is that rubbish song you're singing?"

(bruk dem one by one gyal an' bwoy) "Just a song we used to sing when I was a kid. *(bruk dem two by two gyal an' bwoy)* I don't want to talk about it. *(bruk dem three by three gyal an' bwoy)* Tell me about this love thing. *(finger mash don't cry gyal an' bwoy)* Because I think I'm falling in love. *('memba ah play we ah play gyal an' bwoy)* With Sean."

He turned to look at her. "Perhaps you're not as hard as you seem."

"Do I seem hard?" She was hurt. "I don't mean to seem that way."

"You fuck around like a man," he returned, in his gentle way it seemed no accusation. She mulled on that for a while.

"What does that mean, like a man?"

"You just do it, and it doesn't seem to bother you. How many lovers have you had since you came to London?"

She shrugged. "I don't know. Quite a few. Why shouldn't I?"

He pushed her, teasing. "I'm not calling you a slag, y'know."

She frowned. "No?"

"No." He picked up the bag. "Want another grape?"

"I don't want a grape." She was trying to sulk, but couldn't sustain it. She was too full. "If you think men have a monopoly on bonking you're wrong. I mean, who are the men having one-nighters with then?"

"Women who want them to fall in love," he returned, watching a puppy that was galloping down the incline towards them, its tongue red as cherries and its eyes full of innocence. It bowled into Jeanette and she bent to smooth her hand through silk and spittle. Its owner was a pear shaped woman, with green leggings and big boots. She paused by them, watching her dog. Michael nodded a greeting and they bounced their heads in unison for some seconds.

"What's its name?"

"Calypso," the woman said, smiling as if she had done the world a favour.

"Pretty name," Jeanette offered.

"Yes, I went to carnival and it hit me. He's so excitable."

"Oh," they said. "Oh. How nice." The woman moved on, whistling. They watched her and the dog go over the horizon, steam rising from the animal's back, like whispers.

"You think all women who have sex want love?" she asked.

"Yes, most of them."

"But that's not what I've wanted." She cast her mind back, a golden rope on which she hung memories of lovers, past, present, future.

"What have you wanted?" His back was warm against hers once more, shoulder blades rubbing.

"I don't know. Sex. Is the most honest answer. I'm trying to hear you, I may have other motivations, but I don't know what they are."

"What could they be? Power? Attention?"

"Who's doing the degree in Psychology here?" she asked.

"You, but it doesn't take much." There was a silence as they thought. He, of the first time he had been inside his woman, who he knew would now be in Oxford Circus, quarrelling with customers. She, of Sean.

He felt the change in her. "Tell me about Sean."

She struggled for words. Sean was different. Sean who she wanted in the way that she now recognised Charles had wanted her. Sean, his slender, structured frame and his skin, like a flat, dark sea. He wouldn't take her home. They watched films, she found that he could dance as well as she, and the way he held her face and examined it like a prize was like nothing else. And the way, with him she wanted to wait, there was no urgency to spread her legs. It was strange, she didn't know what to do with the feelings. Like she wanted to kiss his lips for the rest of the year, then kiss his fingers for another. Oh, she wanted him, but slowly.

"I want him to be different," she said at last.

"In what way different?" He knew what she meant, as all lovers do, in a ritual that had no name. Smiled inside himself. She would find no words. There weren't any.

"I . . . I . . . I want to know him."

"And you will." He said it to her until it was a lullaby, long and comforting. "You will."

*

They had collected her life and strung it into a camera, like a neat trick. Nicola liked it. She gave a thumbs up to the editor sitting nearby and turned to Alex for an opinion.

"You go, girl!" Alexandrea was beside herself. Usually Nicola wouldn't have been able to view the feature they had just seen before transmission, but Alex had a word in Ruby Fleur's ear, and the deed was done. "You like?" she asked.

Nicola nodded her head. "It's very tight, but it has some guts, you know? It's strange seeing myself on screen. An actor I once knew told me that the thing that bothered him about being on telly was 'Neck back Syndrome'."

"Huh?" Alexandrea said.

"The fact that no human should be able to ever see the perfect symmetry of the back of their own neck! God, do I really look like that?"

"You better get used to it, girl. There's going to be plenty more where that came from."

Nicola waved a hand. "It's only a screen test. No promises."

"*Only* a screen test, she says! Look, you'll be safe. I just wish I could come."

Just after the new year, Channel Four had approached Nicola and asked if she'd be a subject for a new documentary called *Dreams*. It was a five part programme on normal people who had attained their dreams before thirty. She shared the slot with a lottery millionaire, a young author who'd churned out five books before he hit twenty, a designer who was going on like a bad motherfucker on the Parisian catwalks, and a young woman who spent her time wandering around strange parts of the world documenting something like the dying throes of tigers and penguins.

It was true that Nicola was now the toast of the theatrical world, and the reviews had satisfied even her need for recognition. Julius had reluctantly allowed his personal assistant to take the helm of their lives, and their engagement had been announced to the press with much fanfare. She smiled at the memory of his face when *Hello!* had called for an interview. He certainly wasn't ready for that yet, but she still teased him with it. *Summer Alienates* had ended its season as it had begun, with full houses and critical acclaim. And closing night had been as crazy as opening. The audience had obligingly risen to their feet. Tears and jubilation, the cast hoisting her into the air. Cameras. The flurry of arms and attention, so much of it and she was turning like a human ferris wheel, handing out witty repartee to reporters, kisses to fellow thespians. Everyone wanted to please her. She wanted to please them back.

The man had struggled through the crowd, with white shoes that looked far too big for him and the kind of stomach that only washboards could admire as one of their own. He had asked her for some time, card in hand, and even Julius had taken a breath. The big time had come.

He was expansive, fast-talking, cigar chewing, like out of a comic. But real. And the deal was real. Would she consider auditioning for a part? In a film. Medium budget, but a respected director. They needed a female lead. *And you-all have that cute little accent going on there,* he had said. *We lurve an accent.* She and Julius had gotten stinking, falling down, rotten, off your head and you hate yourself in the morning drunk and stoned that night, laughing at the man and mimicking his voice. She was due to fly out in five weeks.

Naturally, the *Dreams* team had been delighted. They were in mid-shoot, and this was the cream on the cake. With this, she was more than tabloid fodder or serious actress. She was the next great hope of the English theatrical stable. She could become A Star. The documentary was a montage of memories and vignettes: Nicola onstage, emotions flickering across her skin, in an old film of a former production, cheeky one moment, tears glittering down her face the next. In front of photographers, Julius on her arm, their beams clashing and mingling, hands clasped, white teeth. Headlines rostrumed across the screen, the very headlines they had hated and become used to. Nicola and her father, focus on him, telling those old stories, slowly, it took a lot of edit, but there were gems, her first school play, how she was cross-eyed as a child, she saw double, because of a lazy eye, and she would stand in front of the mirror, pretend she was twins and dance, intercut with Alexandrea, memories of first meetings, Nicola long and shy, in a corner, a grazed, bloody knee, Alex offering to take her to the nurse. Then Nicola once more, at home, by herself, recounting what she considered her own first performance.

She had gone to a fancy-dress party one year, when she had been in

Jamaica for the summer. Her little personal revenge, although she did not say as much to the camera. It had been a beautiful moment. She had charmed an invitation out of a youth who was hanging around her. She knew they'd all be there, school enemies, living their little lives. She had made the dress herself. It was ebony, it tasted her, clung to buttocks that had filled out and hips that twanged. She had known her height would do the rest. It did. When she walked in, alone, everyone had stared, the DJ had scratched a record. There were whispers, questions. She was gorgeous, but what had she come as? She walked slowly towards the pool, where the hosts mingled, and had stepped straight into the shallow end, drenching herself. When she stepped out the silence was complete. The dress that had formerly been a statement became her, gave away all her secrets. A pause, and then she spread her arms.

"I'm an orgasm," she'd said.

Men had abandoned girlfriends.

"You want to have a drink before you go?" Alexandrea switched off the machine and stood up. She looked tired. Tiny travelling men had left their luggage under her eyes.

"Sure. Do you have the time before they need you?"

Alex got up. "I think they consider you an asset. This, my dear, is part of the job."

"Getting drunk with an old friend? Give me your job!"

They walked to the elevator, passing several people who did double takes at the sight of Nicola. Alexandrea looked concerned.

"I'm really glad for you, Nick —"

"But?"

"Well, I'm not sure how all of this attention is going to affect our friendship. This is a whole other world."

"C'mon. You're used to being around celebrities. And I'm not exactly in that grade yet."

"I know. But you seem so easy with this, and I feel left behind. And the wedding. It's as if Jeanette handles this better."

They had reached the bar. They slid onto facing seats and ordered. Nicola turned to look at Alexandrea. She had thought Jeanette would come up sooner or later. She seemed to be able to charm everyone but

Alex. And her friendship with Michael, platonic or not, had driven the nails in further.

"Alex, you know I love you to death. Jeanette and me get on really well, but you shouldn't feel that she's stealing Michael or anybody —"

Alexandrea interrupted her. "I don't want to talk about it."

"Al—"

"I wanna talk about something else. Let's talk weddings. What are you going to wear?"

"I wish you wouldn't change the rass subject!"

Alexandrea grinned. "Look, since you've made up your mind about marrying Julie, I've noticed that you're not exactly getting excited by the arrangements. The ring looks pretty, so do the press releases, but . . ."

Nicola looked down at the ring on her hand. Three diamonds and a moon stone. Subtle. Permanent. She had been wanting to talk to Alexandrea about the engagement, about the feelings that confused her, but it was hard to find the words. To marry Julius would be the final commitment. She would drown herself in her needs.

"Alex, I've been wanting to —"

"Alexandrea, I hope you're going to introduce me." He had walked up behind her chair, and she had to fight the urge to panic. Her throat felt very dry. He was too near. He was as handsome as usual, but she found that she couldn't delight in his suits these days. The very sight of him made her feel sick. She was aware of his hand resting lightly on her shoulder, a finger moving back and forth slowly, across nerves and pores. She wrenched her body away and turned to face him.

"Mr Pearson. This is, er —"

"Nicola Baines, Mr Pearson. How you doin'?" Nicola moved swiftly, stretching out her hand so that he had to cross over to her.

"*The* Nicola Baines!" he chuckled and shook her hand. "May I join you ladies?"

Nicola noted the flicker on her friend's face. She smiled, a special one reserved for only the hardest of adversaries.

"I hope you won't hold it against your employee if I keep her for a few more moments, Mr Pearson. And I'm sorry, but the discussion is of a personal nature."

He smiled back. "Of course. My apologies. Perhaps there'll be another chance. Alex and I have become good friends." He began to move away and then turned back.

"Alexandrea, I will expect this to be a *few* more moments." He strode away. Alex put her head on the table.

"Hey —" Nicola stroked her hair. "I know you told me about all this rubbish, but it's getting worse, isn't it?"

Alexandrea raised her face. "It's so subtle, so fucking clever, I could never make a case! He hasn't *done* anything, on the face of it he looks charming, so *charming* and he's said that he accepts my turning him down, but he *hasn't*, not really, he keeps *touching* me, just tiny things and no-one else seems to see it, but he's driving me mad! You saw him, Nicola, didn't you see him, that little finger action, tell me I'm not mad —"

Nicola tried to be reassuring. "Shhh, I saw it. I know what you mean." There was silence between them for a while, Alexandrea biting at her nails, Nicola thoughtful. She slammed the table. "You have to do something. Complain, take it to a superior —"

Alex sighed. She seemed to be getting some control. "There is no superior. He's the superior."

"There must be some kind of legal action . . ."

"You don't understand." She bit a nail. "I don't want to rock the boat. He talks to people. He's respected. He has a really good reputation, Nick. I've been doing some checking since he started this and there's not one person, man or woman, who doesn't trot out the same stuff." She folded her hands, her face taking on a look of exaggerated adoration. "'Tony Pearson is a brilliant, driven, intelligent, wonderful journalist. He gave me my promotion. He talked to me when I was down. Shit, I even sounded out Jenny and she said, totally off the top of her head, that he was at his best when he advised her how she should handle some idiot who was coming on to her!" She looked resigned. "No, at the end of the day I'll have to put up with it."

Nicola tried to argue. "What he's doing is wrong, Alex! There's got to be something we can do. Maybe Julius has some contacts, I'm sure he could get someone to have a word, someone he'll listen to. He's not GOD!"

"He's God here. Look, I got my contract extended. People are seeing what I can do. I won't let him get me out of here."

"But if he's top dog here, you won't make much progress anyway."

Alexandrea reached for her hands. "I know this sounds stupid, but I'm just not going. I'm not letting him get the better of me. I want to stay. Look, I guess a pinch and a cuddle isn't too much when you look at it properly. I just went to bits there. I overreacted, okay? He just took me by surprise. I have to get back. Can't keep massa waiting." She shrugged. "I'll be fine." She squeezed Nicola's hands. "Really. I'm just tired."

Eyes settled on them as they walked back to the elevator.

*

Sean whistled as he walked. He had been doing more whistling these days. And the days were glorious. Now, for every hateful thought he had a hiccup, an interruption that stopped the sodden flow in his mind. Yelled at by the chef he just smiled and continued making stock, or rolling pastry, or lightly moistening fruit with chocolate. Friends had remarked on the difference in him, some of them had met her and approved. He heard music in his head, strange, melodic tunes that she taught him *(go down Emmanuel Road gyal an' bwoy)* they were printing a history on the world, that time with the fireworks, and warm moments when he waited on the college steps for her, feeling the sun on his back, the deeply satisfactory feel of thigh against thigh, an evening at a jazz club, another with her rocking to Anita Baker doing her thing, his arms around her waist, and his games, that were fed with continued urgency as he loved her. One-two-three women in raincoats who he knew were slags, four-five a pair of them walking with a man and they were probably both fucking him and thinking themselves liberal and clever, six, an old lady on the bus who had entertained him from Leicester Square straight into North London, imagining, seeing her withered body, her tits — they probably sagged to the waist, and he could see her swinging them over her shoulders, slack bags of mucous and dry nipples, saddles of fat astride her waist, digging into her ancient, cracked belt. Seven, a baby girl who'll never get to heaven like my Jeanette because she won't keep herself pure past fourteen and he could see her deflowerment before his eyes, probably against some pitted wall at a rave, with a drunk youth who could do better for himself anyway.

Only one incident had spoiled these times. He had known the girl for years, as usual one of those bitches he called friends but who had never thought to really see him. She had told Jeanette that they suited each other physically, it was brilliant to see such a lovely black couple, they looked so alike. He had known then that she was a stupid cow. To compare Her to himself. To suggest that they were anything alike. It was preposterous. It was just that Jeanette's heart could see past his imperfection, she saw the man *(the making of a man is in his might) (fe go bruk rock stone)* and more, and he would love her for that *(bruk dem one by one bruk dem two by two)* and he had plans because she was pure and they would share each other's bodies eventually, soon *(finger mash no cry)* when the time was right and he would have to abuse himself in the meantime, his seed drying on his stomach deep in the night, he would do this for a while more and then they would be together *(remember ah play we ah play)*.

The grip of his hands left tiny crescents in his palms, white marks fading into black. A ginger tom paused to watch him down the road, and then went back to perusing its own backside.

Mavis

De firs' time me tek a customer it wasn't easy. It was funny, but since me inna de business everyt'ing was smooth for a while. Carl start sponsor me wid money, all de girl dem ah pay extra attention, since me is de new one on de block. Of course dere was some bitchiness ah gwaan, but is like is part of de job, y'know?

Den Carl tell me seh him have me first customer. All de girl dem ah laugh, tell me seh me ah go lose me virgin now, but Susan cuss dem, ask dem if dem never 'memba how dem did feel de firs' time dem do it. Me ask Carl how him know is who, den me get to realise dat dem have a likkle man name Missa Simmit, who did get to sleep with nearly all de gyal dem firs'. Him like fe bruk de new ones, even though him have him favourites inna de group. Mos' ah de man dem come back ah de place fe do de business, but some ah dem wan' tek you wid dem, or do it inna de car, but dem haffi careful, 'cause Jamaica is a small place, an' more time a man ah get him t'ings inna de back seat an' car-full ah him friend come on deh.

Carl pick out de t'ings for me to wear, Susan ah hug me tell me seh me mustn't worry, him never las' long anyway. It was funny, 'cause me never 'fraid. Maybe me was jus' tryin' not to t'ink about it. Den de man come inna de room. Me memba him was one dry up likkle man, an' when him tek off him clothes him titty dem jus' ah heng down, an' me feel fe laugh, even though inside me couldn't stan' it. All de time him ah tek off de clothes him ah chat, ah tell me seh him work outta Hellshire, catch fish, y'know, an' dat if me come down dere me can get free fish, him will catch it for me special. Him all smell like fish when him get on top of me, him wasn't heavy, jus' renk, renk like old man, fishy ole man, like him hug up de fish dem ah night time. Him t'ings look funny afterwards, shiny and wet like dog doo-doo, ah lay next to him leg, an' me feel sick, lawd, me did feel sick. All de time him ah work up himself me jus' look up inna de sky, try t'ink of somet'ing else, an' den him look 'pon me an' ask me if it hurt. Me tell you, me never feel nutting. Like de whole ah me bottom part seize up. Me jus' ah lie dere ah wonder when it ah go hurt, when it ah go feel good, anyt'ing, jus' to feel somet'ing, y'know? Me jus' feel seh de man t'ing ah gimme injection, like it ah freeze me up, nuh mek me feel nuttin'. Den me feel like scream, me ah tell meself seh Mavis, you have a decent madda, you ah decent s'maddy, an' look weh you come to, look how you ah gwaan, de man ah fuck you fe money an' all you can do is look 'pon de sky. After him ask me if it hurt, an' me tell him no, him look down 'pon me, smile, an seh 'Dat is because me tek time.' An' den him gwaan again, ah puff an' a gwaan like idyat. Me jus' pray dat Jesus ah go look down an' forgive me.

When him done, him climb off, like me ah donkey, an' look 'pon me, ask me if me okay. Me say yes. Him tell me seh him ah go sen' one ah de girl dem in. Me jus' seh yes. Him tell me seh when me come ah Hellshire him ah go save de nicest fish, fry bammy wid it, 'cause me is a nice likkle girl. Me seh yes. Is only when Susan come in dat me start fe bawl. What ah load ah eye-water me did leggo dat day! Like me ah get mad. Susan ah hush me, pat me, de whole ah de girl dem ah crowd in fe say somet'ing, tell me seh is not nutting, me will get used to it. Me jus' ah bawl. Den Carl come in. Firs' him ah try sweet me up, tell me seh me ah go get money fe buy t'ings, me can all go ah Miami an' buy t'ings, get pon de plane, wouldn't dat be nice? Me ah bawl, an' one ah de gyal dem ah cuss seh she never know anybody go ah Miami yet, him get vex an' box her, den him leggo one box pon me an' me start calm down. Him tell me seh me mus' clean me face an' follow de gyal dem 'pon de road.

Carl love bring flowers. Him give all de gyal dem flowers like it mek up fe de money weh him ah t'eif from we ah nighttime. Him love himself so much him haffi gwaan like sweet bwoy. Flowers can feed Sophie pickney ah night-time when she haffi lef' him inna de yard an' go 'pon de street same time? Mos' ah de gyal dem have pickney, an' dem sen' dem to dem family, or some ah dem have dem at home, cause is not all ah de girl dem live ah de place. Two pickney live ah de house, me know seh Carl never like it, but him never want to lose de girl dem, so we manage. But de t'ings dem woman haffi do fe keep de pickney dem quiet is a shame. One gyal give de pickney rum regular wid de milk, so it drunk off an' don't mek noise. We use to cuss her, but what she goin' do? Carl used to get ignorant if him hear any noise.

Ah suppose de sinful part of me did like de work. When me start get likkle money me bring all radio inna de place, fix up me room, mek it look nice. It was nice to have some t'ings, even though me wasn't rich, 'cause Carl ah tek him rent same way. An' on de street, when ah man pull up an' call me, seh him want me, if him good lookin' me feel kinda nice seh him choose me. Not dat me like de work. Me know seh man ah nuh good somet'ing. Dat is my experience. Dere was one girl name Allison who seh she love one man live round de corner, him carry her out ah weekend. Me nuh know how you can love ah man after you have man ah do dem t'ings deh to you. De customer dem wid money was always wort' it, regardless of whatever bumboclaaht foolishness dem want you fe do. De bes' job I ever get was two weeks in Ochie. De man was a tourist, seh him come from Germany. Hardly speak English, him jus' ah tell me seh how Jamaican girls very beautiful, very beautiful. Him tek me down one hotel an' ah gwaan like me is him wife. Of course him pay Carl a serious breed ah money. You shoulda see de ole neigar dem at reception. Dem did well an' know dat me was workin', an' dem vex to see me an' white man you see. Dem smell me out as we reach. We spend de whole time fuckin' back to back. Some mornins' when me wake up before him me jus' stan' ah de door ah smell de sweet country breeze, me never want to walk on de street wid him because me family never live too far from dere, an' me really 'fraid seh s'maddy ah go see me an' carry news.

One time me ah walk back inna de hotel ah wait pon de man an' dem have one conference, dem call it woman's conference, inna de place. De woman up dere ah speechify up herself, me sure she was a lesbian. She ah talk 'bout how black an' white mustn't sex together. Ah was walkin' back through de door 'cause me nuh have no time fe waste, an' she mussa see me, because she haul up an' yell down de mike how 'YOU ARE SLEEPING WITH THE OPPRESSOR!'. Me kiss me teet', 'cause she never have no money yet, so who ah get fuck? Me did feel fe bawl back an' tell her she better careful. Me hear how two ah dem lesbian did get join together one time, dem haffi carry dem down ah de hospital fe get dem apart, an' de whole ah Jamaica did pile inna KPH fe get a look at dem.

When me come back from Ochie me notice seh me belly ah roll, me jus' ah sleep-sleep like me have dropsy. Susan start get worried, tell me seh me mus' tek a wash-out, Carl ah get vex, ah stamp up an' down ah cuss how de whole ah we love breed up de place. Me never really did t'ink seh me was goin' to get pregnant. T'ink de good Lawd woulda at least answer me prayer. Still, me find out seh me get belly fe de tourist. Dem ah ask me if me wan' dash it weh, but me realise seh me couldn't do dat. Susan ah tell me seh me mus' careful, 'cause if you dash weh too much pickney you t'un mule, cyaan breed again, or you get wash-belly yout', sick-sick an' cyaan tek care ah demself.

When me know me was pregnant me try fe look a likkle domestic work again. Me walk street an' knock 'pon people door, but by den me belly ah show, an' de woman dem ah look pon me like me was dirt. One time me knock a door an' de man who come look like him ah go dead, 'cause me did see him down ah New Kingston ah look we on de weekend. Him look like him t'ink me ah go mek trouble. Me hear a woman voice ah ask him is who, him jus' call out seh is Jehovah Witness, an' close de door inna me face. Me never really look after dat.

Carl did get two more new gyal dat time, so him tell me seh me mus' clean de house up while me pregnant. Me did wan' come off de street dat time because dere was one fool man who look like de belly jus' ah turn him on, an' de whole ah de gyal dem ah support me, seh ah nastiness dat, how Carl mus' tek me off. Him ah grumble, an' me ah clean dutty floor, scrub dutty sheet wid de seven month belly in front ah me. Early mornin' hours when de girl dem come in dem check me inna de room, everybody ah guess if is a girl or a bwoy, dem ah tell me a bwoy because of how me belly point up. One mornin' Sophie come in seh she have joke to gimme. De whole ah dem ah laugh like dem know it, seh she get her special man las' night. Dem seh de whole ah dem run from him, she was de only one who could tek him on. Me ah ask her what him do, so? She seh him always pay fe you eat big dinner down ah one stush place, so me seh what wrong wid dat, nuh nice t'ings dat? She seh him go ah dinner wid you an' him watch you eat an' you haffi nyam all weh him order, den him tek you to a dance or a movie, whatever you want, as long as t'ree hours pass. Me never really undastan' what she was sayin' — is what him want inna de bed? She kiss her teet' an ask me if me ah idyat, wha'appen, you never tek nuh biology lesson ah school? Me start to feel vex an' shame an' seh me never wan' hear, but den she smile an' tell me seh it tek three hours fe de food fe pass through you system. Me ask her how you mean, him want to watch you do dem nasty business? She laugh. Watch? All de time you belly ah grumble fe use de bathroom, him ah get ready fe HIM dinner. Me did get so upset me tell de whole ah dem fe come outta de room, fraid seh if me baby hear dem t'ings it ah go come out look funny.

Me firs' pickney born in de summer, jus' a month after my own birt'day. Dat was how me get her name. An' bwoy, what a pickney pretty! She slide outta me wid puss-eye an' tall hair, an' me jus' look pon her an' tell Susan ah me German pickney dat.

17

"Attitudes have been defined as 'likes and dislikes'. They are our affinities for and our aversions to situations, objects, persons, groups, or any other identifiable aspects of our environment . . ." The lecturer was getting into his stride. Around the lecture room gloomy architecture bent almost double to keep the dying April sunshine out. The enclosed students watched its fight with regret. Jeanette couldn't believe that she had lived in London for eight months. The Easter holidays had left them lazy, but the man at the lectern was holding their attention. His name was Jones. He was one of the most popular professors, tiny, dour, but with an instinct for his material. ". . . this includes abstract ideas and even social policies."

He paused and the class paused with him, twanging with expectation.

"Could someone identify for me the essential ingredient that defines something as an attitude?" He cast small grey eyes around the hall. His students shifted in uncertainty. He settled on a woman sitting next to Jeanette. "Lara? Care to cease masticating your pencil and contribute?"

Lara glanced at Jeanette appealingly. The silence was thick.

Dr. Jones sighed.

"The difference between school and university, ladies and gentlemen, is your ability to *think*, rather than regurgitate. I have been saying this for a long time, and certainly shouldn't be saying it to those who have made it into the second term. Still, I imagined there would be a pause here because none of you have got to this point in the *book*!" He tapped the lectern. "Anybody? Have a *try*!"

Jeanette raised a hand. Jones frowned.

"I am loath to go to Jeanette *again*. Can anyone else move their brains into gear?"

Silence. He sighed. "Very well, Jeanette. What are your thoughts on the matter?"

Jeanette gripped the sides of her chair. "Well, it seems that your attitudes have a lot to do with your emotions . . ."

The lecturer inclined his head. "Thank you. H. C. Triandis defined an attitude as an idea charged with emotion which predisposes a class of actions to a particular class of social situations. We will end the class now, as I see that your cognitive abilities are waning with the onset of *hunger*." A ripple of laughter ran through the room. "The next time we meet I would like someone to tell me the other two components of attitude. Someone who is *not* Jeanette. I have a particular attitude about the rest of you sitting in front of me with nothing to contribute." The ripple again. "That will be all."

Lara leaned forward to Jeanette as the class began filing out. "Made us look like dummies again, huh?" She grinned. "I have a particular *attitude* about that." Jeanette piled her books into her rucksack and pushed her friend's shoulder. "I have a particular attitude about your attitude . . ." They both giggled together.

The walls of the corridor were thin and unappealing. They paused at Jeanette's locker so she could stuff her books into it.

"Do you have a tutorial later?" Lara asked.

"Yeah, at two thirty." said Jeanette.

"Want to have lunch?"

Jeanette hesitated. "Well, I don't want to be funny, but my sister's meeting me and I haven't seen her for ages."

The other girl waved her hand. "It's fine. Another time. Still, is like I can't see you these days, what with your sister and these famous people you're living with, and your new boyfriend."

"Well, you've met Sean, who's not exactly new. And Nikki, for that matter. Actually, bring your man and we'll go to that Friday rave." She grinned as the other girl turned away. "Don't bring that attitude with you either!" Lara laughed and kept going.

Jeanette was looking forward to seeing Maye. They were close, but London had bitten into their time together. Maye's daughter, Simone, had gotten the flu when they had last arranged a meeting, so it had to be cancelled. The time she spent with Sean had compromised other opportunities, and she felt guilty. It was a strange feeling. Her relationship with Charles had never had similar consequences.

Maye was sitting on the steps, her daughter beside her. The six year old was leaning against her mother, each brown plait jostling for purchase on her head. They were playing I Spy.

"I spy, with my little eye —" the child chanted happily, and then saw Jeanette. "— somef"ing beginning with A!"

Maye looked up into the sky, smiling. "Ambulance!"

"No!" Simone put a finger to her lips and Jeanette stood quietly.

"Mmmm . . . aeroplane?"

"No! You're not even warm, mummy!"

Maye concentrated. "A wonderful mum?"

Simone laughed scornfully. "That begins with a W!"

Her mother turned to tickle her and spotted Jeanette. She stood up, smiling. "You're both cheaters! Her name begins with a J!"

Simone ran over to Jeanette and the two hugged fiercely. "Boy, have I missed you, child!" She looked up at Maye. "For your information, my niece does not cheat. Officially, I am Auntie Jeanette. And that begins with an A."

Maye put her hands on her hips. "Alright, alright! Gang up as usual! Y'alright, babe?"

"I'm good. You alright?" She didn't need the question answered. Maye was the picture of health. She reflected again that as sisters, they were like chalk and cheese. Maye so fair, her dark curly hair and light brown eyes making her look almost Greek. It was only around her nose and full lips you could see the touch of Mamma's tar brush. She was dressed simply in jeans and a T-shirt, small and lightly built. They'd shared brassieres until Jeanette was 13 and her breasts had really taken off. She could remember Maye offering her maternity bras, but they had been horrible.

Maye touched her face. "I see the madwoman never cut up you pretty face too much." The scar was small, and had healed quickly. "Good thing you never come up with keloids."

Simone was dancing from one foot to the other, hair bouncing. "Auntie Je, Auntie Je! The lady who cut you up, did you beat her? Did you beat her?"

"Simone!" her mother spoke reprovingly. "No-one in this family goes on like ol' neigar!"

Jeanette bent down to the little girl and picked her up. "I am going to carry you all the way to the park and I'm going to buy you an ice cream and I'm going to beat you up all the way there!" Simone screamed with laughter and tried to get away.

*

Jack Thompson banged a fist down on the table. His editor regarded him gloomily and reflected, not for the first time, that if Thompson didn't keep rolling out the headlines, it would be a great pleasure to fire him. The man was a nightmare to work with. Thompson banged the table again, and the editor was pleased to see a large gob of mucous dangling from the other man's nose. A spring cold, and he couldn't imagine anyone who deserved it more.

"Are you listening to what I'm saying, Stewart?"

"Yes, Jack. I always listen to you."

"You aren't trusting my instincts here! I tell you, that Baines woman is a story waiting to happen!"

Stewart Alderton folded his hands on his pleasantly rounded belly. Outside he could hear the familiar hustle and bustle of his newsroom, and he took comfort in it. The gentle murmur of computers, whispering words and words and more words, endlessly, phones punctuating voices, urgent, lighter, occasional shrieks of jubilation and more often heavily muttered swear words. Lovely. He jerked himself back to Thompson, who was railing again.

"In my opinion, Miss Baines has had her five minutes of fame. C'mon, Jack. If she gets the American role, fair enough. I just don't see what keeps you at her doorstep. There's work for you to do *here*."

Thompson swiped at his nose, missing the globule there. He looked thoughtful. Alderton regarded him with increasing suspicion. When the man roared it was old hat. But a quiet Thompson was dangerous.

"Why don't you wait and see if she gets the part? Then convince her to do a spread talking about the pleasures of banging Julius Fraser. But I can't see that there'll be much more. And her publicist is angling for a *Hello!* spot anyway. After that photo spread Fraser screamed about, I don't think she's got much time for the likes of us."

"Look. I can't explain it. I just know that this woman is going to come good. I feel it in my bones. Did you see that interview with Jonathan Ross? She's full of tension. And she's so sodding talented. And the black press have been getting to her, writing all of this damning stuff about her being involved with a white man. I think she's going to run and run."

Alderton looked at him carefully. He wasn't sure that he'd ever heard Thompson talk about talent. The man was a bunch of cynical nerves, never had a good word to say about anybody. He cleared his throat. Maybe he could spare him another week if he cut back on the time that he was door stepping the Baines woman.

"Alright. You can have another week on her. But cut the hours you spend sitting on her doorstep. I need some more stories from you. A lot more is happening right now." He paused. "So help me, Jack, if you're using this as an excuse to perv just because you fancy the pants off her, I'll —"

Thompson got to his feet. "That's not bloody it and you know it."

"We'll see." Alderton raised a finger. "One week." He hauled a tissue from a box in front of him. "And wipe your nose."

Thompson grabbed the tissue and shuffled out of the office, sniffing. Alderton was a crashing bore. How could someone like him be expected to understand instinct? It was a gut feeling that you developed, pounding the streets. Nicola Baines was gorgeous, yes, but it was more than that. He'd been watching her for months, and he felt as if he knew her intimately. The way she pulled back her hair and piled it on top of her head every time she went to Fraser's house, and yet it was down when she came out, wild and free. He could tell now when she was unhappy, when she was nervous, when she was delighted. All in the body language, and she had bundles of that. He had tried to gain her confidence several times, but that bastard Fraser had tipped her off, and she smiled her way out of it every time.

Alderton had dismissed Jack Thompson's ability to assess talent, but he was wrong. All his working life he had been there, snapping at and grabbing for the world's talent. At 47 he'd seen them all come and go, Bowie, Rod Stewart, the Beatles. There was a kind of indefinable factor there, not merely of talent, but of generating news, controversy, the fuel that fed the media. After all, the Beatles were still going, dead Lennon or not.

He had the strange feeling that Nicola Baines could do much the same. She had the X factor. All he had to do was let it run.

*

Jeanette and Maye watched Simone on the swings in the park. The six year old had made two new friends in half an hour, and was busily chatting to them. Maye was telling Jeanette about Simone's father.

"The thing I can't get my head around is him saying he loves her. I mean, alright, we're not together any more, him have him new woman an' t'ing, and I'm tellin' you, Je, me nuh really business wid dat, still. That's cool. But him won't even check the child for six months and then he comes with all these presents to sweet her up, talkin' 'bout how Daddy loves her, and of course she just takes him on. I don't blame her, is her dad. But he'll have her for a weekend and she comes back mouthin' off an' back-chattin', and everything I tell her, she tell me daddy say something different." She looked exasperated.

"I guess you talk to him, right?" Jeanette knew the story of old. Scott had never been known for his reliability, just his charm.

"Till me blue."

"What him say?"

"Bwoy, foolishness 'bout is not all the time him can come check her, him have him *runnin's*."

"I bet Mamma has an opinion."

"Mi dear. All she deh pon is if me play wid puppy, puppy lick me mout'. Like everything is my fault."

"I know." Their mother was not known for her tact. "If you cyaan hear . . ."

"You must feel!" They chorused together, laughing. Maye pushed back her curls and looked at her sister.

"Me love talk 'bout meself. How 'bout you? Look like you mashing up uni."

"Mmm . . ." It was true that her grades had been good. Four As and a B. She had been pleased.

"And Mamma keep chat-chat 'bout how you cyaan come check we now you ah move wid big-time actress."

"Cho. You know that's foolishness. Still, look like Nicola's heading for big things. See the documentary?"

"Of course. Simone spend the whole night ah look for you on it. We swear seh we see you leg in one shot."

Jeanette laughed. It was true. She'd come out of the kitchen mid-shoot and had to beat a hasty retreat.

"Sean was teasing me about that."

Maye looked sly. "Yes. Sean. Who woulda believe say you dash Charlie away an' come to London to find another man!"

"How is he?"

"Charles? Him deh 'bout. Me hear say him still love you off."

Jeanette moved uneasily. "You lie."

"No. Me see him the other day. You want to see the boy ah cut him eye after me like is me do him somet'ing."

"Too bad." She felt regret about Charles, but it was just the way life went. She'd tried to call him months ago, but he'd hung up the phone in her ear.

"How you so dry? Charlie too fool. Tell me 'bout Sean. Him look nice in the picture you send me. Of course Mamma just turn up her nose."

Jeanette smiled. "Boy, the man turn me idiot."

"Sweet t'ings in bed, nuh true?"

"I don't know." She didn't. To her amazement, they had not yet slept together. Four long months of cuddling, but she was still reluctant to move away from the delicious build up. Maye stared at her.

"You telling me you don't give the man piece yet?"

"We're waiting." She laughed, realising how prim she sounded. "I want to wait."

"For what?" Maye continued to stare.

"Boy, I don't even know how to explain it. Is just that when I check it, I kinda feel that me rush into the sex thing too quick. With Charlie, everybody. Not that me regret it. Just that Sean feels different. Special. I want this to be different."

"Sound like you wah marry off de man." Maye cast her eyes back at Simone, who was dangling off the monkey bars. "Simone! Don't I tell you not to do that?" The child giggled and swung onto the ground, calling back an apology.

Jeanette thought about it and knew that the idea didn't displease her. She kept trying to explain her feelings to people, to Michael, to Nicola, even to herself, but ended up frustrated. Even Maye, who she shared secrets with, couldn't understand. She wanted to be *(new)* everything to Sean. When they finally made love she wanted it to be perfect. She liked his lack of insistence, the way that he seemed fascinated with her, not her body. She wasn't used to that. Even Charles' love had been based in lust, constantly telling her how she looked ready, he had always been touching her up, wanting her to dress sexy. Sean appreciated her everything.

As they watched her niece play, other thoughts invaded. She couldn't help it, there were some things she didn't like about the relationship. She'd never been to his place. He kept telling her how it was just a bedsit, nothing special, she wouldn't like it. He seemed embarrassed. She tried not to pressure him, anxious not to displease, and she resented that anxiety. She'd never worried before. And there were days when she didn't see him, when hours seemed like years. But she didn't want to go on like she was trying to tie him. He always had an explanation. Now that she was with Maye she wanted to voice it all, had hoped that the words would come. But she couldn't explain. Aware that Maye was looking expectant, she opened her mouth.

"He . . . we . . . I . . ."

They burst into laughter again. Pleasurably irritated by her own efforts, Jeanette fell into silence, gesticulating wordlessly.

"You look so worried and so pleased and so vex at the same time." Maye covered her mouth as the mirth threatened.

Jeanette grabbed her shoulders. "Don't you understand, please tell me that you get what I'm saying!"

Maye could only shake her head. "But you nah say nothin'! Look, I'm glad for you, I'm happy that you feel so good."

They lapsed into silence, watching Simone shake hands solemnly with one of her new playmates.

"I have to meet this guy." Maye insisted. "This bloke that leaves you at a loss for words."

"You will, you will."

They sat in the season's light, planning. She would bring him to Manchester. Maye would crack out the champers, or at least a bottle of red wine or something.

"Don't bring Mamma."

"Why, 'fraid she too fas'?"

"I'm not ready for that."

"Does he like kids?"

"Oh, Simone is fine. He loves them, he watches them all the time. The other day we were walking on the road and he was looking at these twins, they were so cute, and he turned to me and told me that the next time we walked there we'd be with our own kids, and Maye, I wasn't even scared, I didn't think about spoiling up the healthy body, y'know? All I thought about was how sweet they'd be." The words, coming fast now, fell from her. "Did I tell you he has the most beautiful skin? I wrote a poem about his skin and I haven't got up the bottle to read it to him yet, but I will, maybe I'll read it to him when we're coming back to London on the train."

"Poetry, to rass! You well want to marry this man!"

Jeanette smiled. "Maybe."

18

The kettle shrieked its way into the morning. Alexandrea poured hot water into the large mug in front of her. The smell of coffee and rum filtered through the living room. She stared at Eamon and Anthea who were talking about what was in and what was out for summer, not hearing their discussion. Her hands shook slightly as she gulped the scalding liquid.

"A bit early for that, isn't it?" Jeanette stood at the dining room door, yawning and scratching her scalp. The problem with sleeping downstairs was that she woke up every time someone moved into the common areas. *The banisters are gorgeous but they creak like a bastard,* she thought. She wiped at her eyes and waited for a reply. Alex said nothing. She heaped sugar into the cup. Took another swallow. Shivered.

"Well?" Jeanette put her hands on her hips.

"It's none of your bloody business."

"Well, *excuse* me." Jeanette sighed. Nobody but her seemed to be noticing that Alexandrea was very intimate with the deadly liquid these days. "Would you be drinking rum at nine thirty in the morning if Nikki was here?"

Alexandrea turned to face her. "Did you hear what I said?" Her head hurt and she didn't want to hear the truth. Not with a team meeting set for eleven that morning. Her brains felt like lottery balls, sweeping and diving.

Jeanette crossed to the kitchen and reached for the kettle. She glanced at the screen where a model twirled, all bones and cotton. "That looks nice. I might get that."

Alex smiled bitterly. "Please, don't try and make conversation."

Jeanette rolled her eyes and dumped a tea bag into a cup. "Snapping at me's not going to change my mind. Girl, you are drinking too much."

"So? Why do you care?"

Jeanette walked over to the table. It had gotten worse as the weeks turned into months. She was tired of the fight between them. Particularly since she had never known what they were fighting about.

"I care what happens to Michael's sister. I care what happens to Nikki's closest friend. What is going on? Do you think that either of them would be happy knowing you're on your way to being a drunk?" She knew it was harsh, but she was concerned. Alex's face remained set in sullen mode. She tried again. "Nicola needs you right now. If she comes back from America without that part she's going to be gutted."

"She'll get it." Alexandrea's face twisted. "She always gets what she wants."

"What she'll want is a friend who's liver is intact."

The other woman glared. "I'm not that bad. For God's sake, it's just a drink!"

"Along with GMTV, eh? The other night when I came in from the pub I thought I hadn't left. I could smell it on you."

Alexandrea stood up. "I don't have to listen to this. You don't know anything about me. You just ponce about stealing all my friends —"

Jeanette threw up her hands. "Oh, it all comes out now, Alex! I'm stealing your friends? What kinda damn foolishness is that? Don't try to tell me this is all my fault! If you're insecure that's down to you. I've tried to be friends with you and you're just not having it. *What* is the problem? You're not stupid!"

Alexandrea smiled grimly. Jeanette didn't know the half of it. What would she know about being stupid enough to lose your man and stupid enough to put up with Pearson's manipulation? She felt ill every time she walked into Endeavour. He was always there, slick, oily, omnipotent. Making little comments. Stripping the clothes off her back with his eyes. Last Friday he had come into the office to speak to Jenny and murmured in her ear as he passed: *No bra today? Tut-tut.* All in a single, confident movement. He was always where she was, and that whole day she felt his eyes on her nipples, her body shrinking back into itself in shame. Choosing clothing each morning had become a burden, heavy jumpers replacing her usual crisp lines. He saw that and smiled at her from across the room. *You can't hide,* his eyes said. *Can't hide. Can't hide.*

She felt diminished, her usual self-consciousness hiked up another screaming hundred degrees. She grasped her own stubbornness as a shield. She would not leave. She would not leave. Not for him and his angry gaze. She could see the message: *Come to me or you're lost. Lost. I have the power.*

She wished she was a different kind of person. Jeanette would have slept with him. She looked at her flat mate, soft and lascivious with sleep. Her sensuality was offensive; it worked on Alex's brain like a cancer. She would have taken what she could and run, probably set herself up in a flat of her own and kept that Sean on the sly. Jeanette was the kind of person who had everything on her terms. So was Nicola, come to think of it. Her tired spirit turned darkly on the women she lived with, because she was exhausted by her own slow implosion. Nicola always left when she needed her. Was probably sunning herself under palm trees, watching them adore her. She hated them both sometimes. For having it all. She wished she could live like that, uncontrollably, for the moment.

She crossed the room and threw the coffee cup into the sink, listening with a kind of cruel pleasure as it broke. The smell grew worse. Jeanette's eyes were wide.

"Want to be friendly? Clear that up." She ran up the stairs.

Jeanette looked after her. She walked over to the sink and began to pick the shards out of it.

*

Mona stepped into the room and she didn't come out until the director had taken breath.

*

The train went clickety-clack clickety clack and Sean nudged her, slid his fingers into the top pocket of her coat, fishing out the tickets she had put there, for the conductor. Sean watched the man smile at his woman, and as Jeanette returned it — wide and beautiful, all her teeth showing, lips drawn back, hair over her shoulders — his eyes curdled. He didn't like it when she did that, but he tried not to show it. Smiling like that made her look too familiar, as if she was on the edge of *(those ripped bitches)* something less than sacred and he had to remind himself that this was *his* Jeanette. Hadn't she showed she wasn't like the others? He tried to calm himself. Today, after all, was the day. The day to meet the family. A day for other things. Today he would offer himself to her. It had taken him a long time to convince himself that she would accept him, accept this body. Convince himself she would not laugh, like the others. At first, her slow pace had frightened him, whipped the slow drip of self-hatred into an old frenzy. Then he had realised that she was seeing herself as he saw her. Precious, untainted. She was clean. Not like the others, who offered themselves on a platter, pouting for the camera. She had been waiting for him. It made sense. They had both been waiting for each other, and when he had woken up that morning he had known.

Jeanette sneaked a look at Sean. He was in one of his moods again. She had romanticised his silences. He was a deep, thoughtful man. Not like some, who felt they had to be talking, talking all the time, trying to impress. They could have comfortable silences. She touched her top pocket. The poem lay there. She had decided she would give it to him when they were coming home. They would be pleasantly drunk *(not like Alex silly sad cow)* and it would be late, and they would kiss, she would kiss those soft lips of his, whilst he held her face and scattered tender kisses all over it. The first time they had kissed he had cried, wiped it away of course, gone on like he was a big bad man, but she had seen them. He seemed so hurt by something. But she would make it better. And when the time was right, perhaps on his birthday, she would tell him she was ready.

Sean reached out for her hand and they leaned towards each other, heads touching.

The train played mechanical music all the way to Manchester.

*

Alex wanted to scream. She had just put forward her sixth idea to the meeting and she was getting nowhere. Pearson had rejected the last five outright, and the studied boredom on his face was clear. Jenny Tasdell looked confused.

"Well, I think that's pretty viable —"

"No." said Pearson.

*

They climbed the hill to Maye's house, Jeanette breathing heavily. She noticed with admiration that Sean seemed unbothered. He was a perfect machine, cogs and wires smooth.

"You . . . you're the one who should be finding this difficult, playing with chocolate all day!" she chided, panting through her mouth.

He pinched her hip. "I don't eat it, I just cook with it."

She stopped, unfamiliar anxiety flooding her. "What do you mean?"

"Nothing." He smiled, his face looming at her. "What did you think I meant?"

"Forget it." She laughed at herself, and started forward again. This love thing made you far too sensitive, she thought.

Sean watched her hips.

*

Nicola's publicist clasped her hands. She was shaking with excitement.

"I think you've got it," she said.

Mona looked at her. She was cool, taut strings of muscles covered with soft down.

"Do you really think so?" asked Nicola.

*

"And this is Simone's room . . . Maye is so good with her, Sean. You should see how close they are." Jeanette picked up a doll from the child's bed and stroked it, put it down.

"I see Maye is politically correct." Sean nodded at the doll's curly head and its ethnic clothing. "Africa according to Barbie."

She turned to look at him. "There's no reason to be so dismissive, Mr Man. I think it's good that she has toys that aren't all blonde and blue eyed." She stepped into his arms. "You won't want our children to be PC?"

He hugged her. "If you want them to be." They kissed and she felt warmth bubble into her veins.

"What time did you say your sister was coming home?"

"Not for hours. I said that I'd put the food on, and she'd finish up when she came in. About eight. Simone's with her father because Maye's on a late shift. Are you starving? Let's go downstairs. I need a drink." She moved off, but he pulled her close to him again. His kisses were slow, but now urgency had begun to peep around their edges. She grinned, took his hand and led him to the door.

"What's the matter?" His voice was cold.

She looked at him quickly. The mood had not let up.

"I just don't feel too great feeling you up in my niece's room, that's all." She pulled at him again. "Come, nuh. You can help me cook."

"I'll be with you in a minute."

She looked at him, puzzled, then headed for the door. "OK. Don't be too long, eh?" She clattered down the stairs.

Sean stood in Simone's room. He picked up the doll and looked at it, placed it back on the covers, gently, as if it were a real child. He looked around the room. It was full of primary colours, stuffed toys, posters on the wall, a tiny desk with a computer screen. The child was obviously bright. He examined a drawing over the shelf. Mummy, Auntie Je and Grandma, black sticks for legs. Mummy done in yellow, Auntie Je and Grandma all hats and jewellery. Big, sparkly earrings.

He was about to leave when he saw it. The magazine lay on a cushion, virginal. Beckoning. He looked away. Not now. Today was different.

But it lay there.

He wanted to touch it.

He didn't know that his hands were shaking. Or that his lips were dry.

He wanted it.

Downstairs, he could hear his woman singing.

The magazine was cool and reassuring. He stroked its sides, as if it were alive. Let out a long breath as the first page peeled easily. A shudder went through him. How foolish it all was. It fell onto the floor from dead hands. He wouldn't. His woman was downstairs. She was downstairs.

*

Pearson smiled at her.

"Good ideas," he said.

They were alone in the corridor, as they often were.

She felt dull rage. "Then why the hell did you reject them all?" she asked.

"Because I can," he said.

She turned to go, furious. He grabbed her arm.

"Don't run away from me, Alex," he said.

She looked down at his hand. Into his face.

"I'll make you regret it," he said.

*

The old lady looked like any other. She wore a red coat over an austere black dress, and sturdy boots that cracked ice pools as she walked through rain. It spat at her disgustedly, and she raised her face to the sky in resignation. The damp seeped into her coat, making dark patterns that criss-crossed over the material. She liked walking, but not in this weather. Like it could never rain honestly, like God was in his heaven practising. She reached out a hand and the drops sparkled against the dark flesh, still taut, still surprisingly young. She could never get used to how icy the rain was in England. The first time it had fallen onto her upturned brow she had jumped in alarm.

She walked her old woman walk.

*

He watched her standing in front of the freezer, reaching for the ice tray, and when she twisted it, the cubes leaped up to her, scattering cold water and ice chips all over her chest, rivulets of liquid dancing into warmth, and he thought that this simple thing was the loveliest moment of his life. Just her, his lady, standing at the freezer like other women, but not other women, cracking ice for a long, cold drink. She turned to look at him, sucking a finger that she had hurt in her efforts. She smiled and he knew that he was wonderful. He could see it reflected in her face.

"What's the matter?" she hesitated, the tray still in her hands. His face was sea tides, crashing. A cube fell to the floor and began to melt.

"Nothing." He bent to pick up the ice cube. He touched it to her neck and she squealed in protest. He put a sure hand under one breast, feeling the fragile weight there. The nipple beneath his fingers hardened, and he could feel her move against him. All her body against him. He felt as if he was life then, life itself, and he leaned into her, propelling her against the refrigerator. She felt the door handle dig into her back, and shifted.

"Hey . . ." She was unsure. Insistent fingers at her breast.

"What's wrong with you today?" She edged away.

"Nothing. What's wrong with you?" He was confused. Wasn't today the day? Why wouldn't she be still? He had to show her. Today was the day.

"Well, you've been quiet all the time." She took courage. "When you're quiet like that I get worried. Like . . ." She plunged ahead. ". . . like you're thinking you don't love me, or something."

"I do love you." His hand slipped under her shirt. She twisted again. He was never this confident.

"I'd really like to talk about it, y'know? Do you really care about me?"

He didn't hear her. He couldn't. The inevitability of the day was heavy on him. It had to be now. Today he'd prove them all wrong. He'd laugh at those memories. She would help him take it all away. If she could shut up. Didn't he bring her letters in his eyes, the way he had done so many years ago? And wouldn't she know that it was him?

"It was me," he said. "Me, Sean." The words echoed in him, familiar, iron in their substance. He closed his eyes and waited for her to say she knew all along, that she had been waiting for him. He waited for permission to take down the pictures. Eyelashes frayed as he squeezed her, and his eyes, tighter. Two or three fluttered to his cheek.

She frowned. "What are you talking about?"

He was trembling. She had to tell him that she knew he was the one. He grabbed her around the waist and pulled her close to him, but now she was protesting, refusing to be still. He held on to her wrists, nails digging into the pliant flesh.

"Oooow . . . Sean, what the hell is *wrong* with you? Let me *go!*"

"Tell me."

"Tell you *what*?"

He dropped her hands, looked at her, standing there vile and snivelling. Disgust bloomed brightly.

"Sean, please, what's the matter . . ." She stepped forward, desperate. "Do . . . do you want to make love, is that it?" *(that look on his face what is that, what is that)* "Yes." His eyes were gravel.

She smiled uncertainly. "I'm sorry, I didn't understand. Well, we can, I mean, we *can*, I've been wondering if you wanted to . . . you don't have to get angry with me."

Still he stood, eyes inscrutable. A slow feeling was coming to her. Slow. And in trying to shake it off, in desperation, she walked away from him into the living room, snapped on the television to do something normal and she felt him behind her and what was this

(feeling)

it felt familiar

(if a gyal man ah run you down)

and he was touching her again and in some part of her she welcomed his hands but there was this feeling

(ah nuh fe you fault)

and she knew what it was and in recognising it she was amazed

(tek 'im, tek 'im gyal)

because it was fear, and it was hot and stinking and so overwhelming that she didn't know how to move and the insistence of his hands was burning into her

(ah nuh fe you fault)

and she had to tell him that she didn't want to, not yet, not now, in her sister's house. Had to calm him. Bring back the Sean she knew, because this wasn't how she had seen it. She clutched at the hands around her waist, began to talk.

"Baby, you know I love you. Don't be mad with me. Don't be this way with me. Talk to me . . ."

His hands began to ease. Her voice was soothing. Perhaps he couldn't expect her to understand. She was trying.

"I want it to be so special baby, I want to take it slow and you want that too, don't you?"

The hands relaxed. Shyness returned to him. He looked at her body hesitantly. Looked for the best way. Perhaps a kiss?

"It's because I love you that I want to wait, because with all the other men I didn't wait."

Something exploded in his head.

"They weren't anything to me. I've never felt this way . . ."

He flung his hands up to his temples. It had all been a trick. There was no refrain, no soft reality.

(all the other MEN)

The rage in him was liberated. It curved from him, hungry. Such rage.

(she's like all the others she isn't mine she doesn't belong to me she's like all the others that tramp the streets, waiting for the beautiful men)

She turned, saw the flare in his eyes. She thought that she had felt fear when that woman had come at her with the knife and she thought she had felt it when he touched her only moments ago, but now

(all the other MEN)

she was no longer a person, she was nerve endings crying and screaming into a rainy afternoon

(all the beautiful men)

and the heavy hand across her face knocked her against the television stand, TV screen exploding, fragments in her mouth

(I don't understand, it was you who saved me, Sean)

and she was wheezing for breath, sobs rattling her whole body, trying to sit up and he shoved her back, head cracking against the wall

(knickers oh my god he's tearing my)

as he brought the pain to her as a gift, the sound of his fists on her body exquisite, rich

(NO NO NO NO)

and every time he raised a fist he looked at it wonderingly, at the dark knuckles kissing her,

(THIS IS THE KISS, BITCH)

bruises on his knuckles and the curious way they broke as she broke, it was magic and so simple, the best kind of magic

(is this what they did to you, the beautiful ones)

the way her eyes closed as he hammered them closed, neatly, like a trick

(all those other men)

and he was bending her thighs back, groping, and

(no no no oh my god Sean no)

she wasn't one woman. He was biting them, teeth sinking

(——————!)

inside all women, knowing that he should have forced them before, it was they who were mistaken not him, and he smiled because his lips were red with blood

(and all the blood is red, my love)

and the sifting dry walls of her body scraped his tender flesh

(O MY GOD IT'S WONDERFUL)

as she tried to deny him but she couldn't she couldn't do that anymore

(why didn't I do this before)

(please please please)

(daddy was right)

and he was laughing

(the making of a man is in his might).

*

Through the window, the old lady watched them for a long time, the rain frozen on her cheeks making patterns and she felt a song in her, a song that she knew well. She bowed her head after a while, hearing the song scream in her bones, her cheap earrings jangling. She watched for a long time, the rain entangled in her eyelashes.

19

Jeanette wanted a scarf. She would get that red one that she had seen Maye wearing. And she needed a big hat. The church hat that Mamma gave Maye last year. That would do.

A hat and a scarf.

The house was dark. She had lain there, looking at the shadows, trying to decide which one he sat in. When she was sure that there was no movement she crawled to the bottom of the stairs. Her gaze settled on the clock, trying to make out the numerals. She watched it move through second after second. The thud of her heart beat time.

There were ten steps and she needed to climb them all. For the hat and the scarf. She had to catch her train. The next train was due at the station in an hour and she would be on it because she knew she had to get out of the house *(Simone will be coming home)* and the steps were just small ones. Not like the ones at home. She placed a knee on the first stair, feeling a secret breeze against her toes. Uncovered. Her shoe had gone missing. She eased her leg back down and sat on the carpet, feeling the pain crackle through her. She pushed it away. She crawled back to the living room, glass cutting into her, bile cold and acid in her throat. She reached for her shoe blindly. She could smell Maye's talcum powder across the house and it drove her on. *(Simone must not see me like this)* On the fifth step she lost her grip and teetered for precious seconds, on the brink of falling, but finally she could grip the banister again and she raised her knee one more time. She began to count. Step number seven.

Eight.

Nine.

The bathroom was the first place. She manoeuvred her body to the sink, bent over it, refusing the coy invitation of the mirror. She washed her hands, watching pink tendrils trickle over the enamel.

She vomited.

Her heart cried for her to wash everything else, but she had little time, there was half an hour left to get out of the house, and she abandoned the sink, not hearing the continuing movement of the water behind her.

The scarf was in the drawer where she had expected it to be, but the hat seemed to mock her and she stirred the carpet as she vainly turned and turned, searching. Until finally she had it on her head, bowing into her face, and the scarf was snug around her neck, hiding her. She went carefully down the stairs once more, listening to the clock. She crawled backwards, toes placing her firmly on each stair. She counted.

It was hard to stand. She used the coat rack to lever, damp hand prints covering the wall. More precious moments flew by, laughing at her and carrying her in their thoughts *(Simone) (did you beat the girl Auntie Je) (Simone)* and finally she stood, her breath coming in short gasps. She knew that she was hyperventilating and that her hands were dripping on Maye's walls. She put on her coat anyway, and stepped out into the road.

On the train, a seamstress stared at the huddled figure curiously. A shaft of light rippled over the carriage and she had an impression of a misshapen face. She drew her shawl more tightly across her shoulders and made sure that she didn't look again.

Jeanette kept on reading.

She had promised herself that she would.

*

Michael yelled at Nicola above the noise. It was a spectacular din, crammed, all varying decibels of it, into the house. The banner stretched across the living room was huge and garish, crafted by friends who had started getting drunk not with the onset of festivities, but the minute they had got the news.

"FEELIN' HOT, HOT, HOT!"

Nicola looked over her shoulder at the crowd. Everybody had let their hair down and it was marvellous to see. She wondered fleetingly what she had done to deserve all this goodwill. Even her father was tucked away in the kitchen, toasting her good health.

"WE FEELIN' HOT HOT HOT!!"

"OLE-OLE, OLE-OLE, OLE-OLE, OLE-OLE!"

She shrugged her shoulders helplessly at Michael. *What did you say?* she cupped her hands over her mouth to make the sound carry. He did a two-step between a couple of revellers and came to her side.

I asked you where Alex and Jeanette are! Oh, and where's Julius?

She bent to his ear and paused as a chorus thundered over them.

"MEK WE RUMB-BUM-BUM-BUM!"

"He's at rehearsal. I wish you would look in on Alex, Michael. I know she's really happy for me, but you know, this shit with Pearson is driving her into an early grave."

Michael looked quietly alarmed. "What's she doing?"

"Drinking too much. She'll say the opposite, and she looks very merry, but, well, you know what she's like." He nodded and made for the kitchen, then turned back.

Nicola smiled and yelled. *Jeanette and Sean are travelling back from Manchester. she's introducing him to the family, mi dear!*

Michael pulled a comical face. "HEAVEN FORBID!" He waded off, stopping to shake hands with someone Nicola didn't know.

She absently responded to yet another rapturous hug from one of the mob. She was pleased with herself. The director had been impressed, he had been trying to hold it down, but the way he had gripped her arms had said it all. She shook her head. The last few days had been terribly tiring, catching Concorde — Concorde, would you believe it — first class, and then the hustle of Los Angeles, some expectations confirmed and others denied. The money they were talking about was staggering. She had known that she could make a packet out of this, but combined with her expenses it would be obscene. She wondered what this meant for her and Julius. He'd met her at the airport along with a motley selection of the press, all eager for a statement, and he had been his usual self, touching her arms, her waist, attentive. And then he'd said he had late rehearsals. It was a new production, and she couldn't help feeling left out. Of course he'd offered her a lead role, but she'd had to take a chance on the screen test, and he'd needed an answer. Part of her felt that he should have waited, suppose she hadn't got the role, but she wiped the thought away. She couldn't see him as her meal ticket. That was exactly the kind of situation she had wanted to avoid. He was becoming increasingly morose about her refusal to set a wedding date. She would have felt better if she had been able to give voice to her insecurities, if she had been able to tell him what her father said, and how all of this had started, but she knew they were words he couldn't understand. How could he be expected to? *(can't very well say darling, I think I love you but I'm not sure you're the one because I've had this insane urge to sleep with white men all my life and you might just be another one of them)* Alexandrea weaved towards her and flung herself into her arms. Nicola could smell beer on her breath.

"God, girl — you're downing it a bit, aren't you?"

Alex looked up into her face with the careful concentration of a drunk. "YOU'RE NOT DANCING!" she yelled. White musk and spittle bathed Nicola's face. She reached out to support the woman, who was grinning maniacally.

"WHY-WHY AREN'T YOU DANCING, NIKKI? ISH YOUR PARTY!" She flung an arm out over the crowd. "THEY ALL WANT YOU TO DANCE, BABES! COME AN' DANCE WIV ME!" She pulled at Nicola's arm and nearly tripped over an ashtray.

"Wait, Alex. I'll dance with you in a minute. Why don't we have some nice coffee first, huh?" She beckoned to Michael, who started over.

An almost comical expression of surprise danced on Alex's face. "WHAT YOU MEAN? COFFEE? AIN'T NO COFFEE HERE, LUV! JUST BEER!" She trailed off, mumbling. "An' wine, if ya want it, champers, there's a lot of THAT, an' BEER, lots of it . . ."

"I'm taking you upstairs." Michael hooked his hands under his sister's armpits, but she pulled away, nearly falling. People had begun to look over, despite the crash of the music.

Alexandrea wagged a finger.

"BOTH OF YOU THINK YOU ALWAYS KNOW BEST!" She put bleary eyes on Nicola, who realised with dismay that Alex was more blotto than she'd ever seen her.

"YOU THINK 'COS YOU'RE SOME BIG HOT SHOT NOW, YOU CAN TELL ME WHAT TO DO?"

Michael tried again. "C'mon, Al. Let's go upstairs. We'll have a talk."

"TALK? YOU DON' KNOW 'BOUT TALKIN'. I'VE TALKED TO BIGGER THAN HER! I'VE TALKED TO WESLEY SNIPES!"

"I know, and that's very important." Michael had an arm around her waist and she was letting him lead her away, throwing shots back at Nicola as her brother spoke soothingly.

"SADE!"

Nicola watched Michael's head nod as they goose-stepped towards the hall.

"BARRY WHITE!"

Another nod.

"OPRAH WINFREY! THAT WAS HARD, NIKKI! VERY HARD!"

Mercifully, her voice was swallowed in the noise. Nicola sighed and allowed herself a small feeling of irritation. She knew that Alexandrea was having a hard time at work, but she really wished that she'd been herself tonight. There was a tiny gap between them. She wasn't used to it. A short, sweaty man tugged at her arm. "Alex alright?"

"Yeah, yeah."

He opened his arms. "So, wha'appen girl? How you ah look like you man lef' you? Come nuh?"

She smiled and stepped into the breach.

*

She gazed into the depths of the house and heard, somehow faraway, the sound of a party. She didn't know how long she stood there, hearing the thing as if on a neighbour's headphones. One of the ends of the red scarf was blown free and she tucked it back under her chin carefully, wincing. The scarf was damp because the blood had only just stopped its steady trickle and she looked down at the stupid stains and wondered why they talked about blood-red, couldn't anyone see that the stuff was brown?

More than anything else she wanted to be in bed. Her own bed. The first bed in which she had been able to do anything she wanted, eat crisps without Maye cussing, fart without her mother's voice asking her to beg pardon, and the other . . . the other things she had done there. Had she smiled when she had done them? She couldn't remember. But she would go to bed. It was important. Important. Because surely when she woke up tomorrow all of this would be gone. Surely.

*

"Nikki! There's the phone for you!"

Nicola got out of the ring of her friends, laughing, and edged towards the kitchen. Her dad held the receiver towards her.

"Oh God, we should have left the answering machine on! It's not the press is it, dad?"

His face looked troubled. "Someone who says her name is Maye. Says she's your flat mate's sister?"

Nicola took the phone and bent over it, plugging her other ear with her finger to block out some of Shaggy's *Boombastic.*

"Hello, Maye? That damn gyal Jeanette too shame to call me herself?"

She could hear a child crying in the background. Maye's voice was tripping over itself, hysterical.

"*What?* Hold it a minute. Dad, lick shot this door for me, please."

The door was closed.

"What? Sorry, Maye. The place here is mashing down as you can imagine. What's wrong with your little one?"

"Nicola, something's happened here, oh my god, I was supposed to meet Je and her man and I've been trying to get you but the phone hasn't been answered and the TV's smashed and there's blood, there's blood all over the place —"

"What?" Nicola cradled the headpiece and strained. She was confused. The other woman's sobs were panicky now, dry down the wire. She injected authority into her voice. "Maye. Listen to me. *Stop.* You're frightening your baby. Listen to me. Calm down."

Her father's anxious eyes were right up in her face, and she blinked.

She could hear Maye trying to stop crying. "Take a deep breath. Let it out."

"Nicola, what's happened? Have you seen her? Have you seen her? I'm so sorry —"

"Sssh. It doesn't matter. Listen, take a deep breath."

Maye obeyed.

"That's good. Everything is going to be alright." The child's wails were becoming strident. "Try and be calm for your little girl." She could feel her own panic rising to the surface. *(what does she mean, blood?)* She heard the clatter of the connection as the woman talked to Simone. The line went clear again.

"I-I'm here. I've sent her into the kitchen. Nicola, I'm sorry, I hardly know you, but I'm scared, is she there?"

"Maye, it's okay. She'll be alright. Now. Are Jeanette or Sean in the house at all?"

"No-no-no. I looked everywhere."

"That's good, that's good." She wracked her brain. "Have you called the police?"

Her father plucked at her sleeve. "Not *now*, Dad."

"Nicola . . ." Michael was at the door. "I need you *now*."

She ignored him, but he took the phone from her. She could hear Maye's voice gabbling from it once again. "Michael! Something's *happened*! Don't fucking *play*!" She tried to grab the receiver, but he shoved it at her father, held her shoulders.

"It's Jeanette."

"I know it's bloody Jeanette! Something's happened to her! Give me the —"

"Nicola, stop! *She's here!*"

"Oh my God, she's here? Where? Is she alright?"

His face was in pieces. "I don't know. She's standing outside looking at the house. I —" He struggled. "I get the feeling I shouldn't go out there."

"What the hell do you mean? Tell her I'm coming." She grabbed the phone from her father and began to yell into it. "Maye, everything's OK. She's *here* —"

"*Nicola!*" She'd never heard Michael angry before and she turned to stare at him. "Go out there *now*, Nicola. *Now*."

*

Jeanette was a shadow under the street lamp. Nicola moved towards her slowly.

"Jeanette, honey?"

"I need to go to bed," she said, but did not turn.

"Jeanette, what's happened?" She stood over the woman and then

sat down on the pavement next to her. Jeanette huddled closer to herself and the wind gambolled around them.

"I need to go to bed." It was a soft statement of fact.

"Alright." Nicola kept her voice gentle. "Can I help you?"

"No. Don't touch me."

Nicola fought back the rising panic. Had they been mugged? Was Sean hurt? And where the hell was he and how had she gotten back to London?

"I won't touch you, sweetie. It's cold out here. Come and be warm."

Jeanette stumbled to her feet and Nicola bit her lip. She was obviously in terrible pain. "Jeanette, are you hurt? Let me help you." She reached for her arm, and Jeanette lurched back, nearly falling. She put her arms by her sides. Her face was obliterated by the scarf and hat and her hair but somehow *(bigger)* different, and Nicola strained to see.

"Can someone else help, sweetie? Where's Sean? Can Sean help —"

Then she saw the woman's face, turned up to the night sky. One eye was swollen shut, a horrible injured orb that throbbed at her. The other wasn't much better. Blood had run down her face like tears and Nicola had a sudden insane thought that perhaps the cut the mad woman had given her had been infected, but as she thought it she knew it was madness, this was much worse and oh my God, what had happened, what could possibly have happened to make her pretty, dark face so full of dull light and dear God, what could she do for her. She moved forward instinctively, hushing and wanting to heal; but Jeanette was walking forwards, like walking on glass, scattered garbage, picking her way through the door and into the house — thank God hers was the first bedroom — and Nicola suddenly knew that the party was over, the party was over.

Mavis

De firs' time me realise seh me haffi come out of de whorin' business was when Carl start talk to me about how me pickney dem look good. Dis time me on de game for a long while. It feel like forever. Me feel like me was a different person, like de likkle girl weh used to nyam condensed milk ah mornin' time, go school an' love off de teacher dem, is like she never exist again. But a part of me couldn't t'ink about how me was ah feel.

Me know seh me wouldn't ah get out of it if Carl never start gwaan. Me did sen' off de firs' pickney go ah me madda yard 'cause when she reach four she start ask all kinda question 'bout her puppa, an' me couldn't handle it, me never know what to say. Den me tell her seh her daddy inna heaven, dat him look down on her every day an' smile how she pretty. But she was a bright chile, so me talk to me madda an' she tell me seh me mus' sen' her come. All dem time deh me feel Mamma did know what me was doin' in Kingston really, 'cause every time me go fe see de chile she ah suck her teeth, shift-shift her foot like she smell somet'ing bad. She never come out an' say anyt'ing though, so me did mek it gwaan. Me was too tired and too long in it to feel shame no more. Life was ordinary, me ah get de customer dem, Susan did lef' de country go ah Miami, seh she ah go try mek new life. At firs' we 'fraid seh dem woulda sen' her back, but me hear seh she find one man to married her so she could get de green card, an' dem time deh de American dem never smart like dem is now, you woulda find it hard fe get in deh dese days, but Susan cousin fix her up wid an American man who owe him a favour, an' she gone. Me did get one letter from her one time, but den me never hear from her again. Me still t'ink pon her sometimes, wonder if she did ever sen' fe her pickney, 'cause she did haffi lef' dem behind.

Is nearly ten years me was on de streets. Ten years. Me lucky seh me madda have good blood, cause after me get pregnant de second time me was frettin' seh

*de titty dem ah go get flabby. But me exercise meself, an' me was still lookin'
fine.*

*As me seh, me nuh believe seh me woulda come out if it wasn't for me child
dem. When de second one born me start wonder if me can breed bwoy pickney,
because is pure gyal ah come outta me belly. Sophie say is because me ah move
wid pure woman. De second girl was for Carl. Him always ah tell me seh ah
lie, but me know. From de firs' pregnancy me did say me nah breed again fe
now, an' me was careful, even though Carl did black up me arm when me tell
one customer seh me nah sex him if him don' wear boots. After me not a idyat.
Dem only ah catch me out once. But Carl was a man who insist seh him nah
wear no condom, an' him still ah come round to we an' look t'ings. An' when de
baby born, you coulda see ah de bwoy chile: she have him structure, him eye, all
him hair too, long, thick hair. Me haffi tek de hot comb out from early an' tek it
to de chile head, because none ah we couldn't handle it, never mind how much
grease we put on deh. Carl even play wid her sometimes, an' me shock, cause
him wasn't a man fe play wid pickney. One day me go inna de room wid
breakfast fe her, an' him ah play, fling her up inna de air. She ah laugh like she
ah go bus'. She was one ah dem pickney, laugh whole heap, love everybody, fas'
inna everybody business. Like me get one of each: one dark an' have de bwoy
bad blood, but she sweet like naseberry, one have de tall hair, pretty like she
couldn't come from me, but she serious like a judge, suck her thumb until she was
twelve. Me try everyt'ing wid dat chile, me madda rub okra pon her han', she
even try put cow doo-doo pon it till she haffi wipe it off quick time because de
pickney ah bring it to her mout' same way.*

*So Carl ah play wid de chile, an' me ah watch. Me all feel good 'bout him for
once, ah watch him nice up de chile. Den him send her downstairs seh she mus'
buy a nutty buddy from de man ah sell. Me smile up wid him. Him ah lie pon
de bed like him is a king. Den him start tell me how she is a wonderful chile,
funny how fe me dry-up body can get pickney look so good, de odder one too, she
ah go have nice hair. De bwoy dem ah go like her pretty eye. Me was jus'
listenin', ah cream me skin wid cocoa butter, an' den me realise what him ah
seh. How you can talk 'bout pickney so, me ask him. Him get off de bed den an'
laugh, tell me seh him is a business man, him is de body inspector. Den dis
bloodclaaht man actually renk fe go ask me what age me t'ink dem coulda start.
Calm, like is a ordinary somet'ing we ah chat. Him seh de firs' one can get out,*

start work an' help me in about six year, depend on how she develop, if she have big titty or what. Tell me seh de youngest one — FE him pickney — can be security fe me ole age. Seh when she turn fourteen me will be forty, den maybe me can all retire, even though me will probably be a good lookin' woman still. Me couldn't believe it. Lawd, me couldn't believe it. Me ah watch de man like him ah go tell me is joke soon, but him jus' ah talk serious, like me woulda ever put me pickney out t'un dem whore. When him leave de room me stan' over de toilet in deh, me never vomit dem way deh excep' when me was pregnant. All de time me ah t'ink, me min' ah race. At least is not now him ah talk 'bout, but time go fast, time go fast. An' right den me realise seh me ah ramp wid me life, me nah t'ink 'bout nuttin, me nah t'ink bout future, me jus' ah walk street ah nighttime ah ben' up me body. Is like me wake up, y'know? An' me start t'ink seh bwoy, if Susan go Miami, maybe me can go somewhere too. Me jus' ah vomit an' ah panic, but where me coulda go, eh? Where me coulda get weh from dis nasty man? Me feel like me ah dead. Den me likkle girl walk inna de room, start bawl when she see me, ask me what happen, if me pregnant again, an' me tun round an' box her before me t'ink, 'cause me did want to know how she coulda know 'bout belly. She jus' a pickney! She start cry tell me seh she hear de odder gyal dem ah talk bout how when woman let man put dem t'ings inside dem mout', dem get baby. Me jus' ah look pon de chile an' de nastiness weh she ah talk, an' me feel sick again. Me ah wonder what else dem hear, what de odder one hear before she go ah country? Me never know seh pickney woulda really hear dem t'ings. Every time me haffi bring back customer me woulda put her in de bathroom fe sleep, put de sheet an' de pillow dem in dere, tuck her up an' turn off de light. Me did do dat wid both ah dem when me couldn't get s'maddy fe keep dem, when de whole ah dem ah work. Me never t'ink seh she shoulda see me wid de man dem. When me do it, me always use to sing to dem, sing loud when de man dem ah do dem t'ings. Funny how de man dem never business. Couple of dem get vex an' ask me weh me ah do, me tell dem seh it ah sweet me so much me haffi sing.

Me start plan up hard-hard after dat. When me put me mind to it, me ah find all kinda way fe jim-screech de dutty bwoy Carl. Me start work all twenty man ah nighttime if me coulda get dem. Tek all de sick man dem, do whatever me coulda do fe mek a money. Me all ask dem fe extra, tell dem seh inflation ah kill me off, if dem nuh see how dem ah marry de goods dem inna de shop, ah sell

173

flour wid rice, together. When me go back ah Carl me hide de extra money inna me crotches, push it up so him don' know. Him ah fool. Mussee t'ink seh me ah work hard for him. Like me business wid him. An' so me ah gwaan. Ah try fe plan up.

One t'ing me know from de good Lawd. We all haffi stan' at him foot an' cry excuse. De whole ah we responsible fe what we do. Me know seh if de Lawd ask me if me tun whore me haffi tell him yes sah, an' tek what him have to put on me head. You don' get more inna dis life dan you can tek. Me know me haffi pay fe me sins but me determine seh me pickney nah go down ah hell an' fire wid me. Dem nah turn no whore. Me want dem fe pretty up an' find husband, try find one decent s'maddy fe deh wid. An' me know seh de whole ah de black man dem wutliss. Dat is when me start realise seh me haffi lef' de rock weh me born. Lef' an' try find decent life fe me pickney. So me ban me belly, start drink peppermint tea again, ah try find a way fe go ah England. Me know seh de whole ah dem mad ovah dere, but dem couldn't mad like dem man yah.

20

The cat's purring got louder. Blearily, Alexandrea pondered on one essential truth: when you were hung over, everything sounded like a chain saw. She slitted her eyes and regarded the animal, who was sitting on her chest, deciding that cats deserved all the bad press they got. It was kneading its claws into her arm. The purring got louder.

"Someone sent you in here to wake me up, you flea-bitten beast," she said.

"Yes." said Michael. She peered over the duvet, wincing at the light. Her mouth tasted as if someone had spread mango jelly inside it and left it there to rot — for five years. She groaned.

Her brother was sitting on the edge of the bed. He didn't look happy. She wondered what time it was. His girlfriend wouldn't like being left alone on a Sunday morning. This probably meant that last night she'd been worse than she felt, if that was possible. And now he was going to tell her all about it. Threaten to tell mum and dad, maybe. The fucking Bobbsey twins. They'd totally freak out. In unison, as usual. *(why can't everyone leave me ALONE)*

The chain saw switched busily to her left ear and tried to bury into her skull. She put her hands over her eyes. "No lectures, please. I don't feel up to it. I'm very sorry for whatever I did last night, a million times sorry and I'll never do it again."

He continued to gaze at her.

She tried to joke. "As long as I'm not pregnant, or HIV positive, as long as I didn't snog Nicola's father, nothing could be as bad as your face." She moved her hands and pain neatly lanced each eyeball.

He still wasn't saying anything.

"C'mon, Mike. I'm not turning into an alcoholic. Chill." *(no I'm not)* He looked at her without seeing her. His voice was overcast. It made him old.

"Jeanette was raped last night."

She tried to understand the words. She couldn't grasp them. She turned them over and over as the cat arched its back against her arm.

(Rape.)

(Jeanette.)

(Jeanette had been.)

(Raped.)

"But — that means she was —" she swallowed the word away. Unwilling, she had meant to say. And when was that bitch not up for it? *(can't say that, little brother will be very annoyed)*

"*Rape*, Alexandrea! You know what that is, don't you?"

Aw, she thought. *He's frustrated*. Michael always wanted to make everything better, best, perfect. Perhaps it was his own personal by-product of their singular upbringing. She didn't know for sure. He had always been like this, pottering around the house as a little boy, watering plants with his baby jug, finding a dead bird in the garden and wanting to know how to bring it back to life. The bird's death had had a certain amount of inevitability for her. She accepted that things would go wrong, be wrong. Not him. He had been *frustrated*. He was active, a doer. He made things better and it killed him when he was helpless.

"I know what it is." Her voice was dull. "Are you sure? I mean, is *she* sure? She does get herself into things . . ."

He stared at her. "What do you mean?"

"I don't mean anything, I just —"

He leaned towards her. "Do you think she blackened both her eyes herself? Bled all over Nikki for the hell of it?"

She shrank away from him. The saw continued to worry at her face. "I'm not going to say I'm sorry for that." He got up. "I know you don't like her, that she pisses you off in some stupid way. I just thought I'd tell you before you went downstairs and asked unnecessary questions."

"Mike, I'm sorry, I'm sorry —"

"*Jesus Christ*, Alex! You're a *woman*. How could you?"

She felt anger. "So? Are you telling me that women don't, well, get the wrong end of the stick sometimes?"

"She's been beaten up! She can't even be near me, me, and I'm her *friend!*" He paced the room, furious.

She didn't know what to say. She was afraid to ask questions. Had Jeanette ended up in the wrong place at the wrong time? Maybe she'd promised something she couldn't deliver *(maybe she wore)* met a man who wouldn't play the game *(those batty riders)* took someone to the point of no return *(one too many times)* and then couldn't return him. She was angry that she couldn't say any of these things *(she isn't like me)* but in the face of her brother's anger she was quiet.

"Does she know who?" she asked.

"It was Sean," he said.

"*What?* I thought she was sleeping with him!"

"Well, she wasn't, and what the hell difference does that make?"

She tried to pacify him. "I just thought . . . well, I thought they were serious."

"They were." His face was sad. "I don't know what went wrong. She's not talking much."

"Where is he now?"

"God knows. Who gives a fuck? I'm gonna fucking kill —" He stopped himself, held onto his head. "I tell you, she's not *talking*. Nikki's been up with her all night."

Alexandrea grabbed at her night robe.

"Shit, poor Nikki. This is just what she needs. Where is she?"

He stopped her. "She's tired. I think she's getting some kip on the sofa. Don't go down there yet."

"You must be mad. Nikki'll need us."

"Jeanette needs her more. Plus *you* did your bit last night."

She pulled the covers up to her chin, chastised.

*

Jeanette looked out of the window. Light crawled over the surface of the world. The sky was the most remarkable shade of blue. She watched its shades deepen, her mind empty. She felt disembodied, as if she had hit a warp in time that had rubbed at the grooves in her wet, malleable brain.

As if she watched a world encased in cotton wool, which made its sounds fuzzy and convoluted. As if she was under water.

Simone had saved her. She'd had to get out of the house so her niece wouldn't see her. This alone had given her a transitory focus. *(aren't those blues pretty when was the last time I was awake for this)* Outside, on the pavement a woman walked, her thick coat a yellow powder puff against the wind, her shoes a brilliant, plastic purple that Jeanette found hard to register *(what kind of woman wears shoes like that what kind of woman wears shoes like that)* and the colours she saw became mixed with the questions in her mind. She could see them, great, bouncy, fat cartoon letters gliding, purple and yellow stripes, festoons of purple and yellow firecrackers *(WHAT KIND OF WOMAN)* and she shook her head. She looked for the sky. The blues faded into a buzz around the horizon of buildings. The pain lingered, waiting. She wouldn't feel it. She promised herself she wouldn't feel it. She wondered if she was still bleeding. She had to concentrate. If she didn't, she would go completely mad *(he held you down)* and the voice whispered in her head, those nasty thoughts, she couldn't let them near her *(he held you down)* they were too close. She shook her head so that the voices would die away.

*

Nicola had been gnawing her lip all night and it was raw. She wasn't used to not knowing what to do. Her impotence mounted the walls in front of her. She hadn't dared to go upstairs to bed, even when Jeanette had given way to sleep. The thought that her friend might wake up in the dark kept her on the sofa. God bless Michael. He had stayed the whole night, hiding in the kitchen. He had been afraid to come out, to speak, lest Jeanette hear his voice and lose it. He had brought her a bowl of disinfectant and warm water after she had coaxed Jeanette into letting her face be cleaned. When he had poked his face around the door, Jeanette's shoulders loosened. Nicola was relieved until she looked closely at the woman. She hadn't relaxed. She was slumped, her face full of resignation.

Michael had seen it before her. He backed away from them, horrified. Their thoughts swirled thick in the room *(she thinks he's going to hurt her too) (she thinks I'm going to HURT her)* and his hand scrambled for the door. He had to get out, he couldn't bear the look on her face. As he disappeared, Jeanette tightened up again.

Nicola dipped the sponge into the warm water and raised it to her face. *(how did she get back to London without walking in front of a bus)* The blood on her face had turned black. There was a bite mark on her cheek, you could count the molars.

Nicola washed her, fighting the need to weep. She reached for the buttons on her blouse.

Jeanette shook her head, clutching the fabric to her.

Her responses were monosyllabic. Yes, she had been raped. By Sean. That was all. Nicola was worried about the injuries. It was hard to know where some of the blood originated. Her clothes were sticky with it, *(what's he done to)* they had to get her to a doctor, but she didn't know who was best or whether Jeanette would go anywhere willingly. *(what's he done to her body)* She seemed to have come to the end of whatever energy had brought her home *(if he could do that to her face)*.

In desperation, she had called Julius. He had wanted to charge over, but she restrained him. It had been hard enough getting all the partygoers out of the house. Michael and her father had taken care of that. There were going to be a lot of people vexed with her this morning, but that was the least of her worries. She was trying to control her own fear. She was glad she hadn't had to beg Michael to stay. Curled up in the long night she had feared Sean coming back. Jeanette didn't seem to know where he was, and he surged through Nicola's thoughts *(suppose he comes here)* and she felt guilty in the face of her fear, because she was scared not only of what he could do to Jeanette *(he's done with her)* but to her as well *(he'll want someone fresh he could come here)* because if he was animal enough to do that *(what could he do to me)* he was capable of anything. Eventually she sent Michael up to talk to Alex. Alex. Drunk Alex.

She sighed, and it was a bitter almond sound. The whole world was coming apart. And this was supposed to be the first day of the rest of her life. She looked at the ragged banner and sobs threatened. Looked at the flowers. Hundreds of them, colours of the rainbow, all over the place, smiling. Her eyes settled on a bunch she hadn't seen before. White lilies and pink carnations. She looked at the label:

I'm not here, but I KNOW you got the part. Congrats.
Love ya.
Jeanette.
P.S. See you soon!

She heard feet on the stairs as Michael tiptoed down. She wondered if he had been crying. His eyes looked red. *(either that or pulling a big head spliff)*

Inappropriate laughter threatened. There it was again.

He sat down beside her. "What are we going to do?" he said.

"I don't know," she paused. "Have you told Alex?"

His lip curled. "Yes," he said.

"We need a doctor," she said.

"Yes," he said again.

They sat. More feet on the stairs. Alexandrea came into the room, looking frail and worried. She stopped in front of Nicola. They looked at each other for a long moment *(forgive me I know it was your special night forgive me I'll only ask it once because I can't do any better)* and Nicola took her hand. They made a circle when Michael took the other.

"Hello."

They looked up. She was something different to all of them as she stood at the door. For Nicola, a broken doll. For Michael, a punctured fruit. For Alex, an empty easel, as she tried not to see.

They went in Michael's uncool VW bug. Because she wanted to, they let her put on a particular pair of shoes. They were purple.

21

Detective Inspector John Aimes stared at the group in front of him. It was obvious what this lot were in for. The girl looked as if she'd had a date with a meat grinder. Someone had been knocking her around, make no mistake. And he could guess what else; there was a man in the group, but he was notably far away from her, the tension palpable. *A friend of hers,* he guessed. A good friend, but not sure now that another man had hurt her. The tallest girl was vaguely familiar, very beautiful. Straight as a willow. Perfectly formed, like a jigsaw puzzle. She was obviously the one that was going to be outraged, confused, do most of the talking. The beat up girl, he guessed was in high-grade shock, there was an apathy to the way she walked. She'd barked her shin on the swinging door and not noticed it. The last girl had seen it and turned away. He wondered why.

They were shaken in a way he had come to know well. There was nothing like the shake-up that came hand in hand with violence, especially in the land of it-couldn't-happen-to-me-guvnor. This was going to be bad. Worse, because it looked like a case of the real thing. He straightened himself and smiled at the tall woman.

Nicola clenched her teeth. "We have come to report a rape."

*

She allowed herself to cry when the doctor's fingers probed her. She found that the more she cried the more it seemed as if she would never again have dry eyes. The tears seeped into her hairline and made tiny puddles there. Puddles of anger. Regret. Bewilderment. Some fell on to the surface of the examination cot, a flat, unheeding piece of furniture. Later they would dry there with the others, forgotten. The doctor asked questions that she answered as the tears fell.

The female police officer assigned to her handed her tissues. She wanted to throw them on the floor, stamp on them, howl. The howl was in her head, so close to the surface. She bit down on it as the doctor kept up his patter. He was a nice old man, she could see that, through everything. But he didn't have a clue. The questions scraped at her skin. *Are you on the pill, dear? Have you ever had an abortion? You weren't a virgin before the incident? Did you have sex twenty four hours before the incident?* That was what he named it, as if he was afraid of the words. They were so loud in her head that she was surprised he couldn't hear her, hear the chanting howl in her head. *(I was raped I was raped I was raped)* It was her mental answer to every question, her heart's answer: I was raped, don't you understand, I was raped, as he took swabs from her vagina, from her anus, from her mouth, as he scraped at her nails, peered between her legs, put a comb through her pubic hair, as if he was on vacation, as if her body was no more than a fascinating holiday destination, to be explored, its secrets forced up. He took clippings of her pubic hair like prizes and she was reminded of Charles, in a time that seemed like forever ago. She had given him a tiny ivory box that she had found in Covent Garden. They had been out on a rare excursion to the capital with his father driving them obligingly. They had laughed all day, eaten stale chips on the side of the road, watched an errant mime artist do his thing, delighted in everything. She had slipped into a public loo and clipped her pubic hair with nail scissors, giggling, placed them, warm and fragrant, in the box, slipped it to him as the mime feigned surprise and lust and love and the drizzle of the West End rain dripped off his face like lonely tears. His father had been nosy, grabbed the box and snapped it open, grinning up at them. She had felt slightly sick as that knowing glance weaved over her, the naughty delights of the gesture that had seemed so grown up and sexy only moments before obliterated by his face.

That had all been before this, before yesterday, before, dear Jesus, she had been raped. As the doctor leaned over her scratches, examined her sore eyes, she felt weary in the face of forever. They said your life flashed before your eyes when you died. She hated the fact that yesterday would flash there too, the fact that she could die remembering yesterday the most.

Making her statement confused and frightened her. The officers were patient, walking in tiny, rhythmic circles around her, but they were probing her too, all of them were probing her, asking her to *explain* herself, asking for *details* that she had not even allowed herself to feel. She had ideas about what to expect, from films, from books, from guesses. But it was like everything else, she realised. You didn't know it till you knew it. She tried her best to remember where he *(Sean, remember him?)* had stood, what had happened after the ice and told them that the bruise in the small of her back was when she kissed him against the fridge.

The decision to report had come swiftly to her. It wasn't born of anger, nothing was as deliberate as that. She knew that she was running on her own expectations of herself. She had expected that she would leave the house before her niece returned, and she had done that. It was the decent thing. The right thing. You didn't lie in a pool of your own blood and vomit and wait for a child to find you. Neither did you shirk your responsibility. You reported. Somewhere she had decided that it was the done thing. She wasn't sure why. She just knew that she needed a mental list. And this was number three on the list. Get home. Go to bed. Report. Like that.

She had heard Nicola and Alexandrea and Michael whispering urgently in the living room, about what should they do, what should she do, and at first she had wanted to go back into that bed and curl around her own spirit, hide it, protect it, it was what she had left, couldn't they understand? But her own questions plucked at her relentlessly, with this new day they were louder. As the officers talked she wanted to say ask him, ask him what was done next, and next, ask him what happened. He knows best. He knows what he did *(his name is Sean)* where he put his hands next, where the furniture was, how she had held up her arms to protect her face but they had been like so much paper. She watched as the solemn men wrote it all down, squiggles curving along the pad. How strange that yesterday could make patterns on paper, could flow through a pen.

Most of all, she wanted to know why. Why he had done this. Why he had hurt her. She loved him. She had loved someone and they had done . . . this. It made no sense to her as they whirled around, as they advised her, like crazy hairdressers casting noble eyes at a badly-done perm. She chanted, hearing it for the first time. *He pushed my legs apart with his hands. He placed his hand on my chest so that he could push himself upward to unzip his trousers. They were nice trousers, nice for a special occasion. No, I didn't hit him with my free hands. I was trying to breathe. Yes, that is correct, he inserted his penis into me. The vagina or anus? The . . . vagina. I was lying there. I was just lying there because I was — Would afraid be the best word? No. Not afraid, even though I was afraid. I couldn't believe it was happening. Shocked, then? Yes.*

Yes. Yes. Yes.

Did you say no?

I said no.

The WPC gripped the side of the chair. The doctor nodded at her. "You should be used to this kind of violence." He was vaguely condemnatory. She watched him walk away, stripping the surgical gloves off. She was used to it. There were times when she was shocked at her own indifference. She had to be. But this. The bastard had *bitten* her.

"Looks like he used the blood for lubrication," the doctor had observed.

*

Alexandrea smiled. She was more intimate with this toilet than her own bedroom. She smiled at the little bottle. Such a small thing. She couldn't help it. It was funny, really, the stereotype that she felt herself becoming. Harassed Woman Hits The Bottle. She put an extra strong mint into her mouth. There was no way she was going to let anyone smell this little nip on her breath. Particularly not Pearson. That would be the final indignity.

She thought she was handling it well. On the surface, she was pleased with herself. She'd remained strong, she hadn't quit. Her presence, she told herself, discomfited him. This was a battle. Every day she tried to let him know that she was fighting him. *(fire me then)* It was the only thought as he entered the room, passed a quick hand over the back of her chair, that was his favourite, just that small, tender touch. *(I dare you to fire me)*

Underneath her bravado it was taking its toll, the silent, constant struggle, hammering at her. In truth, she feared the battle, because there was absolutely nothing she felt she could do. It would always be her word against his. Her own small pieces of research continued as she tried to find comrades in the struggle, but found only a glowing wave on which Pearson rode, jubilant, laughing at her. Her powerlessness overwhelmed and frightened her, and she tried to drown it in whiskey once more, tilting back her head as the liquid trickled down one side of her mouth. She wiped at the mixture of saliva and alcohol and heard her name.

"Alexandrea? Are you in here?" It was another one of the researchers, Julie, a round, white girl who'd never learnt how to apply make-up properly. She'd often looked at the woman in the midst of her sour moods, thanking everything that at least God hadn't laughed when he had created *her* face.

"Yes, Julie, I'm here. What?" She pushed the bottle deep into her bag and popped the mint back in her mouth.

"You got diarrhoea or what? You've been in and out of the place like a jack in the box today."

She forced a laugh. "Yeah, I do have a bit of a tummy bug."

"His majesty's called a meeting in fifteen minutes. Says we're all crap and *he* knows what the next month's programmes are going to be about." The girl sniffed and fluffed her hair. "Says they'll be hard-hitting." Alexandrea slid the door bolt back and stepped out. "Really?" She tried to sound interested. The whole team had given him hard-hitters galore. He wasn't having it. She wondered whether he had turned them all down just so turning down hers didn't look bad.

They walked back to the office together. The other four researchers were already assembled, Jenny in their midst. She was passing out sheets of paper.

"These are Tony's ideas for the next couple months. We're going to have a discussion about them and start deciding on contacts for audiences. Julie and Simon, take the first five. Sharon and Duane, you have the second five, Peter and Alexandrea, handle the last five. That'll end the season, so at least we won't be dredging our brains for ideas."

Alex could see that Jenny was well pissed off. It wasn't the usual thing for an executive producer to hand out ideas. That was the job of the producer and her team. It was, in effect, a vote of no confidence.

"The other big news is that we're going live. That won't start immediately. We'll begin with the last five, so Peter and Alex, you are going to have to get it right. Your mistakes will be seen by oh, about five million people." Tasdell nodded, then turned on her heel. *She is not a happy bunny,* thought Alex. She was proud that she and Peter had been chosen to research the first live shows. *That* was a vote of confidence. She glanced down the page. The madness going on at home was due to continue for a while. She did feel sorry for the girl. She'd never hated her. Not at all. It was a horrible, horrible thing to happen to anyone, and she was sympathetic. Nicola also needed her support because she was stressing more than anyone, but she had her own problems too. Yes, it was all a shame, but she couldn't help feeling that Jeanette had some responsibility in this too. Well, you had to watch out for yourself, didn't you? Any sensible woman avoided certain situations. And that Sean had always been dodgy, you could tell a mile off that he might be that type. Frankly, she was surprised that he'd had to force her. She would have thought they'd bonked ages back, given Jeanette's track record. Of course that didn't mean that he should have raped her, but why the hell did she take him into an empty house, sexying up herself? She felt irritated in the face of what seemed obvious: it wasn't as if Jeanette was in *her* position, dressing decently, being firm, never ambiguous, about what she wanted. It was a hard truth in these politically correct times, but there it was: she could have watched out for herself some more. It was a matter of self-preservation. Men would always be tempted. Of course she'd say none of this to anybody. The vibe was too volatile. Michael would blow her head off.

She looked down the list. Julie, sitting next to her, looked up sympathetically as she drew in a sharp breath.

"Poor love. Tummy cramps, eh?"

She nodded. It had to be a mistake. Surely he wouldn't. She looked up, stunned. Pearson smiled at her from the door jam where he was leaning.

*

Thompson was high. He could feel his tie coming loose as he strode through the newsroom and decided he didn't give a damn. Hysterical laughter bubbled in him. He *had* it, god-damn if he didn't have it. Link, angle, front page god-damn news in the making. He showed his teeth to Alderton, who looked up, irritated, as he burst in.

"What?"

"As they say in the biz, my good man, have I got news for you!"

For once, he was glad to see, the old bastard listened.

*

The line into the Häagen Dazs shop was long, but Sean felt he had time to wait. The day was brittle, the air icy, having a last cold snap before the sun came. You could bite into it. He looked at the line and grinned. Good to be here with all these other insane people who needed ice cream comfort on a cold day. He smiled to himself. He felt liberation. He still wore that same underwear, the blue pair of jockeys he'd put on in preparation for the great day. Oh, but it had been satisfying. He was vindicated. Life was wonderful. He felt superiority for the first time in his life. He looked down at his knuckles, the bruises there hadn't faded yet, but he knew he would mourn their departure. They were an indication of his victory. He had shown them. And it had been so quick, so easy. Perfect. They couldn't laugh at him anymore. He could laugh at them. The might was in him, roaring, and he could laugh. He had been experimenting all day with the new feeling. He had smiled at the cute little thing on the tube platform, and her eyes had passed over him, derisive, and for once he felt none of that blank pain that had become a friend. Simple elation. She didn't know, but the knowledge was his. He could take her now, there, show her his might. He was no weak man, he was a strong man. Other men fantasised this, but them, they were soft, they had never done it, but he had. He had never been more of a man, she had never been more a woman than when he did it to her.

He was not insane. This would have been too simple. He was delighted. Somewhere in his mind he knew that society, as it was, would not admit to his victory. But that was fine. He had always been alone. He had taken a train back to London and walked the streets, strong, fingering his own tall body. He hadn't wanted to go home. It was enough to walk, to feel. He wished that he could tell his father, share with somebody. The bitch had had it coming, and she had got it.

"Excuse me?" The young girl was healthy, all tight jeans and cherry-glossed lips. Long blonde hair. "Have you been here long?"

He smiled easily. "Not long." He gesticulated to the line. "It's been going up."

"Oh, thanks." She hesitated.

"What flavour do you want?" he asked.

"Peaches and cream."

He smiled again. "Just like your pretty face."

She twisted her mouth, delighted. "Wow. Corny."

He nudged her, conspiratorial. "I know. Sorry. It came from nowhere."

"Right." She moved closer. "I'm Rebecca."

"Sean," said Sean.

The line moved up. They turned with the crowd as cymbals crashed nearby. A horde of Hare Krishnas were on the move, graceful, hysterical smiles on their faces, dancing, reaching for members of their audience. He smiled at her. That was it. He felt religious. The world was unexplored.

*

"It was horrible. They kept her there for five hours. And she has to go back, so they can take pictures of the bruises that come up."

Julius stretched, holding the receiver carefully. Around him, stage manager and various hired hands fussed over the theatre. "Hold on a sec, Nicola."

He gesticulated to one of the men who hurried over and spoke softly. "Where's the backdrop?"

The man looked alarmed. "Well, there's some extra work . . ."

"Dammit, man! I expected to see that work today. What are those wankers doing?"

"Well, it is complicated, and the paint wasn't exactly as Jeff liked it —"

"Forget Jeff. I want to see the thing in an hour." He turned away from

188

the man's dismayed face. "Just a minute, Nicola." He glared at the quivering stage hand. "Go *do* it!" He watched him scurry away.

"Sorry, sweetheart. What were you saying?"

Her voice was cold. "I'm aware that you're busy, Julius. But this is important."

He tried to placate. "I'm sorry. It's madness down here."

"It's madness *here*, Julius! I don't believe you are being such an insensitive prat!"

"Nicola, I'm really sorry. I'm listening. How is she?"

A pause. "Much the same. Still a bit shocked, really. Her sister's coming down this morning, with her mum, I think. And she's going to have to go to court in Manchester. They're actually going to haul her back down there."

"Well, if it gets to court they'll have to. That's where it happened."

"How can you be so calm?"

He sighed. She'd been understandably upset by the whole thing. Jeanette was sweet, she didn't deserve the hassle. But there was always something. Just when things had been good between them. He had finally started feeling secure with her. The ring was lovely on her finger. He often found himself admiring it on her long hand. Then she would turn and smile at him and all the dissonance seemed worth it. But now this. Still, it was why he had fallen for her. She was brilliant, beautiful, difficult.

"Julius, are you there?"

"Yes, I'm here. Will I see you tonight? You must need to get away from that situation for a while. I'll pick you up after rehearsals. We can go out, stay in by the fire, whatever you want."

"Oh no, I can't do that."

"Why not? I haven't seen you since it all happened for you in Hollywood. I got you a little pressie."

"Well, I can't leave Jeanette —"

"You say her family's coming up? She'll be fine."

"I can't, Julius. She's clinging to me over this. I'm not sure how I'm helpful, but I am. What's the matter with you? It's only been two days!"

He felt disappointment. "You can't take total responsibility for this,

Nicola," he took a deep breath. "I know she's your friend. I respect that. God knows this is awful, and I'd like you to give her my best. But we have things to discuss. You'll have to be off to America soon, and, well, I thought you might want to do the knot-tying before you le—"

"Give her your *best?* I can't believe you just said that."

"C'mon, sweetheart. It didn't come out right. I'm sorry. Its just that this is all making me feel —" He strained for words and let his uncertainties free. "— a bit insecure. I mean, what's going on with us?"

He listened to the dial tone in his hand and put the phone down gently. He stood for a while, staring at the naked stage. "JEFF! WHERE THE BLOODY HELL IS THAT BACKDROP?"

*

Nicola met Maye at the door and gave her a weak smile. The two sisters didn't look anything like each other. Maybe around the chin, the shape of the face, but not much more. They shook hands. Maye looked drawn, as if sleep had been eluding her.

"I'm sorry we have to meet like this."

"I know." Maye's shoulders trembled. "Where is she?"

Nicola guided her into the hall. "I gave her a sedative, so she's knocked out. She . . . she really needed it. She's not . . . herself."

They sat in the living room, awkward. Nicola made coffee. Maye sat on the edge of the sofa, clutching the mug. She looked around the room nervously, at the cards on the mantelpiece, at the careless beauty of the room. Nicola marvelled once again at the two sisters. One so vibrant, the other tremulous. She wondered at the mother.

"Your mum —"

"It's a —"

They spoke at the same time, and laughed laboriously.

"You go first," said Maye.

"No, you," said Nicola.

"I was just going to say it's a beautiful house. Did you decorate it yourself? I mean, Je told me how beautiful it was, she was really glad when she hooked up with you both, I mean, she liked it . . ." She fell silent.

"Could your mother not come?"

"Oh, she said she'd try, but, well, Mamma's not good with things like this, she's . . . easily upset."

Nicola guessed suddenly that Maye was glad Mrs Abrahams hadn't travelled with her.

"And your little girl? What's her name, Simone?"

"Oh, she's with her dad. She's been staying with him, since . . . you know. I'm not with him anymore, but well . . . I didn't want her to be in that house. They — the police say they'll be coming around to have another look. They say I'm not to . . ." She quivered. ". . . not to *clean* anything, and Simone, well, she *trod* in it, you know, the *blood* and I thought I'd have hysterics." She took a deep breath. "And the police said we shouldn't touch the evidence. I'm sorry —"

Nicola reached out to touch her arm. "Don't be. It must have been hard."

Maye sniffed. "She was always the strong one, you know? Even though I was the older one? She used to protect me, and I couldn't protect her —"

"Shhh. You couldn't be expected to do anything about it."

"But if I'd been home earlier, it wouldn't have happened! I could have stopped it, called the police, well, he wouldn't have done it if I was there, would he? I can't believe it. She was so in love with him. The last time I saw her it was Sean this, Sean that, and if I hadn't invited them . . ."

"Maye, you're not responsible. Is that bloodclaaht . . ."

"Where is he, anyway? Why haven't they arrested him? He's still on the streets!" Maye's face tightened. "I know I sound selfish, but I don't know how to help her, Nicola. She's always been the strong one. I don't know if I can even see her, I don't think I can see her weak. It was her who told Mamma when I fell pregnant, she protected me from all the aggro, I don't know if I can see her like this. And Simone keeps asking me what's wrong with Auntie Je, and I don't know what to tell her, I've only just started telling her about how babies are made, there's no way she'll understand this."

The phone rang. Nicola squeezed Maye's arm reassuringly and picked it up. "This will probably be my boyfriend. I'll be just one second."

"Hello, this is WPC Arthur. May I speak to Jeanette Abrahams please."

Nicola winced. "I'm sorry. She's asleep. This is Nicola Baines, her flat mate."

"Ah. Ms. Baines, I need to have a word in your ear as well."

"Yes."

"Er . . . you are an actress, Ms. Baines?"

"Yes." Nicola was irked. What did that have to do with anything? She had a sudden irrational fear. If she was an actress by trade would the police think Jeanette was too, think it was all a glorious fiction? She sucked her teeth. She was being silly.

"Well, first of all, we need Ms. Abrahams to know that we've made an arrest, taken Mr. Boothe in."

"Mr Boothe?"

"Mr Sean Boothe. The man Jeanette said attacked her."

"Yes, I'm sorry. I never knew his last name. I forgot, or somethin—"

"Ms Baines, you should turn your television on."

"What —" She gesticulated at Maye. "Turn the television on. What's this all about?" Suddenly she could hear the bleep of her call waiting service going into action, a banal squeak on the line.

"Oh my God." Maye was staring at the television news. The news reader was brisk and serious-faced. "Today a 23 year old London man has been charged with rape. The particularly brutal incident is said to have taken place in Manchester. Police are suggesting that the man in question may be connected with at least three other incidents in the Manchester area. At a press conference at Metropolitan Police headquarters this morning, Detective Inspector John Aimes said that the police are presently questioning the man, said to work as a chef in the north London area. We have this report from . . ." Sean's face flashed up on the screen. Nicola felt the receiver slip from her hand. It dangled on its line, a tinny squawk emitting from it.

"Ms Baines? Are you there? Miss Baines?"

22

The garden was white. Nicola stood in the middle of the lawn, speckled with sugary ice. Crystalline smoke came from her lips. She hated the cold. The winter had been a bitch so far, and it wasn't as if they'd had a good summer, either. Rain and sunshine had fought for months. After ten years in England she still resented the turn of the seasons. It took her by surprise, the slow refrigeration that crisped the leaves golden-red and burning with chill. Her exhaustion made her indifferent to the temperature. She could not feel the throb in her arms, and the numbness was a luxury. They had all felt too much in the past months. It was as if Jeanette's rape had heralded in the worst of times, and all the summer had been able to do was die before it had lived. Thank God Los Angeles would be hot. All the time.

She had thought she could handle the press. She could answer their inane questions about Hollywood as the time for her to go drew nearer: what would she eat on the sunny beaches, Bovril and toast? Would Julius be following her? Did she know who her leading man was to be, Costner, Cruise, De Niro? She could field these, make jokes, laugh with them. Alex had begun to call her the black Princess Di; every time she left a function, went shopping, stepped outside the door they were there. Julius had become an optional appendage. She was a celebrity in her own right, complete with an entourage and a best side. And a hook. Alongside questions about the movie there were others. Especially when Jack Thompson was there. She would look for him in the crowd, waiting for his cracked voice and the heavy jowls that gave his formerly handsome face maturity. He would open his mouth, rising above the others, and it was always the same thing. *Nikki, what's your reaction to Black London's continued condemnation of your interracial relationship? Have you heard the expression 'coconut'? Could you explain it to us?* She could hear herself babbling whenever his sycophantic blue gaze settled on her. She knew his ingratiation was a game.

The pungent sound of her laughter echoed into the cold noon. Bounced off the fence. How she had wanted them! She had thought she could control them.

Mona wasn't up to it.

Her ability to hold the shape and feel of her alter ego was dying every day. It was too early for others to notice, but she felt it. On Friday she had dressed for dinner with Julius' family. She had strained through four hours of preparation. The expensive trouser suit seemed too small on her tall body. She looked at her dreadlocks in the mirror and nearly cut them off. She tried to walk in the high heels Mona had bought, and couldn't. She was forced to send Alex out to buy flat evening slippers. It hadn't been meeting his parents that she had worried about; she was a pro at that. No, she had felt her own self fighting, returning, making her too tall, turning the charm of her clumsiness into disorientation. Mona had resurfaced and she had stimulated the Frasers, smiling regally at Mr Fraser's two references to coloured people, balancing the salmon on her silver fish knife, drinking from the right glass. She even played them a haunting tune on Mrs Fraser's piano. She was wooden. She felt like a performing seal. She was a hit.

Julius had been thoughtful on the way home.

"Did you wear the flats to please my mother's sense of proportion?" he asked.

"Huh?"

A November traffic jam throttled the streets. He put his head to the side, puzzled.

"It's the first time I've been out with you shorter than me."

She laughed unsteadily. "Don't be silly." It was true. She always calculated well with her lovers. She had known that Julius would be aroused by her unapologetic height, and usually wore shoes that at least matched her to his six foot two.

"I like it." He stroked her arm and leaned forward to the taxi driver.

She stared after him. He had changed something and she hadn't noticed. It was worrying. She kept her men because she predicted their every move. She studied them to be with them. She left them when she would break their hearts the most; she left them wanting her for years.

As she loved him more, as the press recreated her, Mona shrank from her. As if the outside world had created a mirror of its own, a grotesque expanse of glass that picked up every pimple and open pore. In normal circumstances she would have been able to escape. She would have left Julius, as much as it would have pained her. Withdrawn into the smaller world of back street theatre. These were all options. The challenge would have been great, but not impossible. But for one thing.

Jeanette.

It was Jeanette that called most compellingly for her real self. Jeanette, alternately distant and clinging. Jeanette for whom frustration, with herself and everyone else was the most constant denominator. She railed at the world, at her inability to explain her feelings and her anguish. In one moment she would be in front of the mirror, minutely examining the fading damage to her body. Then she would talk and talk, retelling the story. This inventory was soaked with guilt: how could she not have known? Was God punishing her? Had she done something to invite him to behave this way? Could she have done something to stop it? Endless details of the legal procedure jangled through the house, ruffling the grain of their carpets, official statements, cross-examination, forensic evidence, scene of the crime muttering at them through the ceilings, hugging the covers with them in bed at night, breeding in the corners of the soap dish and the night stands, peeping at them from behind lamps and corners of cushions. They smelled it in their clothes and on the air. Nicola heard her as she chopped onions, sewed a button, could not escape from her even in the warmth of Julius' bed. Jeanette's voice was everywhere (*no-one understands how I feel*) and they ducked their heads before her misery (*none of you can know*) the anger making her voice queer, an accusation. (*why not one of you why me*) Jeanette had always suspected her subterfuge. From the beginning, when she had walked into the house and into the row. She had felt the woman's free eyes on her. It was part of their friendship. Knowing, secret glances between them. Until now it had been a laugh. A release. Someone else saw Mona around her edges, tucked so tight that the two were one. Jeanette had teased her, she could remember the night they had gone to see some stand-up comic, spent an hour roaring with laughter. Mona's sound had trickled through the auditorium, so luxuriant that all had turned. One of the comedians had bantered with her from the stage: *Bwoy, when a black woman go fe beautiful . . .* he had sighed, and every man craning his neck to see her had sighed with him. She felt the triumph, in waves, as her due. Jeanette had bent forward.

"Do you enjoy this bullshit?"

She had thought she meant the comedy, and nodded.

"I don't mean that. The fan bit. You need it?"

She hadn't known how to answer. Froze. Inclined her head, trying to hide behind its self-assurance. "I don't —"

Jeanette grinned. "You could still be an actress."

"What?"

"You could be an actress without acting every day of your life."

Jeanette had seemed content to watch her play Mona with amused affection. Until she was raped. The secret reasserted itself as Jeanette began to demand of her. She would not be held until Mona slipped away. She would not be comforted unless Mona was banished, until Nicola was bare. Every time Nicola touched her she could hear it in her heartbeat. *(I know that you are as scared as me, skinny, taller than your teachers red-brown like the leaves be here with me be frightened with me I know who you are)* Wrapped as she was in the curious darkness of a constant despair, Jeanette had clarity. She saw it in others. She was calling to Nicola to join her in a dark dance, to be herself, see the pain, throw off Mona. And there was fury in her secret demand *(you think you nice join us down here where it's dark and deep and let it all envelope you you ain't nothing special you feel it like the rest of us)*

To accept the whisper was to confront her own pain, to throw off Mona's capable sassiness, to walk rather than shimmy, to speak rather than throw out a practised throatiness. The challenge to be without pretence. The more Jeanette demanded *her* the more she realised that she was living a hypocrisy. A life-saving habit. Mona had gotten the movie role. Mona was to take it up. Mona was to be married. And to keep

Mona alive Julius could be no more than a cardboard cut-out white man. She would have to be black paper beside him.

Jeanette promised acceptance as she was. Jeanette believed, even throughout it all.

And Alex. Nicola saw the furtive bottled gifts in her bag. In one way, she could deal with Jeanette's pain. More and more of it came out in the open, and even though the flood was oppressive, it was there, they tried to handle it together. But Alex had closed in on herself. She had become compulsive. More than once they had had raging arguments about stupid things: who cleaned the bathroom last, why there was no bread. She kept going on about the need for order. Didn't Nicola understand, she had a bloody hard time at work, and she didn't need to come home to disorganisation? And Jeanette stood there between them. Alex hadn't said it, but they both heard the accusation in the air: *You think she's more important than me.* And in between all of this, images of Sean floated along their screens, in the papers. They said they had evidence of serial rape, that he was responsible for more than Jeanette. He had made statements himself, through his lawyer, to the tune of the offended: *the truth will out,* he had said. Nicola didn't know what to think. Others did. One Morris Oakley had spearheaded a campaign, and his face was up there as much as Sean's: he had been banging on about the press treatment of Sean Boothe. *Whether or not this young man is responsible for three rapes remains to be seen. What I am concerned about is the way the press in this country scapegoats young, black males, as muggers, animals, rapists, yardies. Look at the most recent comments of Police Commissioner Paul Condon that statistically, most muggers are black. Look at that. This is a sign of the times.*

Whether or not Sean was a serial rapist wasn't important to her. What was real for her was the fact that one of his victims lived in her home. And she felt the strong arm of obligation. She felt the stain of pain in this house. It chased after her wherever she moved, even here, in the sharp wind. It filled her eyes and ached along her shoulder blades.

She stamped her feet into the frosty ground. Julius saw the artifice in his own way. He seemed to think that something would change if they married. More than once he had complained about her reticence, insisted that she was holding something back. He too, peeled at the layers of her, demanding, all of them demanding.

She had only been able to see him sporadically in the past four weeks. He was under production pressure and she didn't want him to drop in unexpectedly the way he had done before. Jeanette had developed a genuine fear of the men around her, even Michael. She would smile at him across the room now, but if he came too near she would flee inside herself, that curious crouched look of resignation taking over. Michael continued to be overwhelmed at her response and had suggested that he not come around at all, but Nicola had thought this counterproductive. She knew that Jeanette still loved him, and that his absence would increase her trepidation. She bounced from identity to identity for all of them. It was beginning to tire her.

She heard a movement behind her. Dishes rustled together. She turned around, walked back towards the kitchen door and peered inside. Jeanette was standing at the sink running hot water into the basin, the liquid brushing food stains aside. She was wearing thick leggings, and under the wool her haunches looked reduced. Withered.

"Hi," Jeanette said, cracking a smile that was one size too small.

"Hi to you," Nicola responded with a smile of her own. It was too big, she knew.

"I just thought it was time I started washing dishes again," Jeanette said.

"You don't have to," Nicola said. "You don't have to —"

"No. I want to. It's . . ." A slight shake danced off her fingertips, setting the few cups a-tremble. "It's *normal*."

"I suppose so," Nicola said. *(You'll get bedsores if you go on like this)* She stood, hesitant, not knowing what to do.

"Close the door," said Jeanette. "It's freezing."

She turned to do just that and missed the moment when Jeanette's nerveless fingers lost their grip on the cup. The crash echoed through the house and the cats fled off the sofa, blinking reproachful golden eyes at them. Nicola turned sharply, and both women dropped to their knees, in front of the shards.

"Get the dustpan and brush." Jeanette said in a tight voice.

"It's OK, I'll do it."

"No, just get the dustpan —" her voice wavered and tears threatened. Nicola reached for her.

"What is it?"

Jeanette swiped at her watering nose. "Nothing, nothing."

"Tell me," she coaxed. " What?"

"It's just the, the, *(ICE)* ice. The ice. It reminds me . . ."

"Of what happened, sweetie?"

Jeanette brushed aside the euphemism. "Yes. It reminds me of the *rape*. Why don't you ever *call* it that?"

She bolted, and Nicola could hear a door bang. She got up and slowly swung the kitchen door closed, scooping up the mess, using damp newspaper to chase the slivers of china.

After she finished, she headed for the phone. She threw off Mona, and it brought her terrifying relief. She listened to the phone ring. The agent remembered, many weeks later, that she'd had to ask the owner of that voice to identify herself. It hadn't sounded like anyone she knew, certainly not the brash and breezy client who she expected to line her pockets for years to come. But at the time she had been too distraught to register the change. She had pleaded, cajoled, argued and after a long while, relented. Yes, there was local work around, she'd look into it. Something simple. Fine. Some, she reflected, went the distance. Others burnt out. It was a great pity.

23

Thompson watched Michael walk through the crowd. He had been following him for a while. Just looking. The tall black man wasn't hard to miss, even in this crazy melee. He walked on cotton wool, his strength was way under the surface. Nevertheless, people moved out of his way as he walked. Presence. And honesty. It shone off him. It was good to know all the players in this thing. He had recognised Michael as one of the regular visitors to Nicola's house as he hovered on the outskirts of the demonstration. Wasn't it a fine bloody thing, this demonstration. Obligatory placards and tempers being waved in the air. He supposed he couldn't blame the lot of them. From what he had heard through his contacts at the Met, they didn't have much to pin on the kid. Except perhaps Jeanette. He knew her name now, and much more. Photocopies were such a helpful invention. A word in an ear, a couple of pounds, what the hell, he was on a budget, and pow! One statement. He could feel some sympathy. It rang true. If it was, she'd had a hard time. This Boothe sounded like a right nutter. Multiple contusions, extensive facial injury and a ripped fanny. It all added up. Unless this Jeanette liked her jollies hard and fast. He grinned. Only he knew her connection to Nicola Baines. Him. Headliner. But he had to know how to play it.

*

Michael felt like kicking his way through the crowd. He held it at bay. He and Marisa had had a furious row that morning. He had to admit he'd been astonished. She wasn't one for keeping it in, but she'd obviously been screwing for a while. It had all come out that morning when he'd said he was taking just one more day off work to go and check out the demonstration.

"Why would you want to do that?" Her voice had not been pleasant. He was sitting in bed, stripped to the waist, startled by her.

"What's the matter?"

"The matter? What do you think?"

He knew he'd been insensitive. It was okay for her to feel confused, envious even, of the time he spent away. With the other women. And they were a household of beautiful women. He knew that she could have insecurities about that, that Alex's problems weren't enough of a smoke screen for his concern for Jeanette. But he had been honest. He searched his mind for alternate realities. He always told her where he was going. Hell, they had discussed it, his concerns about Alex's drinking and *(JEANETTE)* everything else. How he was needed. But of course they hadn't *discussed* it, not really, he had talked and she had been there *(and that's the way it's been)* saying nothing about how she felt, a silent audience. He hadn't noticed, or, well, he had, but who could find words to bridge the gap? It had been happening for a long time *(since you met Jeanette, guy)* but it was a whirlpool in their relationship, not a flood. A moment, a fillip, not important. They had loved for a long time. There were going to be highs and lows. All the books she owned on relationships said so. He read them at night to help him know her mind. Perhaps he wasn't knowing it so well these days *(since you met Jeanette)* and the words from her this morning had been twisted, risen to the surface like angry wraiths as she'd yelled at him.

"Why the hell can you never fight for me, never raise your voice, never get pissed, always bloody calm and wonderful, Mr Bloody Wonderful Michael Watson!"

He had tried to calm her, but it had added salt to the wound, and she had shrugged her jacket on, clipped her little name badge on, ran out of the house and wasn't there a lot of *(wish I could talk to Jeanette about it)* damage control to do.

"Hey, you want a placard, mate?"

He looked across at the man. He was ordinary enough, spiky dreads on top of his head. A grizzled beard, peppered with premature age. Short, clumpy body. Hands clenching and unclenching.

The placard read: 'I'M NOT A MUGGER . . . OR A RAPIST'

Michael smiled and it hurt.

"You don't look it."

"Eh?"

Michael pointed at the sign.

"Nah, mate. I'm not. You ain't either. Look, I got plenty. Have a few. Hand them round."

"No, thanks."

The man looked at him, puzzled, and moved on. His voice disappeared into the fray: "Anybody want a placard? Placard? My brother, you need a placard?"

*

Sean listened. If he could close his eyes hard enough he could hear them outside.

Calling for him.

He felt strong, even in the reality of the lifeless cell. He fingered the swelling on the side of his cheek. It was true then. The screws didn't take kindly to rapists. Or black men. He had only asked for a glass of water. The warden had informed him that this wasn't no fackin' hotel, what the fack did he expect, and then they'd come in and thumped him. It had not hurt. Not much.

He missed his magazines. His lawyer did bring some in, but he missed the excitement of choosing for himself. They couldn't be expected to understand what he needed. And he missed the ones at home, he knew them, laughing down at him.

He knew their ways and their wiles.

He had received many visitors. His parents, friends. They all told him he was innocent, that he should keep his chin up, he would be out of there. Already the mass public outcry had pushed forward the court date. Apparently someone up in government didn't appreciate having all these black people on the streets. It didn't matter to him. He was grateful for the support of the crowds. They knew he was right. She had shared the experience. Hadn't she been goading him from the beginning, inviting him to be a man? Only he and she knew, in the quiet times, what it had meant. He was sure of that. At night he remembered her face. He knew he had hurt her. He had wanted to hurt her. He knew what they were writing about him, his lawyer had found a black psychiatrist and there was talk of insanity as a defence, of the age-long grind of racism as a defence, but they called it Black Rage. How it had become *de rigeur*. They told him she was loose, pulled her knickers down for every man, and that could be a defence too. He was sure they were right about it all. Their complex miasma of theories and sub-theories, jargon and polished puzzles, the need for a new suit and the tears of those who called themselves his friends filtered over his head. It didn't matter. They could use what they liked. He would say it all, and then some. He wanted to be home. With his memories. He would tell them anything to go home. Still, it would have been nice to tell the truth. The truth was simple. It wouldn't have wasted taxpayers money, or confused anybody. He recited it as he walked the cell.

He knew why he had done it.

It had been fun.

Fun.

There was a thud on the door.

"Oi! Someone here to see you, nutter!"

The face of his lawyer loomed forward. Sean heard muttered voices. The man was probably being told off. He laughed. The door ground open. The dainty man stepped inside. "Hello Sean." He looked at his client's face grimly. "Have they knocked you about?"

Sean fingered his face indifferently. "Don't worry about it." He smiled. "You're not going to worry about it, are you?"

"Your mum's not going to like seeing that."

"Is she here?"

"Yes. Didn't you remember she was coming?"

"Yeah, yeah. Just thinking about other things."

The lawyer put a hand on his shoulder. "You don't have to worry, you know. We are going to get you off." He felt an odd affection for this young black man that he couldn't shake. It made him feel sick some evenings, sitting with his daughter. The man was a rapist, it was obvious, and thank God he'd done it with a bit of a good time girl. That was helpful. He was usually stoic in the face of his violent cases. Stoic was about all he could run to. Despite the evidence, he found it difficult to dislike Sean. He was so charming.

*

She spent most of her time trying to hear music, make it more than some glacial substance in her ears. She walked around the house when she was alone. Spoke her own name aloud. Jeanette Alicia Abrahams. She practised her signature in the air. After she was better she would change it. Take out the curlicues that had prompted more than one cashier to smile at her. Make it a big woman's signature. She would specialise in victim counselling (*now that you know, ha-ha*) make other people's lives better. That was it. This would sustain her. She was appalled into tears when she awoke out of dreams about Sean. Not the ones that re-enacted, in colourful detail, his violence. The tears came whenever she dreamed of the poems she had not been able to write for him, when her dreams had him gentle, laughing, bringing her small things, strawberries dipped in marzipan. There were two Seans. The one she had loved and the other. She strained to understand their synchronicity. One had waited for her in the other. She was a fool. She should have seen it in his silence. He had been planning it. Planning it all along. If the question of love had astonished and confused her before, now it was incessant. She had examined its sorcery and been unable to dissect or explain it. Where had it come from? And why did it stay with her, even now (*why do you fantasise different endings*) calling her, grinning (*a bottle of bubbly Simone on his knee and a big white frock to fuck with Mamma's head*) showing her all the ways it could have been (*and to see him again how are you going to feel when you see him across the courtroom don't let me cry for him don't let me cry for him*) all the ways it should have been, a pretty little girl for Simone to play with, then a boy with his cold skin and my nose (*go down Emmanuel Road gyal and bwoy*) old age that wouldn't have mattered, him grinning when her tits stopped looking at the ceiling and what would he have looked like grey (*fe go bruk rock stone*) and how could she still think of him this way every day when she got up and couldn't feel her body anymore *(bruk dem one by one two by two)* and he was in a cell, he would miss his cooking and she hated him, hated him, hated him *(finger mash no cry)* still wished they could have made new tomorrows *('memba ah play we ah play)* all those new tomorrows. Could she stand them?

Mavis

De firs' time me really try fe get weh me didn't know whether me coulda mek it. All Carl do is pure cussin', how de whole ah we always ah tek time off like we ah sport. Seh him want to see more money ah come in, not de whole ah we ah walk ah go country.

Still, me plan it good. Me was convince seh de firs' time was goin' to be de las' time. Is true, too. Me know seh if Carl get one piece ah news seh me ah step him woulda mash me up. Is not a man dat wrap up fe put him fis' inna you face. An' me know seh if me leave me haffi do it quick, because him know weh fe look fah me. Since Susan go 'bout her business him was like mad man, ah storm 'bout ah tell we seh him ah go kill any bloodclaht gyal who try fe do it again. Das why me never get a chance fe say goodbye to anybody. Never want anybody fe slip an' tell him, never want de odder gyal dem laugh wid me like dem know anyt'ing ah gwaan.

Him hardly ever mek me tek him pickney fe see her sister or her gran'mammy, because him never fool. Him mussee know seh me couldn't stay like Susan, walk an' lef' her pickney. But de Tuesday weh me lef' out dere me was workin' him hard, fe mek me tek de chile to country. She was gettin' older, an me tell him seh she granny never see her from time. Me never tell de chile dem say we ah go anywhere. Dem nuh haffi know dat, mek dem chat it out.

De mornin' come, an me ah look pon de room, feel like bawl. me never have much t'ings, but ah me t'ings y'know? T'ings me ah work fah. Sophie use to call fe her room de pum-pum palace, seh is her crotches give her de bedspread an' de radio weh she have. Even after ten years in de game, me couldn't laugh bout dem t'ings deh. Just 'cause we a mash up we body don' mean we haffi laugh 'bout it. All mornin' de chile ah excite up herself. Me so anxious me wah t'ump her down. Me was 'fraid seh Carl ah go see how she ah gwaan an' t'ink good

206

about what him really ah do. Me madda bredda seh him woulda tek de odder one down ah de airport an' meet me dere. Him did haffi meet me an' gwaan like customer fe get de money from me. Me nearly piss up meself when we count it out. Me feel shame, feel like him woulda smell me body 'pon de paper, 'cause more time me haffi put it up inside me body fe mek sure Carl nuh know. One time him come fe check me inna de room, ah move on me body, an him start cuss how somet'ing scrape him, an' me haffi tell him is new way fe nuh have baby. Me was 'fraid seh him woulda reach inna me fe check what kinda obeah business me ah use. True seh him don' know seh over two hundred dollar him a brush 'gainst. When me give me uncle de money me realise how much it was. Was so much. Mek me wonder how long Susan did tek fe save up. Still, de man who she ah married to woulda want piece for fe him contribution, so me guess him get back on him investment.

De chile ah chat, chat, ah tell de gyal dem seh she ah go pick ackee wid her gran'mammy, how she goin' to see her pretty sister, sister have tall hair like baby dolly own. Jus' as we ready fe go me notice seh Sophie ah screw wid me, like she vex. Me was mekkin' it gwaan, but her face look like she swallow lime, so me ask her what happen. De gyal look inna me eye an' tell me seh she know me ah run weh. Me nearly dead, ah try keep me face straight, try drop joke wid her, Me whisper tell her seh me WISH me coulda run weh from it, but pum-pum palace haffi keep up. She still ah screw, tell me seh ah NOW she know me ah go run weh, because in all de time me deh-deh. she never hear me crack joke yet. Den one odder gyal come up. She did name Mercedes, like de car. She was new, come 'bout six month. Pretty, long mout' t'ing. She ah squeeze up Sophie han', ah tell her fe jus' cool. Seh she mus' shut up her rass mout' if she nuh want a box. Me look roun' an' see de gyal dem ah eyes me up, an' ah den me know seh de whole ah dem sight up de rake, me know seh dem know me ah run. Dem ah gimme smile-smile. Ongle Sophie ah screw like she wah kill me off. Mercedes start push her weh, an' she start bawl out like somebody kill her off. She ah call out seh me ah idyat, Carl ah idyat, me nah go no country, an' me ah sweat, me heart ah beat, me was promisin' de Lawd Jesus if Him could jus' let me out me woulda never sin again, never do anyt'ing wrong again, Sophie ah bawl, an' de chile ah pull me han' ask me if we not goin' country, weh we ah go, an me see Carl up de road, ah do some runnins', but him ah look roun', me could see him ah wonder weh de rass de whore dem ah mek up so much noise, an' me sweat, *me ah try move off, wave to him like everyt'ing sweet, an' me could see him ah talk to de man, seh him soon come, him ah go check a t'ing, an' den me see Mercedes grab up a knife from inna her bosom, ah hol' it nex' to Sophie side, gentle like, ah whisper seh she ah go cut her if she don' shut her mout', tell me seh me mus' run, run, see cab dere, run, an' de whole ah dem whisper like de sea, run, run, run, run.*

Me run.

24

"Alex? There's a call for you. Shall I transfer it?" Jenny stood at the door of her office, splitting her face with a yawn. Alexandrea nodded and picked up.

"Hello?"

"Wha'appen, sis?" Michael's voice was cheerful, but tired.

"Oh. Mike." She took one large earring out and shifted the receiver. "I'm alright. To what do I owe this honour?"

"Nothing much. I'm taking pictures around your area and wondered what time you're getting off."

Alexandrea smiled. He always seemed to know when he was needed. "Fancy a model?" She loved the pictures Michael took of her and kept several of them on her wall. Gerry was off in never-never land with the rest of them. She sometimes wished she could see him just to get them back. Michael had a light touch and had captured her in many stages, from the shaken photographs of his first camera to more sophisticated renditions, sepias and greys with only her lips a vivid red.

He had the patience and the eye; in many ways she felt they did the same thing. He saw souls through a camera's eye and brought them to the surface, as if through mist, for any who would see. She dug under the masks and found their wishes.

"Nah. Been there, done that." He laughed. "So, what time?"

She glanced around the office. It was nearly eight and most of the team had gone home.

"I'm just writing a brief. I could get off in an hour." *(we could go for a drink)*

"I'll be there. Wait for you at the desk, right?"

"Yeah, they'll buzz me. Do you have the car?"

"No. You know I don't take it with me when I'm shooting."

"Don't know how you expect to get the girls if you haven't got wheels."

"I've got one, remember? And the sixteen piece harem of course."

She hung up the phone and bent across the keyboard. She was glad that Michael was coming around. She would be able to get her mind off work. Not that she thought about anything else. Not since that bastard's programme sheet. Her fingers fluttered across the keys, her mind working two steps behind, nearly as quick. Sexual harassment. A programme on sexual harassment. It was unbelievable. Pearson's arrogance was unbelievable. The fact that he had been capable of handing the idea to the team, much less with her in it, was astounding. They had been instructed to make it juicy. She wished she could make it juicy for him, *(instead you make it juicy for yourself orange juice and vodka bloody marys ooh pina coladas are nice we're doing the cocktail thing these days)* but she had given up on all hope of revenge. It was too late. Too late for everything. Her contract ended in a month and then she would be out of the place. Back on the dole. He had won, and that was the way life went. Resignation was not in her blood, *(hey I'm still hoping and dreaming on the love of my life and damned if it makes the slightest bit of difference)* but she admitted defeat. He was too strong, too perfect. There were no cracks she could wrench open. The man's life was steel encased heaven. She'd been lucky enough to be in the wrong place at the wrong time, and *(isn't it the story of my life)* now she was used to the crawling nausea that went with the everyday grind. Recently it was a relief when he snaked his way behind her, a secret hand down her body. It usually meant he wouldn't do it for the rest of the day, and the waiting was the worst. He knew she went off to the loo regularly, and had been waiting for her at the door several times.

"Don't you know what they say about perverts who hang around women's toilets?" she had snapped.

His face was neutral. "Don't you know what they say about women who drink in toilets?"

So he knew that too. It was just one more thing. Part of their sick underworld. He had stepped towards her, gliding two fingers between her legs. She pushed him away, nauseated.

"What's it today? Rum? Vodka?" He took a deep breath. "Ah. We're going up market. Smells like liqueur." He laughed out loud. "Dear me. Is there anything you *don't* drink, Alexandrea Watson?"

"Anything that comes from you!" She stepped back into the toilet, spoke through the door. "Fuck off, Pearson!"

He laughed again. "Such a *stubborn* child."

She had listened for his retreating footsteps. The strain of the secret had smashed into all the reserves she had left. The need to drink was vast. To forget everything. She found herself hovering at the doors of pubs and off-licence stores, grinning madly *(they all get what they want)* pressing her nose to the glass, looking at the rows and rows and rows of bottles, cans *(need to get a little of what I want)* and finally, finally, her nerve had broken *(going to get what I want)* and she had slammed her money on the counter. The finest, she wanted the finest, and she wanted it all: rum, vodka *(hair of the dog that bit you baby)* wine *(biting you oooh biting you so hard)* and all her anger was poured out in the glass which she abandoned eventually, put the bottle to her head, fierce and defiant. *(God let me defy somebody)* She choked on the first swallow, didn't feel the liquid soaking the front of her blouse as she headed for oblivion.

Michael rose when she came out of the elevator and hugged her. She pushed him away.

"My God, you stink! What have you been doing?"

He looked injured. "I'm not that bad. I had to get behind some bins to get this —"

"Perfect piece of the inner city?"

He patted the camera at his hip. "All for the art, mi dear."

"Mmmm. So, what are you working on?"

He was vague. He hated talking about his work when he was trying to get his head around it. He was preparing for his second exhibition, but had not been able to work full speed for a while *(Jeanette keeps bumping around your head)* what with Marisa giving him hell. She had always been capable of holding a grudge, and she was getting into Academy Award winning stuff. She wouldn't talk to him properly. She held her resentment up as a shield.

"How's Marisa?" Alexandrea seemed to read him.

"Not good," he said shortly.

She sighed. "You're not going to be break up, are you? You're our last hope."

"What do you mean? Julius and Nikki are proving a model mixed race celebrity couple. And you having that fool out of your life can only be a good thing."

She pulled on her coat. They had never talked about Gerry, but Michael's dislike of him had been obvious from the beginning. She knew that Nicola had told Michael about Pearson, but nobody seemed to understand what it was doing to her. Her efficiency always got in the way. Capable, uptight, Alex. Surely no-one could keep *her* down. She longed for Gerry, if only for his recognition of her weakness. He knew she was a mess. Hadn't he scraped her off the living room floor *(oh but he liked it baby)* left her in a pool of her own vomit to teach her a lesson *(he liked it because it made him feel like a big man)*.

No-one knew about the programme. In a convoluted way she had thought that people could help, but it wasn't so. She was ashamed that she couldn't help herself. She rarely asked people for anything. She had learnt that it did nothing but create stress. If she asked, they would worry. She felt responsible for that worry. She had learned that she had been born alone and would draw final breath in the same way. And she would not have them know she was weak. She could handle life, she and a beer. She could handle life.

She linked her arm in her brother's. "Julius and Nikki are good, but they're arguing as usual."

Michael groaned. "Not *again?* I know they check for each other, but maybe they should just give it up! What's the problem now?"

"Well, her quitting the States."

He stared. "You lie."

"No. I thought she would have told you. She called them up and said she wasn't going."

"She's got a lot more to worry about than telling me her business." They paused, Jeanette between them. "How come the papers haven't been going mad?"

"Well, she's hoping to keep it quiet for a bit longer. She's having a press conference at the weekend to announce it."

"Is it because she wants to be around for the trial?"

Alexandrea shrugged. "I dunno. I suppose so. When is it, anyway?"

"I don't believe you." He looked down at her, eyes a cocktail of tender reproach.

"What?"

"You don't know when the trial is? You live in the same house."

She sighed. "Please don't be angry with me, Mike. I've got other things on my mind."

He was pulling away. "Like what? The trial date's in a fortnight. At the very least you could read the press. You're supposed to be a journalist."

"I don't pay any attention to it."

He sucked his teeth. "It's happening in your house!"

"And I get enough of it every day!" Her voice echoed through the reception room, strident. He looked at her, softening.

"Alright. Calm yourself. Just tell me. Why are you avoiding this?"

(because if she's careless it's not my fault) "She's not my friend."

He put an arm around her shoulder. She leaned against his warmth and sniffed him in. Cologne and dustbins. It was alright. He squeezed her close. "What is happening to you?" His face was serious. "You never used to be this hard. You used to give a shit. It doesn't matter if she's not a friend. You used to get just as mad about violence as me. Whether you like her or not, she's been hurt. She must feel horrible when she turns the telly on. Her ex, the guy who raped her, always there."

She tried to turn away from the words. She knew it was true *(but something died in me it died in me don't any of you get it)* but she refused to let it touch her. Stubbornly she held on to her world. Jeanette was one of the lucky ones. She never got hurt. She dumped them all the time, she screwed them and left them, she acted as if she was God, and look where it had got her, down here with the rest of them.

Men had left Alexandrea all her life. She couldn't understand why. She couldn't understand the women who got them, the ones who got them to propose, to be vulnerable, she couldn't understand that power. Gerry's departure had left her with questions that had ruled her life for what felt like always, since Troy Bennett scooped her off the ice. How did you make someone love you? What spell did you cast? What part of you did you open *(Mum has the answers just ask Mum)* what scent did you trail, what words did you speak? It felt beyond her. It had always been beyond her *(stop touching each other you're married married married)* and it still was. It didn't matter that Jeanette had been raped. What mattered was that she had been successful before, and Alex hated her for it, she wasn't bad looking, she had more brains in her little finger than *her* with her Psych degree *(left that behind you now haven't you)* and yet she could not keep, please, hold a man. It made everything else nothing at all.

"You don't want to hear what I have to say. You'll get vex."

"I won't. I promise."

She took a deep breath. "Mike, she went with him to an empty house. I know you love her, but I have to say that I feel she has some responsibility for this. She gives the impression that she's up for it. No, wait, you asked." She held up a hand as he tried to interrupt. "I am not saying she should have been raped. But she does put it about. She gives the wrong impression. You have to take care of yourself. I think she was stupid." She could see he was trying to be calm.

"You don't think she should have trusted him? He was her man."

"Yes. But every woman knows that she has to be careful. Call it damage control."

He looked at her sadly. "Is that what you think of men? Do you think I could rape?"

She was shocked. "Of course not. I know you. But I would still think a woman was foolish if she went off with you with a dress cut down to her nipples. She must expect to be felt up. *She* doesn't know you."

He shook his head. "So when does she decide she knows me well enough? Tenth date? The marriage bed? Does she ever get to be around me with her . . . tits hanging out?"

"I don't know. You have to choose well. You would be a good choice. Others wouldn't. Come on, Mike. It was obvious that he was a bit doolally from the start."

"It wasn't obvious to me." He walked away from her. "She was in love with him."

"Well, she picked the wrong person to love."

He turned around. "So have you. So do you deserve to be dumped by some wanker who left you a note and the rent?"

She stared at him.

*

Becky Teller peered around the door. The crowd in the room puzzled her. She could see that they weren't all from the press. The room was vivid with civilian clothing. She stepped back and looked carefully at the couple in front of her.

"Something about this smells," she said.

Nicola looked up from lacing her shoes. The bronze sandals on her feet wound black threads around her arches and up the back of smooth calves. Totally inappropriate for the weather. She gifted herself with a ragged grin. She was going to be Mona to get these idiots off her back. She hoped it would be one of the last occasions. In the meantime, she still couldn't wear the footwear.

She felt Julius looking at her. There had been a fight. Not a bad one, given their history. But he had seemed to realise that something had changed. After several hours of holding his head in the face of her nervous insistence, he had relaxed. She was not going to America. She planned to try and explain it to him one day. Not yet. But soon.

"What's the matter? I'm on in five minutes."

Becky continued to knit her brow. "Just a feeling. The crowd out there aren't all hacks."

"Who are they then?" Julius looked concerned.

"I don't know." The publicist plucked at her cellular phone. "Nikki, I don't want you to go out there yet. I think I should make a call."

Nicola shifted impatiently. "Please, Becky. I want to get this over and done with."

The publicist waved her hand, dialling with the other. "I appreciate that. But I know these things." She swore and hung up. "Janet isn't there. Maybe she's on her way."

Janet was Nicola's agent. She wasn't usually late, especially when a protégée was about to give up possible international recognition. Nicola felt a prickle of discomfort, but was too anxious to dwell on it.

"Well, I'm fine to go up by myself. Or you can come."

"You don't understand." Becky peered again, increasingly anxious. "I can't put my finger on it." She started. "Shit. Morris Oakley is out there. Back row."

"*What?*" Nicola stopped fiddling. "That's the bloke who's been leading all the demonstrations. What the rass is he doing here?"

"Who?" Julius looked confused.

"He's been on everything talking about that man who attacked Nicola's flat-mate." said Becky.

"Jeanette? What would he be doing here?" said Julius.

"I don't know." Becky was dialling again. "Take it from me. Something's happened. Has anyone heard the news, seen a front page?"

Nicola put her hands in her hair. "No, but what —"

"They know something we don't." Becky dialled once more. "I'm calling a friend."

Julius tapped a watch. "She's on *now*."

"No she's not. Not yet. Give me five minutes." She sighed in relief and spoke rapidly into the phone. "Wayne? Becky. A word in your ear. Is there anything new on the grapevine about Nicola Baines? What do you mean, don't I know —"

Nicola gripped Julius' arm. "What *is* it? What's happening?"

The door flew open. Panting, Janet burst in. "Oh thank Christ I caught you! I've been running from Oxford Circus. Have you heard?"

"*What?*" Nicola glared at her. But she knew before Janet opened her mouth. She knew from the woman's pallor and from the fact that Oakley was out there and the fact that things were tearing to pieces. They had made the connection.

"It's all over the news." Janet was still breathless, chest heaving. "Jeanette and Nikki, it's all over the news."

Julius grabbed her. "Make some sense, woman! What do you mean?"

Nicola sat down on the floor. "What's the headline?" she asked.

25

Jeanette ran her fingers through the cassettes in her bag.

The WPC smiled at her reassuringly as the room loomed down at them. She raised her head as the sounds outside crescendoed. Jeanette squared her shoulders.

The other woman smiled again. "It won't be long now."

"That's him, isn't it?"

The WPC nodded. Jeanette ducked her head back to the bag. Music. Mamma had disapproved of everything she brought into the house: rap, reggae, blues, you name it, she had a problem. She and Maye had often been sent to their rooms to practice the hymns for Sunday service. It wasn't enough to let them pick it up as they went along, like everyone else. Her mother's precious children had to be tone perfect. So it was rock of ages cleft for me, you are the rose of sharon to my heart, and all things bright and beautiful from eight Saturday morning until ten. Then they could go out to play. As they got older, the ritual stayed the same. Mamma would not have sinners in her house. The only advantage was that once she could hear them singing, Mamma left them alone. They would play gin rummy and poker, Maye's sweet contralto mixing with her smooth bass. Mamma could never understand where she had gotten a female child who sang so deep. It was surely a curse from God. Jeanette beat Maye all the time. Her sister's voice would always rise to a crescendo on the chorus when she had a good hand.

For weeks she had been searching for a piece of music to replace the song in her head. *(bruk dem one by one, gyal an' bwoy)* It was on the end of her consciousness all the time. Like a threat.

*

It had been a struggle to keep her identity secret after the story had broken. She had become a prisoner in the house as cameras peeped and pried, as her community raged at the doorstep. She could not believe that it had become such madness. Nicola had been following her around, pleading forgiveness for the press revelations, their insistence on connecting her with Sean, but that was the least. She could feel it all going terribly wrong. Lara had showed her how much. She had managed to creep into her university to retrieve her personal belongings and had bumped into her classmate. The other woman stepped back, as if burnt.

"Lara! Hi. I —"

A long look. "I know it's you."

She shrank from the certainty, the condensed condemnation. "I don't —"

Lara looked up at the ceiling. "Spare me, okay, Jeanette? Spare me. Just tell me how you could do it."

"What —" She wanted to die. Lara's confidence hurt her more than anything else, the nightmares, the icy roads, the pictures in her head.

"How could you do that? How could you? Your feelings might have been hurt, but is that any reason to put a man in prison? A good man, a good black man who was making something of his life. How will he live his life now?"

"How do you know —" Her name hadn't been in the papers. Surely no one had put her name in the papers. It was against the law, the police had told her.

Lara sucked her teeth, a wet, complete sound. "Not hard to work out." She put her face close to Jeanette's. "Unless Nicola Baines has another slag living under her roof."

"Please, Lara . . ." She was shaking, the small breakfast Nicola had coaxed down her throat threatening to rise from her stomach.

"Don't talk to me. You make me sick."

Jeanette had watched her hurt, righteous back swim down the hall.

*

She sifted through the tapes, looking at the names. Would this be the one, or this one, or this one? She sorted, shaking her head occasionally, like an old woman with a tremor.

Outside, they clapped and beat the walls.

*

The room was packed. Suede against leather. Cotton against silk. Shades of humanity, chewing gum, chattering like birds, rows of curious eyes and whispers, exclamations, I-know-it-all declarations, united and divided in their fascination. It seemed to Nicola that they all had identical smiles. A swell ran through as she paused at the door. She turned to Julius.

"We shouldn't have come. This is going to make it worse," she said.

He looked at the faces looking at them. "You could be right," he said. "But she needs you. Who else does she have?"

"She has Michael." He was coming towards them, and she waved.

Julius shook his head. "She needs you. There's not long to go now."

She rubbed at her eyes. She was afraid. He touched her.

"Hard without Mona, isn't it?" he said.

"Yes," she said simply. "It is."

His eyes were soft. "You can do this. You, Nicola."

She was still afraid. She had told him about Mona, knowing that the time had come. At the press conference she had watched, as if from afar, her mirror image shatter. The final moment had come before she was prepared for it. She heard herself stuttering and stammering in front of them, wanting to weep, clutching Jack Thompson's exclusive in her fist — *THE REAL REASON NICOLA BAINES IS GIVING UP ON HOLLYWOOD* — wanting to beg forgiveness for her real self that stood before them finally. She had barely managed to read the statement Becky and Janet had hurriedly prepared for her. *(I have decided to pursue my career in Britain)* and she was a child again, cringing in their faces, afraid of their voices, feeling the awkward lines of her body, *(This decision is for the moment, final and has been made for my own personal reasons)* reaching for the reflection in the mirror but finding it irrevocably gone, beauty gone, rebellion lost, *(I would ask the press to respect my need for privacy at this time)* only she, herself, left, so tall that she could see her head brushing against the ceiling, *(as well as the privacy of my partner, Julius Fraser)* feeling her knees growing knobby looking down in the way she had looked down at them when she was small, a smear of blood on one, and the knowledge that it was her mothers blood and O please, daddy, please, promise me that when we get home and I have to cross the road again, promise me the blood will be gone, *(That is all)* promise me, promise me, and as they were driven back to Julius' house she curled up next to him and told him about the mirror that had kept her alive, the image that had given her strength to approach him, to arouse him, the quiet ritual in her room, every morning. She showed him photographs, velvet with dust and heavy with shame. Pictures of what she had been and feared she still was. *(I was ugly, ugly, and they hated me)*

(Don't)

(Can't you see it)

(Don't)

(I wanted to use you)

(Yes)

(and now I can't)

(Yes)

(you're not a trophy anymore) Now all she could do was reach for herself. Today they had waded, knee deep, through cameras, to the courtroom and she felt as if she had been crawling through inches of demanding bodies for a long time, today was no different, it was a circus. Ever since Nicola Baines had been linked to the notorious Sean Boothe. The rapist and the actress. Lives of the rich and famous. Who would have thought that they had crossed paths? The gossips had lovingly honed it on the streets. Boothe had been at her house. Been at her parties. Rumours fell around them like small animals, whining for attention. Boothe had become obsessed with Nicola Baines and dated his victim to be close to her. Boothe had a photograph of Nicola Baines on the wall at his home. Shots of his bedsit were livid across the pages. Wall to wall women. He had a voodoo altar, it was said. He had worshipped Nicola Baines on it. The press drank it like wine. Sean Boothe's alleged victims had been whittled down to one for lack of evidence. It didn't matter. Shots of Nicola and Sean on a dance floor. The club where he had saved his future victim to

get Nicola Baines' attention. Murmurs, virulent with authenticity. He had planned to make her next. Thank God he had been caught.

*

Whites vied with blacks. One felt the undercurrent of the other as they judged and were judged. It was a soap opera for all *(The Real Reason Nicola Baines is giving up on Hollywood)* and Jeanette was no longer the main player. She gave way to celebrity. There were no prayers offered up for her. Black skins prayed for Sean Boothe despite everything. He had been the sacrificial lamb.

*

Alex looked into the crowd as she arrived at the courtroom steps. Police were vainly trying to keep order, brittle and condescending. In the sway of black faces she saw that an argument was going on. A small group of mainly white women were hurling anger at the majority.

"RAPE HAS NO COLOUR!"

"FREE SEAN BOOTHE!"

"RAPE HAS NO COLOUR!"

"FREE SEAN BOOTHE!"

The women kept their chant as loud as they could. A man squared off with one of the few black women standing there. The movement of the crowd flung her into the shoulder of the woman next to her and she righted herself to look into his eyes.

"Why you with these fools, eh? You don' see what's going on?"

She stared at him. Oceans between them. Alexandrea strained to hear her answer, but it was lost in the roar.

*

A silence fell on the courtroom.

Alexandrea slid into the seat between them. Michael put a hand on Nicola's shoulder. "It's time," he said.

*

Jeanette looked at the men in front of her. *(underneath their clothes they're all naked)*

"Do you swear to tell the whole truth and nothing but the truth . . ." *(go down Emmanuel Road, look at the naked men, bruk the rock stones, bruk them on them)*

She fingered the Bible and wondered if they knew she was born a Christian child.

*

Alexandrea shifted uncomfortably in the chair as hours went by. Her eyes were on fire. A million pins danced on her skin, wild.

"Keep *still!*" Michael hissed.

She shifted, shifted as she listened to Jeanette speak.

*

She watched Charles walk into the room and stared at him, not understanding. Why was he here? What could he know? Why had no-one told her?

He was fine today.

Fine in his suit.

*

Alex watched Sean's eyes, his hands on his lap, silent. Watched him examine them minutely, holding them up to the light. She arched her back in pain. She knew what he was doing.

He was admiring them, the hands that had hurt Jeanette. She watched him steal a kiss from his own palm, sank her fingernails into her wrist and rocked, knowing.

*

She listened to them like a child.

They were telling her who she was.

Sean, flat, still dark and beautiful as the sea.

Charles, shorter, rounder, browner.

The insane little ditty danced in her mind, giving her no relief

(but they were inside me they were inside me)

as they told her who she was

(silver batty riders, your honour)

(she was in a fight and I saved her)

(those are very short shorts, your honour)

(a fight about a man)

(a vulgarism, your honour, street name)

(underwear hardly there)

*

Michael held her hands tightly. Alex looked down at their locked fingers. She could not stop the tears. They ran rivulets down her neck, dripped on to her knees. She leaned forward.

*

"It started slowly," said Charles. He stretched back in his seat. "A little tap here and there. She liked being held against the wall." He swallowed. "Stuff like that. 'Hit me harder,' she said. 'I like it like that,' she said."

His eyes rested on Jeanette. "It made me sick."

She watched her lawyer try to make it better.

*

Lawyers bleated around her, coaxing, cajoling. *And then, what?* they said. *Explain it to us, tell us what happened. Paint it in detail. Give us the negative. Imprint it on our brains. Hold nothing back. Tell us everything.*

She spoke, in the high necked frock that she knew her Mamma would have been proud of.

Alex became so congested that Michael took her out into the hall, pushing past the other people in the public gallery.

"Why are you crying?" he asked.

She couldn't speak. It was too familiar. He pushed.

"They're lying, they're *lying*," she said.

He put his lips next to her ear, breath making her earrings tinkle into the empty hallway.

"How do you know?" he said.

Her mouth worked. She knew people. Had made it her life's work to know them. The blind girl she had interviewed when she had just started out, telling her what it was like, *(you all think it's like being in a dark room it's not)* the confidence with which the woman had manoeuvred her way through the office where she worked, a light touch here and there, guiding her *(Is blindness like being in the dark?)*

(No, no, no. Imagine your arm, does your arm see that there's nothing there? Nothing. No darkness. That would mean I could see. There's nothing. Hold your arm up against a window, do you understand, there's nothing) and hearing that young girl, her fascination had begun. She wanted people to tell her their lives, all of it, she had been open and receptive *(sink into me let me feel what you feel let me be you)* and as she listened in the courtroom that hunger and instinct for other people's lives had come back to her, blinding brilliance. And until it came back, until the light came streaming to her, she hadn't realised it had been gone. Gerry and Pearson had taken it, thieves in the daytime and she knew she had been stripped of what made her real *(do you see now, do you see when you hold up your arm)*, her ability to imagine the lives of others *(hidden body language, secrets in between the words, secret tears, I used to see them all, I'm not a writer I'm a watcher)* and she was crying for what she hadn't allowed herself to see *(the sound of vomiting late at night)*

(what must it be like to be invaded pried apart punished his sweat mingling with yours)

(she used to dance and I hated her because I couldn't dance never learned how to be free)

(to be free and then to lose that freedom) and she climbed the rungs of Jeanette's ladder as fast as the light, reached the top, she knew, knew, knew *(what must it be like to have his fingers between your legs, pulling, parting)* she knew more than anyone else there, and she let go, let go the time clock, the neat piles, the sadness as the jury rose together, went away to collect their thoughts, memories, knowledge, prejudice, childhood, adulthood, lessons learnt, judgements.

26

Alexandrea packed her bags. Neatly, like she always would.

Sean pulled his hands over his collection.

She unclipped the identification badge on her jacket.

He looked down at his feet. They stank of prison. He would have to wash them off.

She smiled.

He smiled.

Ruby Fleur knocked at the door.

He looked up at Bill Waivers' face.

"You're here very late," Ruby said.

The meaty fist reached into him. He was driven back against the wall.

Alex looked down at the computer screen. The guest list stared back at her. Twelve women who had been harassed by their bosses. A sales assistant. A doctor. An administrator. A student. A woman who had worked in a grocery store, it had been her cousin. A secretary. Someone who had been on the dole and got it from her client advisor. A gymnast. A stage manager. An orthodontist's assistant. A nursery nurse. A lawyer, who had taken him to court.

The blood caressed the wall.

"Yes." Her finger hovered over the delete button. If only she could do it. If only Ruby would go away she could do it. Delete it all. All the programme notes.

He watched Bill step towards him.

*

Jeanette stood aside and let her mother come into the house. She looked at the coat, slightly decayed. It had been the first coat Mamma had bought for herself when she came to England. After coats for her and for Maye. Mamma had taken them to the seaside one day and showed them the tide. She had told them how water was warm in Jamaica, didn't they remember, and the three of them had watched the waves, breaking into the cold air, the spray freezing and breaking across the sky, mid-air, crashing rhythmically into the water and Mamma said it was time to go, too long looking at foolishness, but she had not forgotten.

Her mother stood, arms akimbo, looking at her. "Me see de papers," she said.

Jeanette moved towards the kettle. So here it was.

"Would you like a cup of tea?"

"You have peppermint? Me nuh know whether you keep those t'ings."

"You can have anything you like, Mamma."

"Alright. Mek it peppermint. Me have likkle wind 'pon me chest."

Her mother sat, heavily, coat still on.

"You can take off the coat you know, Mamma."

"Don' worry 'bout me. Ah don' come to stay long." She folded her hands along her bosom.

Jeanette looked up in the air, helpless. Same old Mamma. In an odd way, she was glad that some things never changed. Same coat, same earrings. The ones she always wore. She wondered who had given them to her mother. A man who was courting her? *(lick dem one by one gyal an' bwoy)* Had mamma ever loved a man? She could see her mother's disapproving gaze on the room. She poured boiling water and handed over the cup. She could take anything now that he was innocent in the eyes of the world. Nothing could be worse.

"Me see the paper," her mother repeated.

"Yes."

Sean had been acquitted. By the end of the trial she had expected no less.

"You go church?" her mother inquired.

"No, mamma."

The older woman tutted. "You should go."

"Why, Mamma? I got enough church to last forever."

"To ask forgiveness."

Jeanette looked at her. The words boiled in her. "Why should I ask forgiveness?"

Her mother was stern. "Me always know seh you woulda come out bad."

"Thank you."

"Gyal, don talk to me so speaky-spokey, like you smell somet'ing bad. Me know how you stay."

Jeanette waited. She had known her mother would never understand. Known in the long silences as she had waited for her to ring, to reach out and she had never brought herself to do it. In the silence she had known.

"If you gwaan so, bad t'ings will come to you."

"Mamma, I don't want to have this conversation —"

"Me see you."

"I don't —"

"Me see you a sex de man inna Maye house."

(bruk dem one by one)

"What?"

(bruk dem two by two)

"After you do dem nastiness inna you sister yard you expect any decent s'maddy to believe you?"

(bruk dem t'ree by t'ree, gyal an bwoy)

She heard the words in her head. She had seen. Her mother had seen. She sagged against the chair. Dug her nails into her face. "Mamma —"

"You never learn, eh? You never learn. Well. Me know seh you woulda vex up wid me. Imagine how me shame, me own daughter gwaan wid nastiness an' den *shame* tek you inna courtroom go chat you business!"

"You *watched* him? You watched him *rape* me?"

Her mother rose. Old woman in an old coat, features like dough, withered prettiness peeping, body slack from hard work, but the skin still taut and young on her arms. She shrugged. "If you cyaan hear, you mus' feel."

Jeanette watched her pick up her bag, a careful hand at her hip checking that her stockings were on straight.

It was that easy. Easy to hurt. *(finger mash no cry)*

The enormity of it shook her as the jingle in her head chuckled at her, insidious, constant, clashing *('MEMBA AH PLAY WE AH PLAY)* and as her mother slid the gloves on those young hands *(GO DOWN EMMANUEL ROAD, GYAL AN' BWOY)* the small memory that had been there, all along lit into flame, burst into unforgiving cries *(tek de odder sheet mek pillow, cho gyal, me know de bathtub cold but Mamma have t'ings fe do, you ah go listen to me sing like a good girl)* and her mother was stepping away, the Lord's angel *(what was I doing in the bathtub)* and she wanted to know so badly that she thrust her mother's revelation to one side, grabbed at the old coat, plaits in disarray, what had she been doing in the bathtub, Maye hadn't been in the bathtub with her, why had she been in the bathtub *(BRUK ROCK STONE)*

"Mamma, what did you do when I was in the bathtub?"

Mavis' eyes were huge. Spittle worked at the side of her mouth. Her earrings jangled. Those earrings. She could remember them singing, making pretty noises, every time her mother had put her in the bath and gone into the other room, and yes, that was where she'd heard that tune *(bruk them one by one)* heard her mother hum it every time she hoovered, every time she cooked a meal, and she had always wondered which words went with that idiot tune, but she knew, she knew, she knew because her mother had sung those words every time a man came up the stairs, it was her oldest memory and she could see that it was her mother's oldest memory too, else why was she looking so terrified? *(Ah comin' to you, Carl. Jus' puttin' down de pickney)*

"WHAT WAS I DOING IN THE BATH, MAMMA? WHY WAS I IN THE BATH? WHERE WAS MAYE?" *(Me don' know why you nuh send de pickney go ah country wid de odder one)* and the rustling of sheets, creaking of the bed, and Mamma singing, singing into the night air while her daughter gazed at the black ceiling with the mosquitoes biting her. She remembered slapping at them while Mamma sang.

Mavis pushed at her arms, but she clung, convulsively, memories dawning in her face, how could she not have remembered, she had *told* Michael when they were in the park, how could she not have remembered her mother's earrings?

"Let me go!" The older woman's face was panicked, tears threatening.

"What were you doing, Mamma?"

"Tek you han' offa me! Me nuh want you nasty han' dem 'pon me!"

"What were you doing, Mamma? Why did you sing? Did you sing for Maye too?"

Their faces were close. She watched her mother's eyes get wider, wider, and she still didn't know who the man had been and what Mamma had been doing while she and the mosquitoes sung like a choir, but my God, she was losing it, Mamma was losing control and she felt huge, raging fury, and she was shaking her now, with all the strength in her body.

"This is what you sang, Mamma."

They were so close that they breathed the same inch of air.

Jeanette's voice played bass through them. "Go down Emmanuel Road, gyal an' bwoy, fe go bruk rock stone. Go down Emmanuel Road, gyal an' bwoy, fe go bruk rock stone . . ."

Her mother trembled, but she didn't care. She sang. "Bruk dem one by one, gyal an' bwoy —"

"No!"

"Bruk dem two by two, gyal an' bwoy, finger mash no cry, gyal an' bwoy —"

"No . . ." It was a plea.

" 'Memba ah play we ah play —"

Mavis wrenched herself out of her daughter's arms and hit her across the face. Once. Twice. And then the energy ran out. They looked at each other. The older woman's chest was concave, breasts withered, head slack, voice hollow. "Dem time deh me did stay like you. Jus' a whore." Her head came up. "Jus' a ole whore." She picked her bag up from where it had fallen. Jeanette watched her walk down the hall. Open the door. Step out into the evening rain.

*

Michael turned the ignition off and reached into the back of the car. The picture lay there, framed and wrapped. It had been the last straw for Marisa. She would not have pictures of Jeanette in her house. Like everything else, he had ended it gently. It was better this way. They were hurting each other. He didn't want to hurt anybody.

He rang the doorbell and then saw that the door was ajar. He stepped in, and heard the music.

*

Ruby sat down beside Alexandrea and studied her face.

"How come you're here so late?" She looked at her watch. "It's nearly nine. Everybody else is gone."

Alexandrea moved her hand, defeated *(please go away, Ruby, go away let me do this, let me fuck him up)*. She shrugged *(please go away Ruby, go away, go make love to who you make love to at night time, go drink some wine, comb your hair anything)*.

Ruby touched her shoulder. "What's wrong?"

Alex started to move away *(please don't touch me I miss him so much and you all invade me when you touch me please)* but Ruby grabbed her shoulders and turned her back towards her. They stared at each other for what seemed like a long time.

Ruby touched her cheek. Tender, soft. Alexandrea felt the anger surge inside her, impossible to hold anymore. She wailed, hot, bitter, juicy with rage, and the words began to spill over her lips, her tongue, fast, flecks of spittle in Ruby's face that the other woman seemed not to feel or see.

"You won't believe me, no one will believe me, but he touches me all the time, he puts his *hands* on me — Pearson, he makes me sick, when he does it I want to be sick — and I can't get away from him so I'm going to *screw* him up, Ruby, don't stop me, I'm going to get rid of the whole programme — how can he be such a lying *bastard, bastard, bastard*—"

Before Ruby could stop her, she pushed at the computer in front of her. It teetered and then fell heavily onto the floor, plastic exploding, screen whirling crazily, an insane eye that leered at them.

Terrified, Alex stared at Ruby Fleur. Her face was grave.

"I know," she said simply. "He did it to me."

*

She wanted to breathe the bass, like she had before. It took time. Every place that she lost herself she turned back to the CD player and hit the tune again. She would dance. She had to.

She was slow. Her body was stiff. But she had to. She moved her head from side to side, hypnotising herself, trying to feel the pulse, the heartbeat. It sidled to her, nudging her to know it once again. She could feel it climb into her, coaxing. A slow growth. The muscles in her back creaked and loosened. Her hips curled, shook themselves out and she could feel it coming, faster now. She reached her hands out, eyes shut, and felt the horns tremble over her. A guitar riff, throbbing, picked at her feet, lifted them. Urgency made her ankles ache, and she felt blood and bone crackle as the music took her and asked her to play. Waist an undulation. Groin in time, following, lips rolling back over white teeth, bursting, and she had it, heard the music no more, heard her own music, and it was terrible, terrible in its force and she knew that she could go with it, be with it, felt the cracks come together, neatly, pushing the shadows away, the glow and the warmth taking her away from her whole body. This was her religion, her praise and if the whole world had been watching, she would have laughed, surely you have this too, you have this, find it, breathe it, take it back, take it back.

Michael watched her, wrapped her fever around his soul.

27

"So what will it be, tea, coffee, something stronger?" Ruby had changed into a soft robe that flowed around her. Her flat was smaller than Alex had imagined it would be, stuffed with colour: purple mats, yellow sofas, overflowing bowls of potpourri, red walls. Fat lilies laughed at her from the shelves, the table, in the toilet, perched on a surface above the cooker. Music played low on the stereo.

"Tea, please." She was starting to calm down, but tremors still ran across her shoulders. Ruby's movements had been swift. She had called someone to clear the broken computer from the floor and a taxicab that rolled them through the damp streets. All the way she had not let go of Alexandrea's hand, keeping its stiffness warm in her lap. Each time Alex had tried to speak she had hushed her, tender steel running under the words. She put a tray, bright with dots, onto the table in front of the couch and began to pour.

"Ruby, I —"

"Hush." Not asking what Alex preferred, she added sugar and milk to a cup and handed it to her. "I once had two dear friends who nearly broke up over the word 'hush'. Shows you how humans can't communicate to save their lives." She leaned back and sipped at her cup. "Mmmm. Lovely. These two friends of mine, she was Jamaican and he was American. Well, Kevin kept complaining to me that she was unsympathetic. Angie kept telling me in the other ear that he never let her comfort him. They seemed to be talking about the same thing, right? So I finally sat them down and they were going at it like hammer and tongs, cussing each other, blah de blah, bollocks. Suddenly I worked it out. I asked what exactly she said to him when he was upset. She finally figured it out. She was like, 'hush.' And then he started yelling again about how she always told him to *shut* up when he tried to share his feelings." She smiled. "See? Language. She was saying 'Hush, baby'. But he heard 'hush' as 'hush up, hush your mouth.' But they were trying to love each other."

Alexandrea looked at the floor. The stereo throbbed at her *(face the music)*, and she tried to catch the words *(if me cut you)* but the singer was indistinct and American *(all the blood)* and she didn't know the tune.

"So." Ruby moved forward, putting the cup down. "First I have to tell you that I'm leaving Endeavour after the sexual harassment show in two weeks."

Alex raised her head. "I wish you'd leave before that. If he did the same thing to you, I can't understand how you can be around him —"

Ruby sighed. "That's just it. I played the game. I could tell you that I fought and raged the way you've been doing, but I was stupid and it seemed a small price to pay for getting what I wanted." She laughed at Alex's face, and then lowered her voice. " I watched you and Pearson. I saw that look in his eye. Years ago I would have told you that you were an idiot, screw the man and get what you can. I wouldn't have had any sympathy."

Alex felt another tremor of the anger. "So what's changed?"

Ruby looked surprised. She crossed over to the stereo and turned the volume up. The music swelled over them. Ruby patted the plastic. "Obscure little Prince track that hardly anyone's ever heard." She grinned. "Listen to the lyrics. 'Face the music. When I cut you, all the blood is red.' We're all the same. We're not in a competition over who's pain is the most important." She crossed back and reached for Alex, hugging her fiercely. "Poor little controlled, self conscious Alexandrea. You really don't know the power you have, do you?"

Alex struggled. "But I don't have any power! And you're not doing anything! I might have smashed the computer, but the information's still in there, the show's going on, you're *hosting* it . . ."

Ruby smiled. "I tell you what we're going to do . . ."

*

Julius glanced over at Nicola. He was glad that he could see her in the gloom of the theatre. He chuckled to himself as he studied her face. It was set, intent, concentrating on the play in front of them. It was here that they were one. In the theatre, the place they lived the best. Where they re-created themselves. It was here that they had begun to know each other.

He pondered on what their relationship had been. He, desperately peeling back all her guardian angels, asking for the truth. She, always fighting. How ironic that when she had finally given up the last of her secrets, it was to end.

He supposed this was how it felt when the heart broke. Dull aches in his calves and an emptiness that neither good wine nor her kisses could fill. Each one was a goodbye. They felt so final. They were one in so many ways, and because they understood most of what there was to understand about each other *(but not all, no, not all and was it necessary to understand all, but that is what she needs)* the finality between them had needed no words. But he had said them anyway, just to be sure, a week after the trial. A week of goodbye kisses that were really mementoes she was giving him for the long nights ahead. *(You're leaving me then? Yes.)* There had been tears in her eyes, every time they walked, played, loved, and he asked again, just to be sure, every time she kissed him *(You're leaving me then? Yes.)* She had left the ticket on his bed. An open return, dated a month in advance. And every day they smiled sadly at each other, and he thought of asking for an explanation, but it wasn't necessary, who needed to know more than he knew? So the questions and kisses had gone on, as the hours passed and he counted down.

She sneaked a look at him from under her eyelashes. She knew that she was hurting him, but she had to leave. Perhaps she would come back to him, when there was enough strength inside her, when she knew herself. She was glad that he had not asked. She needed to walk the footsteps that her mother had walked, feel the same breeze once more. When her father told her that he was heading back to Jamaica, asked her to come with him, she had agreed, surprising herself. But it made sense. It was the only way to answer her questions. It had all started there. And she needed to go, if she was ever to have an answer for her father or herself. She had never said if she could love a man who looked like him. She leaned her head against Julius in the theatre and felt his arms surround her. She only knew that she loved a man who looked nothing like her father. Perhaps one day it would be enough.

They rose to applaud with the others, ducked the respectful glances from the crowd as the lights came up and they were recognised. Outside, as they climbed into a cab, he pulled at her. "Must you leave?" She could feel the burnished surface of his cheek against hers.

"Don't —"

He couldn't stop. "Say you won't."

"Please —" She held him close. "We don't have long. Don't spoil it. Don't spoil it."

He put a finger into the curve of her waist as the cab pulled away from the curb. Looked up at her, resolute. "You know I love you."

"Oh yes," she whispered. "Oh, I know."

*

Alex fumbled for her keys at the door. They had stayed up nearly all night, Ruby admonishing her to keep the tea in large supply, phone attached to her ear, cajoling, talking, sometimes pleading. By midnight they had two women. By two am they had five. By the time they left the tea and started on the coffee they had seven. Seven former employees of Endeavour Productions.

The door swung inwards and she stepped into the hall, scooping up the mail from a tidy pile on the floor. She snapped on the light and glanced at them, not seeing *(we're going to get him get him get him)*. Then she heard the low murmur of voices from the living room. She cocked her head, surprised. It was late, and she knew that Nikki was staying over with Julius. She walked forward.

Jeanette and Michael were sitting on the sofa. Except they weren't just sitting. She caught the softness in Michael's eyes before they pulled apart, startled.

"Sis, we have to talk —"

She stared at him. They were together. She knew that look on her brother's face. She looked at Jeanette. The lines on her face were still weary, but fainter, somehow. Her eyes were dark, watchful. Alex put out a hand to steady herself. *(Was I so cruel, do they fear my disapproval so much?)* Michael had straightened his back, reared himself for battle.

"Alex, you're just going to have to deal with this, babes. I think —" He turned back to Jeanette, unsure. "Well, we're talking, we've been talking and —"

Alex sat down on a cushion and let her handbag fall from her shoulder. "Have you left Marisa?"

Her brother frowned. "Yeah." He looked at Jeanette again. "You know I wouldn't do that, be with them both, try to be with them both —"

Alex inclined her head. "Give me and Jeanette a bit of time."

"I'm not going to let you —"

"It's okay, Mike." Jeanette hadn't taken her eyes from Alexandrea's. "Go away."

"But —"

Jeanette reached a hand up and patted his thigh. "I mean it."

He wavered, unsure, and let out his breath. "I'll be in your room, Je." She nodded.

The silence between them spun into the night. Jeanette raised her chin and broke it, haltingly.

"I can't deal with a fight, Alex."

"I know."

"I can't promise you I'm not going to hurt him, I can't promise I'm even going to be with him, I can't — promise anything . . ." She gesticulated helplessly.

"I know."

"Why are you so calm?"

Alex bit her lip. "I owe you an apology."

*

Thompson rolled over in his bed and put the phone back on his nightstand. The young woman next to him moved sleepily.

"Who was that?" she asked.

"Nothing important. An old contact in America. Go back to sleep." He had been celebrating his headline with this young thing since it all broke, but he was beginning to get bored. With her and the headline. He'd heard that Nicola Baines was running off back home, and he wasn't about to follow her there. If she headed for the States, he'd take up the old trail again. In the mean time, he had a new scent. It sounded juicy. And it wasn't every night that Ruby Fleur chased down his number and called him up at home. She was small potatoes, but this could make her very big. Sexual harassment. He laughed, running a thumb along his bristled face. He was getting to be quite the one for the sexual scoops. It might be nothing, but he'd be there. He laughed again, and burrowed under the covers, put his mouth on the woman's thigh. Her moan was sleepy but he was sure he could have her awake in no time.

"You changed your mind quick." She arched her hips towards him. "Was it good news, then?"

"I think I'm becoming a feminist," he said, and buried his face between her legs.

*

Somewhere in the night, a man eased himself from the wall of his one-bed room. Examined the colour of his own blood, on the carpet, walls, a splatter across his magazines. He dragged himself to the bed and lay across the white duvet. It hurt to laugh, but he did it, choking on the water in his mouth, spitting bright red again and again. He would heal, he knew this. Heal and show some more of them his might. Wincing, he reached into the pocket of his jeans and uncrumpled the piece of paper he found there. He wondered if Miss Cherry Lip Gloss watched television much. He would tell her he had been acquitted. She would understand.

Mavis

So you hear me life. Me nah ask nobody fe feel sorry for me. Is not de way me do t'ings. Me come ah England, wid me two girl pickney dem, come fe struggle. Sometimes when me put on me old coat and walk in de rain me use fe bawl fe me country. How me couldn't mek no progress dere. Wonder how de whole ah de gyal dem ah mek dem life, if dem still ah work. Me never even get to talk to me Auntie Myra again. All me have left from her is a pair of earrings she give me before me did go to Kingston. Me wear dem all the time to remember her. Is practically de only t'ing me have to remember Jamaica.

Me go back to de domestic work. Haffi mek a money. Clothes nuh cheap, rent nuh cheap, pickney haffi go ah school. Me bring dem up in de ways of de Lord. Das' all me coulda give dem. Sing hymn every day inna dem ears, warn dem how life hard an' man nasty. Me couldn't mek dem know seh dem Mamma ah ol' whore, so me tek dem go ah church. Tell dem seh dem mustn't fornicate.

Me scrub out white people toilet till me hand dem renk, always mek sure me wash it before me touch me pickney. Hope say dem would walk in de eyes of Jesus, say him will watch over dem. Life hard, but me fin' out seh me coulda care fah me pickney. Never want another man, never find one. Part of me wish seh me never breed no girl pickney. Me know seh dem woulda get tempted into nastiness de same way like me. Me warn dem. Warn dem seh if dem cyaan hear, dem will feel. Tell dem seh dem puppa dem was righteous inna de Lord, hope seh dem woulda look a man like dat.

It never work out. De firs' one get up an breed like she ah dog, lay down with wutliss neigar like she never have a God-fearing bone in her body. De crotches sweet her till she get diabetes to rass. Askin' you pardon, Lord. And de odder one. Well. What a disgrace. It nearly kill me when she realise weh me used fe do. Me couldn't tell her dat, though. Couldn't tell her how much it burn me. Now she know dat is bad genes mek her do what she did do, lie on the man,

239

tek him inna de big-big court and talk out de business dat spose to be between a man an' him woman, maybe she will change. Maybe she will tek it to the house of de Lord. Maybe she will all come deh one day, wid me.

Me know seh de Lord is a gracious Lord.

Alexandrea, June 14th, 1996

I saw Gerry the other day. He was walking along Brixton High Road, looking at the girls. He looked healthy. I was surprised that I didn't feel anything. Just recognition. He was wearing a shirt I bought him, and I remembered the watch he had on his wrist, knew where he had bought the shoes. It was kind of sad, but funny at the same time. He didn't see me, but that was okay too. I don't think about him so much anymore. Sometimes I see his eyes in the faces of nameless joggers and the ache hits me. But I carry on, regardless. I think I've gotten over him. It comes to all of us. I'm so glad. Nikki was right.

The drinking is still a struggle. Once an alcoholic, always . . . they say. But I've been dry for a while. We'll see how that goes. Ruby does a lot for me. It's brilliant to work with someone who knows what you want to do and trusts you. We make documentaries. It's not much money, but I feel like I'm doing something worthwhile at last. And the last Ruby Fleur show was excellent for publicity. I wasn't there. I suppose I'm not perfect. I couldn't go up there with those brave, brave women to point the finger at him. I just couldn't. I hear that he nearly hurt himself trying to pull the plug on the director, but as they say in this business, it was good telly, and they kept on going. Not that he could have done a thing about it. It was live and kicking and by the end of it the big wigs who fund Endeavour *(good to know that money rules over everything)* had him in the office for hours. There was no way they could do that much damage control, what with the press baying at the door. I was watching it with Jeanette, Nikki and Michael, and right after the show hit it was all over the news, Ruby purring at the journalists that she'd tipped off. I guess Pearson could have cried conspiracy if Ruby hadn't stood up at the end and told the entire country that he'd done it to her too. We laugh like hell about that. Ruby says that if she hadn't left she would have become an Oprah clone, sobbing about her fake hair-do and her collection of bootleg Prince music and her single status on national television. They offered her a packet to stay. But she says she's developed some morals. Our work is getting so much praise. Every time I pluck another secret out of thin air she looks at me and says *god-damn girl, you're good.* I guess I am.

Nicola faxes me like a madwoman. Julius faxes me about her faxes. Says she's on his mind a lot. Well, she would be, Julie, I fax back. You love the woman, or what? I went to his latest play the other night. He's never going to get as good as Nikki again, but they all try. I've been several times. He keeps teasing me that the press will start rumours. I hope not. Still, I think they've had their fill of all of us. I hope it runs their bellies. Imagine, me with a white boy. That would seriously damage my rep. I don't think anyone would believe that.

Michael keeps laughing at me. He says he can't understand how his finicky sister can have unwashed dishes in the sink. There were only one or two. Damn cheek. Like I have time to wash dishes.

I have to tell Ruby that slavery days are over.

Nicola, June 14th, 1996

I'm going to be so fat when I get out of this place. Auntie Joy keeps ramming plantain and fry dumpling and stew peas down my throat like it's going out of style. Keeps asking me if I don't see how me foot dry up and I look like I need nourishment. I had to run down to the gym and sign up, quick-time. Still, it's nice to know that my boy will take me on any size I get to. He keeps telling me in his letters that if I discover any new sides to me while I'm here he's going to strangle my rass if I don't tell him. He keeps telling me that he'll be there any time I get back.

I don't do Mona anymore. I'm trying to find me.

Janet keeps the phone very busy. She sighs and complains, telling me she'd keep my career going if only I'd put some effort into it. I think she does it for effect. People in good old LA still seem to want to take me on, but I'll get to that. I do still want to act, if I can manage to do it. Julius insists that the talent is still in there, fighting to get out, I don't need Mona or anything else to access it. I suppose I'll find out. There are things I've been dealing with here. I can feel myself becoming an old cliché, to rass: Young Actress Returns To Rediscover Her Roots. They actually printed that in *The Gleaner* when I got here. I suppose it's true. I needed to come back for a good while, watch black people busy being doctors, madmen, beggars and teachers. It's gradual. I sit in Half Way Tree and watch them all whiz by and I try to guess whether they feel the same alienation I have felt. Maybe not. Maybe it's just me. I'm a spectator now. Maybe there'll be a day when I feel like joining in. For now, it's cool to watch.

I saw a girl who used to go to my school. She sat down beside me in a bus and started chatting. I couldn't believe it! She was gabbing on about how she used to admire me when we were kids. What a way people lie to themselves. All I could do was laugh. I think I offended her. Too bad.

Jeanette wrote me a long letter. She told me that she thinks her mother used to work as a prostitute. That maybe that's the reason they never knew their fathers. That blows my mind. All I ever used to hear was that her mother was a God-fearing woman who wouldn't dream about talking about sex, much less *doing* it, and for money as well! I wrote back and said that she shouldn't condemn her too much, if she's able. Probably a stupid thing to say. I get the feeling that's not all, but I suppose everyone has their secrets. I remember that when I wrote Mona she was a prostitute.

I can't say all the bullshit's left me. But I've got time.

Jeanette, June 14th, 1996

I can't sleep at night. This blasted child keeps kicking me like he's ready to come out and stand up and face the world, and he doesn't seem to understand that he has to stay in there for at least a couple more months. Like he's eager to get out and look around.

Michael insists on walking on the road and buying girls' clothes. Like him and God have a pact that this is going to be a girl child. The doctor knows but I don't want her to tell us. Mike was not happy. He keeps dancing around on one foot and saying how the hell are we going to prepare for this child if we don't know what to get? I've told him that at the rate he's spending, if it is a boy, we're going to have to kit it out in pink and yellow dresses until we're rich, which will probably be never.

When I fell pregnant I had a moment when I almost went crazy. Thought it might be Sean's.

God.

But of course it's not. I didn't give a damn about the gender. I was just grabbing the doctor and asking *how many weeks am I?* And she looked astounded, and then said: *eight*. Of course it was an insane thought. It all happened so many months before, and I would have been pushing it out by now. If it had been his.

Maye came round to tell me I could re-apply for my degree. I'd like to. I will, when I know this child is safe. Michael tells me he'll be a house husband, but I know the boy just want an excuse to be lazy. He's good to me, though. Can't understand when he started fancying me. What a boy lie. I feel safe with him. He's my friend. That's one of the only things I know when I wake up. There are times when I look at his sleeping face and it's the only thing between me and the broken morning. Mamma's voice keeps coming back to me. Remembering how every time I went out with a boy, she would caution me. *Don' gwaan like a wetty-baggie gyal,* she would yell as I went through the door. Don't act like a wetty-baggie gyal, a cocktease — hard to get, get left! But all of us are wetty-baggie gyals to somebody. All of us. In the mornings I watch everything be born again and it's corny and real at the same time, and her voice in my head is only a whisper. I listen to the traffic outside, telling my belly that whether it's a boy or a girl I want it to learn how to drive quick, get a degree, always listen to its parents. Never listen to its grandmother.

I'm going to like this child. It dances inside me.

ooooo

AUTHOR'S ACKNOWLEDGEMENTS

*Soroya, Zak, Jenne, Karlean, Gareth, Claudine, Amba, Abena, Claude,
Roger, Paul, Carla, Simone, Helen F, Marcus, Nick A, Llewella G, Taitu,
Anjani, Mark O, Soraya, Ayesha, Janice, Peter N, Michael O, Jameela, Vivia
G, Philip, Terrence L, Tonia, Sarah, Warner, Tanya, Yemi, Janey, Jennifer,
Bobby, Maria, Carol, Mauline, Martin R, Mechel, Ricky, Marion,
Shirley, Alafia, Denise, Joyce, Benjie & Daniel, my family,
Angela & Tony, Jamie Starr, Terri
and D.I. David Ryan.*

*You all know
why.*